The room ... she felt as if she belonged there, which was absolutely ridiculous.

Karly turned to go back into the kitchen to wait for Blake, and walked right into his broad chest. Stumbling backward, she would have fallen if not for his big hands encircling her upper arms to steady her.

"I'm sorry. I didn't mean to—"

Her voice failed her as she gazed up into his sexy brown eyes, and for a split second, she thought she caught a glimpse of the warm, compassionate man she'd thought she was in love with. But just as quickly as it appeared, the glimmer was gone, replaced by a closed-off stare.

"You'd better watch your step," he said, his deep baritone sending a shiver coursing through her. "One of these days those ridiculous shoes are going to cause you to fall and break an ankle."

Before she could find her voice and tell him that she didn't need his input on what she should or shouldn't wear, he released her and motioned toward a door across the room.

"Let's go into the office for this talk you seem to think is so important."

She took a deep breath and followed him. Now she had to find a way to tell him she was still his wife.

THE RANCHER'S
ONE-WEEK WIFE

BY
KATHIE DENOSKY

First Published in Great Britain 2016
By Mills & Boon, an imprint of HarperCollins*Publishers*
1 London Bridge Street, London, SE1 9GF

© 2016 Kathie DeNosky

ISBN: 978-0-263-91875-5

51-0916

Our policy is to use papers that are natural, renewable and recyclable products and made from wood grown in sustainable forests. The logging and manufacturing processes conform to the legal environmental regulations of the country of origin.

Printed and bound in Spain
by CPI, Barcelona

Kathie DeNosky lives in her native Southern Illinois on the land her family settled in 1839. Her books have appeared on the *USA TODAY* bestseller list and received numerous awards, including two National Readers' Choice Awards. Readers may contact Kathie by emailing Kathie@kathiedenosky.com. They can also visit her website, www.kathiedenosky.com, or find her on Facebook at Facebook.com/Kathie-DeNosky-Author/278166445536145.

This book is dedicated to my editor, Stacy Boyd. Thank you for being my cheerleader and for waving those pom-poms when I need them the most.

One

Blake Hartwell shook his head in disgust when he heard the low-slung sports car bottom out in first one, then another of the many potholes pitting the dirt lane leading up to the foreman's cottage. As he brushed the sorrel gelding he'd tied to the side of the corral, he decided right then and there that whoever was behind the steering wheel of that little red toy couldn't be from the area. Folks in rural Wyoming had better sense than to drive a vehicle that sat that low on unpaved mountain roads. It was a surefire way to knock a hole in the oil pan or tear up the exhaust system on a car.

"Whoever he is, he'd better be prepared to hitch a ride on the back of an antelope if he breaks down because I'm not driving his fool hide back to town," Blake muttered as he glanced at the afternoon sun sinking toward the taller peaks to the west.

The car stopped at the side of the foreman's cottage next to Blake's truck. When the driver's door opened, a leggy blonde stepped out, causing his heart to stall and the breath to lodge in his lungs.

Blake clenched the grooming brush he'd been using on Boomer so tightly he wouldn't have been surprised if he left his fingerprints in the wood. He swallowed hard as he watched her walk toward the corral as fast as her spiked heels would allow on the uneven ground.

Slender and sleek in her formfitting black dress, her delicate body moved much like a jungle panther on the prowl. Blake's lower body tightened and he wasn't sure if it was in response to the sight of her now, or the memory of how those long legs felt wrapped around him when they made love.

"Aw, hell," he cursed under his breath. "What does *she* want?"

Boomer stamped one of his front hooves, then looked over his shoulder as if to ask if Blake knew her.

Reminding himself to exhale, Blake released the breath he'd been holding and went back to brushing the gelding's rust-colored hide. He knew her all right. Back in December, he'd met Karly Ewing in Las Vegas. She'd been on vacation from her job— whatever that was—and he'd been in town to compete in the national bull-riding finals. He'd accidently bumped into her in the lobby at Caesar's Palace and barely managed to catch her before she fell. As a way of apologizing for his carelessness, he'd convinced her to let him buy her a drink. They'd ended up talking for hours and the chemistry between them had been explosive. By the end of the day they'd been lovers. By the end of the week they'd been husband and wife. And one week after that, they'd been filing for a divorce.

When she stopped a few feet from the horse, she looked a little uncertain, as if she wasn't sure what kind of reception she'd get from him. "H-hello, Blake."

Her voice flowed over him like a fine piece of silk and reminded him of the way it had sounded when she'd said his name as he pleasured her. Blake gritted his teeth against the heat building in his lower belly and continued to brush Boomer.

He wasn't about to let her get to him. Not again. It had taken months after that fateful phone call on New Year's Eve, when she told him she wanted a divorce, for him to get a decent night's sleep. If possible, he'd just as soon avoid repeating that.

She'd made the choice to end things between them and although he hadn't agreed with her, he had accepted it. The way he saw it, there wasn't anything they hadn't already covered and there was no sense in rehashing it now.

"What brings you to the Wolf Creek Ranch,

Karly?" Without waiting for an answer, he added, "Eight months ago you weren't even willing to come here to see it. In fact, you said you weren't the least bit interested in learning anything about the back-side of no-man's-land."

As long as he lived, he would never forget the sting of her rejection, or her scorn for the land he loved. The ranch had been in his family for the past hundred and fifty years and he'd spent the majority of his adult life trying to get it back from his gold-digging stepmother after his father's death. He'd finally accomplished that goal almost two years ago and once he'd made Karly his wife, he'd been looking forward to showing her the place that he was proud to call home. But she hadn't cared enough about him or it to even see the place before she refused to live there with him.

Meeting her startled gaze head-on, he did his best to ignore the effect she had on him whenever he looked into her incredible blue eyes. "Why the sudden interest in a place you had no desire to learn anything about?"

Color rose on her cheeks and it seemed as if she might be slightly embarrassed. "I, um, I'm sorry if I left you with the wrong impression, Blake. It's not that I didn't think the ranch would be beautiful…"

When her voice trailed off as she looked around, Blake stopped grooming the gelding and rested his forearms on the gentle animal's broad back to give her an expectant look. "Then what was it?"

As he stared at her, awaiting an answer, a slight breeze fluttered her long, honey-colored hair and reminded him how the silky strands had felt when he'd threaded his fingers through them as he kissed her. His body came to full arousal and he was damn glad the horse stood between them. At least she wouldn't be able to see the evidence of how he still burned for her.

Turning back to face him, her eyes couldn't quite meet his. "I've always lived in the city and I was…" She shook her head. "It doesn't matter."

"What are you doing here, Karly?" Seeing her again was heaven and hell rolled into one neat little bundle, and the sooner she laid her cards on the table and went back to Seattle, the sooner he could get back to the business of trying to forget her.

When she took a deep breath, he did his best to ignore the rise and fall of her perfect breasts. "We need to talk, Blake."

He shook his head. "I don't know what you think we need to discuss now. We pretty much covered everything that needed to be said eight months ago. I wanted you to give us a chance to make our marriage work. You didn't want that. End of story."

"Please, Blake." She took a step back when Boomer blew out a gentle breath through his nose and turned his head to gaze at her. Looking a little apprehensive, she continued. "I wouldn't be here if it wasn't important. Could we please go somewhere we can sit down and talk? I promise I won't take up too much of your time."

Blake sighed heavily. It was clear she wasn't going anywhere until she'd said her piece. And truth to tell, he did need to talk to her. He hadn't yet received a copy of their divorce papers and he needed them for his records.

"The door's open," he finally said, motioning toward the foreman's cottage. "Make yourself at home. I'll be in as soon as I put Boomer in his stall for the night."

She opened her mouth as if she intended to say something more, then with a short nod she turned on her black spiked heels and slowly walked toward the back porch. Watching the gentle sway of her slender hips as she navigated the hard-packed, uneven ground in those ridiculous shoes, Blake shifted his weight from one foot to the other in an effort to relieve the pressure in his now too-tight jeans. He'd spent the past eight months trying to forget how her soft curves had felt beneath his hands and how her kisses were the sweetest this side of heaven. Seeing her here—where he'd wanted her—was bringing back all the memories he thought he'd left behind.

Shaking his head, he untied the gelding's lead rope from the top fence rail. He had no idea what she thought they needed to discuss, but if it had brought her from Seattle all the way to his remote ranch in Wyoming, it had to be pretty damn important.

Leading Boomer into the barn, he decided to get

this meeting over with as soon as possible. Then, after he watched Karly drive off his land and away from him for good, he had every intention of getting his brother, Sean, to come over from his ranch on the other side of the mountain and go with him to the Silver Dollar Bar in the tiny community of Antelope Junction. Sean could be the designated driver, while Blake finally finished the job of forgetting he'd ever met the petite blonde who'd turned his world upside down from the moment he'd laid eyes on her.

Karly opened the back door to Blake's home and walked into the kitchen on shaky legs. It had taken every ounce of courage she possessed to face him again, and although she had thought she'd put their brief relationship in perspective and moved on, his effect on her had been no less devastating today than it had been eight months ago, when she'd agreed to become his wife.

Blake was every bit as handsome, every bit as masculine and even sexier than she'd remembered. With wide shoulders, narrow hips and long muscular legs, he had a physique women drooled over and men spent endless hours in a gym trying to attain. But the steely muscles covering his tall frame had been honed from years of ranch work and competing in rodeos, not from lifting weights or working out on fitness machines. He was the real deal—the epitome of every woman's cowboy fantasy, and then some.

That was something she hadn't even realized she

possessed until they ran into each other in Las Vegas. But when he caught her to him to keep her from falling, all it had taken was one look at the cowboy holding her to his wide chest and she'd come close to melting into a puddle at his big-booted feet.

A delicious little shiver slid up her spine when she remembered how it had felt to be held in his strong arms, to taste the passion of his masterful kiss and experience the power of his desire as he made love to her. Her breathing grew shallow and her heart sped up. She forced herself to ignore it.

The hardest thing she'd ever done had been making the call to tell Blake she thought it would be in both of their best interest to call off their brief marriage. But when she had returned home, she'd thought about how little they knew about each other and she couldn't think of a single thing they had in common besides not being able to keep their hands off of each other. Her breath caught and she had to swallow hard against the sudden wave of emotion threatening to overtake her.

"Get a grip," she admonished herself. "Nothing has changed. He lives here and you live in Seattle. It would have never worked."

To distract herself, she glanced around Blake's neatly kept home. Even though the appliances were ultramodern, the rest of the kitchen appeared to be as rugged and masculine as the man who lived there.

A wooden butcher-block island sat in the middle of the kitchen with a variety of copper bottom skillets, pots and pans hanging above it from a wrought-iron rack. The cabinets were a warm oak with hammered black hinges and door pulls; the countertop was polished blue marble. A wagon wheel suspended from the ceiling with old-fashioned-looking chimney lamps served as a chandelier over the round oak dining table, while the windows on the wall behind the dining area framed a panoramic view of the Laramie Mountains, which surrounded the ranch.

"Beautiful," she murmured as she gazed at the picture-perfect landscape. It was as rugged and fascinating as the man she was here to see.

Wandering into the living room, she wasn't at all surprised to see a stone fireplace with a rough-hewn mantel surrounded by a grouping of heavy leather furniture and rustic wooden end tables. The room was so cozy and inviting, she felt as if she belonged there, which was absolutely ridiculous. She belonged in Seattle, in her own apartment with its modern decor and view of the city. And try as she might, she couldn't imagine how it would have been living here with Blake. If that wasn't enough to convince her that she'd made the right decision, she didn't know what was.

But as she looked around at the colorful Native American throws on the back of the large leather sofa, and the pieces of vintage tack and Western accents hanging on the walls, she had to admit that Blake's home had a warm, friendly feel to it that her place had never possessed. An uncharacteristic loneliness suddenly invaded every part of her. She did her best to tamp it down.

She loved her life in Seattle. She had a great job as buyer for a large import/export dealer and although she didn't have much of a social life, she did occasionally go out with some of her coworkers for happy hour after work. But as she thought about how long it had been since that had happened, she took a deep breath. She really couldn't say she had a lot in common with any of them anymore. They were all either married or in committed relationships and were more interested in going home to their significant others than hanging out to talk shop.

It was odd she hadn't noticed that before she met Blake. And she had to admit that when she did realize it, she might have had second thoughts about her decision to end things with him. In the end, she hadn't let that sway her and resigned herself to being the only one in her office with no one to go home to.

But the more she thought about it, the more her loneliness increased. Shaking her head to dislodge the unsettling feeling, Karly turned to go back into the kitchen to wait for Blake and walked right into his broad chest. Stumbling backward, she would have fallen if not for his big hands encircling her upper arms to steady her.

"I'm sorry. I didn't mean to—"

Her voice failed her as she gazed up into his sexy brown eyes. For a split second, she thought she caught a glimpse of the warm, compassionate man she'd thought she was in love with. But just as quickly as it appeared the glimmer was gone, replaced by a closed-off stare.

"You'd better watch your step," he said, his deep baritone sending a shiver coursing through her. "One of these days those ridiculous shoes are going to cause you to fall and break an ankle." Before she could find her voice and tell him that she didn't need his input on what she should or shouldn't wear, he released her and motioned toward a door across the room. "Let's go into the office for this talk you seem to think is so important."

Blake stepped back for her to precede him into a study off the living room, and as she seated herself in the burgundy leather armchair in front of his desk, Karly forced herself to stay calm. The heat from his calloused palms through the fabric of her dress when he caught her had set her pulse racing and made breathing all but impossible.

She tried to calm herself as she stared at the outdoor scene intricately carved into the oak desk's front panel. She'd just as soon face off with the bear fishing in the stream as she would having to deliver the news she'd traveled over a thousand miles to give Blake.

"So what brings you all the way to Wyoming, Karly?" He removed his hat and hung it on a peg by the door. "I'm betting you didn't make this trip by choice."

He wasn't going to make their meeting easy and

she really hadn't expected him to. When they'd decided to dissolve their marriage eight months ago, they had both said things out of hurt and frustration that she was sure they both regretted.

"Please, Blake. Can't we at least—"

"What do you expect from me, Karly?" he interrupted, sinking into the chair behind his desk. "I haven't seen or heard from you since just before the first of the year. After we spent Christmas in Las Vegas, I came home expecting my wife to be joining me here for New Year's Eve. Instead, I get a call telling me you'd changed your mind. If I wanted to stay married, I'd have to give up my life on the Wolf Creek Ranch, quit riding bulls and move to Seattle because you decided you couldn't live out in the middle of nowhere."

"That isn't exactly what I told you," she said, defending herself.

"Close enough," he stated flatly.

"You were just as adamant that you couldn't live in the city," she reminded him, feeling a little guilty. He hadn't been as insulting in his assessment of Seattle as she'd been about where the ranch was located. But dredging up what he said and what she said wasn't getting to the point of her visit. When they continued to glare at each other for what seemed an eternity, she sighed and shook her head. "I didn't come here to argue with you, Blake."

"Why *are* you here? I thought we settled things when I signed the papers without contesting the divorce." He frowned. "By the way, I'd like to get a copy of the final decree. You said your lawyer was supposed to mail that to me, but like everything else you promised, it didn't happen."

Karly stared down at her tightly clasped hands. She supposed he was right. She had made several promises that she hadn't been able to keep. She'd meant to keep them at the time. But once she went back home to pack her things and close her apartment, her sanity returned and the fear of failure had her second-guessing everything that had happened in Las Vegas.

"When I took the documents back to Mr. Campanella after you signed them, he suggested that I file for the divorce myself in Lincoln County on the eastern side of the state," she finally said. "Which I did."

Blake frowned. "Why?"

"The dockets in Seattle are filled with other domestic matters and it can take up to a year or more just to get a court date," she explained. "All I had to do was mail the signed documents to the courthouse in Lincoln County and after the ninety-day cooling-off period the divorce would be final."

"Mail them?" His frown darkened. "I thought a lawyer and at least one of the petitioners had to go before a judge for a divorce. At least that's how I think it is here. Is it different in Washington State?"

Rubbing her temples, Karly tried to concentrate. This was what she'd come here to tell him. It was also where everything got extremely complicated.

"If the petition had been filed in Seattle, Mr. Campanella would have been present. But Lincoln is one of only two counties where residents of Washington State file uncontested divorces by mailing the paperwork to the county clerk. Neither petitioner has to be present, nor do they have to have legal representation." When she noticed his skeptical expression, the tension headache she'd been fighting began to pound unmercifully. "It's really quite simple. The judge looks over the papers, signs a final judgment and sends it back."

"That sounds out of character, for a lawyer to pass up a case like this," Blake said, frowning. "Most of the ones I know would jump at the chance to make some easy money."

"Mr. Campanella is the grandfather of one of my coworkers," she explained. Karly really appreciated the woman's offer of help. When she'd come back from Vegas and realized the enormity of what she'd done, she'd been in a panic to fix her mistake. "Jo Ellen asked him to guide me through it all and he agreed. He suggested that I use the courts in Lincoln County since ours was a simple, uncontested divorce. He said it would save time and cost a lot less than going through the court system in Seattle. I agreed, and followed his instructions."

Blake nodded. "I guess that makes sense if you're in a hurry to rid yourself of an unwanted husband."

His words were bitter and cut like a knife. She had to swallow around the lump forming in her throat. He had no idea how hard it had been to make the decision not to follow her heart and move to the middle of nowhere with him. She had witnessed the unhappiness and resentment created when her mother followed her heart and it had ultimately ended her parents' marriage. Karly had reasoned that it was better to end things before it came to such hard feelings between herself and Blake. But there was no sense in dwelling on the mistakes and heartaches of the past now.

"I never said I was in a hurry to get rid of you."

He stared at her for a moment before he shrugged. "That's debatable, but it's not the issue. I need a notarized copy of the final decree."

Karly nibbled on her lower lip as she nervously met Blake's fathomless brown eyes. The time had come to lay out the reason for her visit and apologize for making such a mess of everything. "Actually, I don't even have a copy of it myself."

"Didn't they send you one?" he asked, his frown turning to a scowl.

"No, but I'm sure they will," she said evasively. She needed to explain what happened before she told him the reason she'd traveled all the way to Wyoming. "The import company I work for sent me to their offices in Hong Kong for several months shortly before the ninety-day cooling-off period was up and I wasn't able to check on it from overseas." Her head pounded as she thought about how badly she'd handled something as important to both herself and

Blake as their divorce. But she'd been sad and unsure as to why she'd felt so badly about a logical,
sensible decision that should have brought only relief. "When I got back last week, I called to inquire
about our copies of the final decree."

He must have been able to sense that there was
more to the story because Blake's scowl darkened.
"What did they say?"

Shaking her head, Karly took a deep fortifying
breath in order to tell him the rest of what had happened. "I called the Lincoln County courthouse to
see if I could get a copy of the final decree…"

When she let her voice trail off as she searched
for the right words, he prompted, "Yeah, I got that.
You called about the papers. And?"

Karly briefly closed her eyes as she tried to gather
her courage for what needed to be said. Opening
them to meet his suspicious gaze, she did her best to
keep her voice steady. "Apparently the papers were
lost in the mail because the court clerk has no record
of us ever filing for a divorce." She had to take a deep
breath before she could finish. "It appears that we're
still husband and wife, Blake."

"We're still married," he repeated as if he had a
hard time grasping what she'd said.

"Yes." She hurried on as she reached into her
purse to take out a new set of divorce papers. Her
hand trembled slightly as she placed the envelope on
the desk in front of him. "I'm really sorry for the in-
convenience. Once you sign these, I'm going to fly to

Spokane and drive over to the Lincoln County court-house to file them with the clerk myself."

"So all this time, I've been thinking I'm a free man and I wasn't," he said, sitting back in the desk chair.

"Have you met someone?" she asked before she could stop herself.

He raised one dark eyebrow as he stared at her. "Would it matter if I had, Karly?"

Yes! "No," she lied. Thinking quickly, she added, "I was, um, afraid this snag might have derailed plans you might have made with someone else."

He continued to stare at her for a few moments before he smiled, shook his head and opened the envelope to remove the document. Reaching for an ink pen, he signed where she had flagged the papers with colored sticky notes.

"Well, you're stuck with me for at least another ninety days," he said, sliding the pages back into the envelope and pushing it across the desk's shiny surface toward her.

Karly winced at his acidic tone. She knew he was disillusioned and extremely unhappy with the situation. "I'm really…sorry, Blake. I never meant for any of this to happen." At least, not the mishandling of their divorce.

"Yeah, well, it did," he said, sounding resigned. "When you file these at the courthouse, make sure they send me copies of everything."

"Of course," she said, nodding as she slid the envelope back into her shoulder bag. She hesitated a moment as she tried to think of some way to say goodbye. Deciding there wasn't anything she could say that wouldn't make matters worse, she rose to her feet. "I'll be in touch if there's anything else we need to do."

"Did you drive all the way from Seattle or is that little toy in the driveway a rental?" he asked, standing up.

"I rented it when I flew into the Cheyenne Regional Airport," she answered, wondering why he wanted to know.

"I'll check under the car before you leave to make sure you didn't do some kind of damage to the undercarriage," he said, taking his wide-brimmed hat from the hook as they left the room. "You hit quite a few potholes on your way up the lane. Drive slower on the way back. You'll be less likely to damage the car."

"Who's responsible for taking care of the roads around here?" she asked. "They're in terrible condition."

"The county is responsible for the roads leading up to the ranch property lines, but ranchers have to keep the roads on their land plowed in the winter and graded in the summer," he explained. "We took care of grading the road after the snow melted off in the spring. But once the rainy season hit it washed out a lot of places. We were waiting until it dried up to work on the road again, when we have time."

"I think it's safe to say it's dry enough," she said

as they walked out of the house. She didn't know much about caring for a ranch or tending to roads, but she did notice the red sports car was coated with a thick layer of Wyoming dust.

His deep laughter sent heat racing through her veins and reminded her of the carefree man she'd met eight months ago. The man he'd been before she'd told him she couldn't be his wife after all. "It won't be an issue much longer," he stated. "The new owner is having it asphalted all the way to the county road."

"Why didn't the previous owner do that?" she asked, walking across the yard with him to the rental car.

"After her husband died, she wasn't interested in anything but trying to sell the ranch to a land developer. When she tried for a couple of years and failed to find a buyer, she finally sold it to one of her husband's sons from a previous marriage," he answered, sounding a little angry as he kneeled down to peer under the car.

She briefly wondered why he would be upset by a property dispute between the owner's heirs, but she abandoned her speculation when her cell phone chirped. Taking it out of her shoulder bag, Karly looked to see who was texting her. Her heart sank as she read the message. It was an alert from the airline, informing her that due to a contract-workers strike at the Denver airport, all flights had been canceled until further notice. Since the only commercial airline going in or out of the Cheyenne airfield was from Denver, she wasn't going anywhere until the labor dispute was settled.

"Lovely," she muttered sarcastically. Now what was she supposed to do?

She'd packed light because she hadn't expected to be away from home for more than a couple of nights. And she certainly hadn't planned on having to find a local place to stay indefinitely while the strike was settled.

"Looks like everything is intact," Blake said, unaware of her dilemma. He straightened to his full height as he dusted off his hands. "When does your flight leave?"

"It's not leaving," she said disgustedly as she opened the browser on her phone to see what lodging was available in the nearest town. "All flights in and out of Denver have been canceled due to an airport workers' strike."

He remained silent for several long moments and when she looked up, he was staring at her. "Looks like you'll be spending some time on the Wolf Creek Ranch after all," he said, folding his arms across his wide chest.

"No, I'll get a room in town," she said determinedly. It had been hard enough to see him again, to sit across the desk from him. She couldn't imagine spending the night in the same house with him, knowing he was so close and not being able to touch him or have him hold her.

He pointed toward the mountains to the west.

"Not tonight you won't. I can't, in good conscience, let you drive on unfamiliar mountain roads in the dark. Hell, it would be a miracle if you didn't get lost or end up hung in the top of a tree after missing a curve and going over the side of the mountain."

"You *can't allow* me to drive back in the dark?" she demanded indignantly. "I have news for you, buster. If I choose to go, you aren't going to stop me."

He closed his eyes and shook his head as if trying to gather his patience. When he opened them, he looked directly at her. "I realize we won't be married for much longer, but right now, I'm still your husband," he finally said. "I take my vows seriously. It's my job to keep you safe until a judge says otherwise. I'd feel a lot better if you would at least wait to make the drive until tomorrow morning. It's safer."

Karly was surprised by his grudging admission that he thought he should protect her. There hadn't been anyone who'd cared about her safety since her mother passed away several years ago. But as nice as it was to have someone worry about her well-being again, she needed to remember that Blake was only doing it because he felt it was his obligation. He'd signed the divorce papers. He must be as ready to undo their mistake as she was.

Sighing heavily, she tried to decide what to do. Everything about this trip had gone awry. Her flight from Denver to Cheyenne had been delayed for over two hours due to a dangerous storm front moving through, the drive to the ranch had taken three times as long as she had anticipated due to the car the rental agency had provided and her meeting with Blake hadn't gone as quickly as she'd thought it would. The way her luck had been running, it was very likely that she'd end up in one of the disastrous scenarios he mentioned.

"Eagle Fork is only twenty miles away," she said, glancing at the sun rapidly sinking behind the mountains to the west.

"It takes a little over an hour in the daylight to drive down the mountain to get there. How long do you think it would take you to get back at night?" Blake pointed toward the road. "Do you really want to drive on unfamiliar, rough mountain roads in the dark? At least stay tonight."

"If I take it slow, I shouldn't have a problem," she hedged. Sleeping in the same house with Blake—even if it was in different rooms—wasn't a good idea. He was six feet two inches of male temptation that had proved almost impossible for her to resist in the past. It had taken going all the way back to Seattle for her to realize the effect he'd had on her good sense. What crazy decisions would she make if she stayed here with him?

"And what happens if you have a deer or elk run across the road in front of you?" he persisted, oblivious to her inner battle. "I've got news for you, sweetheart. If you hit one of those in that little toy car, you're going to lose."

Karly stared at him as she weighed her options. Driving up through the mountains during the day with all the switchbacks and ninety-degree curves had been a challenge. And of course, there had been the last several miles to the ranch, which had become a dirt-and-gravel road pitted with more holes than a piece of Swiss cheese. But at night?

She hated to admit it, but her choices were extremely limited. Since she didn't know another soul in Wyoming, she either had to risk going down the mountain in the dark to find a motel room in Eagle Fork, or stay with Blake.

As she watched the evening shadows begin to overtake the high mountain valley, she decided she had run out of time. There simply wasn't enough daylight left to make it back to town before it got completely dark.

"I suppose I could spend the night here and then drive back down to Eagle Fork tomorrow to get a room for however long it takes the strike to be resolved," she said, talking more to herself than to Blake.

"Then it's settled," he said, walking to the back of the car. "I'll carry your luggage inside."

"I wasn't expecting to spend more than two nights away from home and only have an overnight case," she said, using the keyless remote to open the trunk as she walked over to take the small bag from him. "I can bring it inside."

He shook his head as he lifted it from the trunk.

"Grandma Jean would have my hide if she got wind of me letting you carry your luggage yourself."

"Does she live close by?" Karly had never known what it was like to be close to a grandparent. Three of hers had passed away before she was born and her paternal grandmother had lived so far away, she'd only seen her a handful of times.

"She lives down in Eagle Fork," he said as he placed his hand at the small of her back to guide her into the house. "There were several of us who lived with her during the winter when we were still in school."

"Because of all the snow?" she mused as they climbed the stairs to the second floor. If the roads were so difficult to navigate in the summer, she couldn't imagine trying to get around in a heavy snowfall.

"It was easier to stay down there where we could get to school than have to miss and make up all of the schoolwork when we were finally able to get back to class," he said, nodding as he stepped back so she could enter a bedroom. When he set her small suitcase on the bed, he hooked his thumb over his shoulder toward the door. "While you get settled, I have to drive over to the main house to see about a few things the owner needs me to take care of."

"Was that the huge log home I passed just before I got here?" she asked, unzipping the overnight case to remove her flip-flops. She loved wearing heels, but she had been in them all day and her feet were beginning to hurt.

Blake nodded. "The owner had that built a couple of years ago. Right after he bought the ranch."

"It's beautiful," she said, removing the heels to put on the flip-flops. "And it's perfect for the rugged surroundings."

He stared at her a moment before he turned and walked out into the hall. "I guess I'd better go on over to the main house. Make yourself at home. I won't be long."

As she heard him descend the stairs, she began to realize just how little she knew about the man she had married. In Las Vegas, Blake had literally swept her off her feet and charmed her into a fairy-tale week of romance, lovemaking and a wedding. But as idyllic as their time together had been, they hadn't talked about their families or jobs, their hopes or their dreams.

"It would have never worked between us," she murmured as she sat down on the side of the bed.

The realization was not a new one. So Karly had no idea why the words made her feel so sad. This was what she'd chosen—the way it had to be. She wasn't about to make the same mistakes her mother had made. She wasn't going to give up everything— her home, her lifestyle, her job—for a man and then resent him for her choices.

No matter how beautiful it was here or how cherished and safe Blake made her feel when he took her in his arms, she couldn't live on this ranch with him any more than he could live with her in Seattle. And the sooner she accepted that truth, the better off she would be.

Two

Blake glanced over at his backpack, the thermal food carrier and the jug of iced tea on the truck seat beside him as he drove away from the main ranch house. *His* house.

He had never lied to Karly, not eight months ago and not today.

But he hadn't been completely honest with her, either.

When they met in Las Vegas, he'd told her that besides competing in rodeo, he was the boss at the Wolf Creek Ranch in Wyoming. She had assumed that meant he was the foreman and he hadn't bothered to set her straight. For one thing, they'd been so hot for each other, they hadn't talked at length about their jobs or much of anything else. And for another, he didn't go around flaunting the fact that he owned the Wolf Creek or that he was a multimillionaire.

He had firsthand knowledge of how the lure of money could influence people and he intended to avoid that kind of shallowness at all costs. He didn't want the money to affect his relationships, and he'd been especially careful about what he'd shared with the woman he'd married so quickly. In the past, both he and his father had seen the ugly side of women hell-bent on getting their hands on a hefty bankroll and once had been enough to leave Blake more than a little cautious.

But he was fairly certain Karly had no knowledge about the size of his bank account. She had fallen for him—without the influence of his money. He had figured that when she joined him at the ranch it would be a nice surprise to let her know that they would never have financial worries like a lot of other couples starting out. Unfortunately, he hadn't had the chance to tell her the truth because she'd decided that living in a big city without him was preferable to living on the ranch with him. She'd made that decision without the influence of his money, too.

In hindsight, he wished he'd told her right after they got married in Vegas. He didn't want her thinking that he had been trying to hide his assets because of their pending divorce. That wasn't the case at all. And he had every intention of telling her the truth, as well as providing her with a nice settlement for the very brief time they'd been married. He just needed to figure out the right time and way to go about doing that.

He could have told her about his wealth when she called from Seattle to tell him she thought they'd made a mistake and that ending the marriage would be for the best. But he'd decided against that because she might have assumed it was a desperate attempt on his part to get her to reconsider their divorce, to give them a chance. Him begging for a second chance was something that would never happen. Even if his pride had allowed it, it probably wouldn't have made a difference. She'd had her mind made up and nothing he could have said would have changed it.

So he'd kept his secret and signed the papers. But he could have told her the truth today, too, when she'd mistakenly assumed the foreman's cottage was his house and that the main house and ranch belonged to someone else. But he'd held back without really knowing why.

All he knew was that his ego had taken enough of a hit eight months ago, when he'd learned that while she might have been the woman of his dreams, he obviously hadn't been the man of hers. And if he was perfectly honest with himself, there had probably been a little fear holding him back, as well. He hadn't wanted to tell her he was rich and end up finding out that he'd been wrong about her—that Karly could be swayed by the temptation of his money.

As he steered his truck up the lane leading to the foreman's cottage, he reached up to rub the tension building at the back of his neck. He wasn't sure how something that had originally felt so right had gone so wrong. When he'd married Karly after only knowing her a week, the decision had seemed as natural as taking his next breath. Their whirlwind wedding carried on the Hartwell family tradition. Blake's Grandma and Grandpa Hartwell had been married three days after meeting and his father and mother tied the knot two weeks after their first date. Both couples had successful marriages until death separated them and Blake had been sure it would be that way with himself and Karly. It was obvious now that he had been wrong.

Parking his truck beside the little red sports car, Blake took a deep breath and reached for his backpack, the thermal carrier full of food and the gallon thermos of iced tea he'd had his cook pack for their supper. There was no sense in trying to figure out how he could have misjudged Karly's commitment to their relationship. He had and there wasn't anything he could do about it now. Besides, he'd never been one to dwell on his mistakes.

As he walked toward the cottage, she opened the door and stepped out onto the porch. His breath caught and his heart thumped against his ribs. He felt the same pull that had drawn him to her the first time he'd laid eyes on her in Vegas. He forced himself to ignore the feeling. She might be the most exciting woman he'd ever known, but the sting of her rejection and her disdain for his lifestyle told him in no uncertain terms just how unimportant he was to her. She'd walked away from him once. He wouldn't give her another chance to do it again.

Distracted by his turbulent thoughts, it took him a moment to notice the frown on her pretty face. "Is something wrong?" he asked as he climbed the steps.

"Where do you keep your food?" she answered his question with one of her own as they entered the house. "I was going to make something for dinner, but the refrigerator and pantry are both empty. If you live here why isn't there anything in the house to eat?"

"I usually eat down at the bunkhouse with the single men or over at the main house," he said truthfully as he set the cooler and jug of iced tea on the kitchen island, then turned to hang his hat on a peg by the door. He did eat with his men at the bunkhouse occasionally, just not as often as he ate what his cook made for him in the main house.

She looked doubtful. "Even in the winter when you're snowed in?"

He couldn't help but laugh at her erroneous assumption. "Sweetheart, there's no such thing as getting snowed in around here. A ranch is a twenty-four-hours, seven-days-a-week operation. It never shuts down because the livestock are depending on us to take care of them. If it rains we get wet. If it snows we wade through it no matter how deep it gets or how cold it is."

"I hadn't thought of that." Looking a little sheepish, she shook her head. "I'll be the first to admit I don't know anything about ranching."

"Don't worry about it." He motioned toward the thermal carrier. "And don't worry about cooking. I had the cook over at the main house pack up what he made for supper. Why don't you set the table while I go wash up?"

He didn't mention that he'd had to endure an interrogation and a stern lecture before old Silas finished loading the carrier with containers of food. A retired cowboy turned cook after his arthritis prevented him from doing ranch work, Silas Burrows had some definite ideas on how Blake should conduct his life and he didn't mind sharing them every chance he got. Having a wife show up unexpectedly, one that Blake hadn't told Silas about, definitely got the old boy started. As sure as the grass was green, Blake knew he hadn't heard the end of what Silas had to say on the matter, either.

"I'll have dinner on the table by the time you return," she said as she started removing the food from the carrier to set it on the butcher-block island.

Blake watched her for a moment before he gritted his teeth and left the room. Karly had changed into a pair of khaki camp shorts and an oversize T-shirt while he was gone. She shouldn't have looked the least bit appealing. But he'd be damned if just seeing her in the baggy shorts, shapeless shirt and bright pink flip-flops didn't have him feeling as restless as a range-raised colt.

Disgusted with himself, he marched up the stairs and down the hall to the master bedroom. How could he want a woman who had rejected him? Who had rejected his way of life and the land he loved?

Setting his backpack on the cedar chest at the end of the bed, he walked into the adjoining bathroom to wash up. As he splashed cold water on his face to clear his head, he couldn't help but think about the irony of the situation.

When Karly called him a few days after they parted in Vegas to tell him that she had changed her mind about being his wife, she hadn't even been willing to discuss coming to Wyoming in order to see if they could save their brief marriage. Yet almost nine months later, here she was—in the very place she said she never wanted to see—with papers to end the union.

But as he dried his face and hands with one of the fluffy towels from the linen cabinet, he couldn't help but think there had to have been something that happened when she got back to Seattle that had caused her change of heart. But what could it have been? Was there someone else she hadn't told him about? Maybe an old flame or someone she had been seeing before they met?

He'd asked himself the same questions a hundred times—and just as often told himself to forget about solving the mystery. He had no way of knowing what went through her head. And no reason to ask once she'd been determined to end things between them.

But now that Karly was here, he had a golden opportunity that was just too damn good to pass up. All he had to do was convince her to stay at the ranch a few days, until the strike in Denver was settled. That would give him time to ask her what had happened, to find out what had changed her mind and why.

It might not be the smartest thing he'd ever wanted to do. And he knew that whatever he found out wouldn't change the state of their marriage; he'd already signed the papers and let her go. Hell, he'd probably be better off not knowing. And he certainly wasn't expecting anything about him or his ranch to change her mind, even if he did learn the answer.

But some perverse part of him felt that it was his right to know why she'd refused to even try to make a go of things with him.

With his mind made up, Blake went back downstairs to the kitchen to help Karly set the table. "I've been thinking. It doesn't make any sense for you to spend money on a motel room when you can stay here for free," he pointed out as he got two glasses down from one of the cabinets.

"I can't do that," she said, looking at him like he had sprouted another head.

"Why not?" he asked, pouring them each a glass of iced tea from the thermal jug.

"I don't want to impose," she said, placing a container of country-fried steaks on the table.

"How would you staying here be an imposition?" He carried the glasses to the table, then held her chair for her to sit down. "We're still married and the last time I heard, a husband and wife staying in the same house isn't all that unusual," he added, laughing.

"We're not going to be married that much longer," she insisted. "We're practically divorced already."

"It doesn't matter." He shrugged as he seated himself at the head of the table and reached for the container of steaks. "You're still my wife and that gives you the right to stay here."

"We really don't know each other," she said, taking a bite of a seasoned potato wedge.

"That didn't seem to be a deal breaker when you said 'I do,'" he pointed out, before he could stop himself. He felt like a prize ass when he saw the wounded expression on her pretty face.

She stared at him for several long moments before she shook her head. "I think it would be best if I get that motel room tomorrow as planned."

"Look, I'm sorry about what I just said." He took a deep breath. "That was out of line."

She stared at him for a moment longer before she shook her head again. "Not entirely. We were both—" she paused, as if searching for the right words "—caught up in the moment in Las Vegas. And I don't think one of us was more at fault than the other."

Maybe she had been caught up in the moment, but he had known exactly what he was doing and the commitment he was making when he vowed to take care of her for the rest of their lives. But arguing that point wasn't going to accomplish what he had set out to do.

"That's all water under the bridge now," he said, shrugging. "But if you stay here, I'm sure you'll be more comfortable than in a motel room. And you won't have to drive the mountain roads more than once to get back to the airport."

She gave him a suspicious look. "Why are you being so persistent about this, Blake?"

"I figure it will save you a few hundred bucks or so," he said, thinking quickly. She obviously had to watch her finances. Otherwise, she wouldn't have mentioned that by filing the divorce herself instead of having a lawyer do it for her she was saving money. But he wasn't going to point out that he knew she was on a tight budget. She had her pride, the same as he did, and bringing up the state of her financial situation would probably send her back down the mountain as fast as that little red car could take her. "Besides, staying here beats sitting in a motel room for several days with nothing to do but stare at the four walls."

He almost groaned aloud when she nibbled on her lower lip as she mulled over what he'd said. She wasn't trying to be seductive, but it seemed like everything about her had his libido working overtime.

Maybe it was due to the memories of making love to her that haunted his dreams at night. Or, more likely, it was the fact that he hadn't been with a woman since they'd parted ways in Las Vegas. Whatever the reason behind his overactive hormones, he had every intention of ignoring them.

"I suppose not having anything to do would be pretty boring," she finally conceded. "But I wouldn't have anything to do here, either."

"Sure you would," he said, careful not to sound too eager. "There's never a lack of things to do around a ranch. You could help me feed the horses and a couple of orphaned calves. And tomorrow afternoon, you can ride up to the summer pasture with me to check on a herd of steers we'll be moving back down here in a couple of weeks."

"You mean ride a horse?" When he nodded, she vigorously shook her head. "That's not an option."

"Why?"

"Other than a pony ride at the grand opening of a grocery store when I was five, I've never been on a horse," she said, taking a sip of her iced tea.

That explained her skittish reaction to Boomer when she'd first arrived. "Don't worry about it. I've got the perfect horse for you and it won't take any time to teach you how to ride her."

"I don't think that would be a good idea," she commented, reaching for a roll. "Horses don't like me."

"Why do you say that?" he asked. "You just admitted that you've never really been around horses. How would you know if they like you or not?"

She frowned. "Your horse snorted and stomped his foot at me this afternoon. If that wasn't an indication he didn't like me, I don't know what is."

"Hoof," he countered, correcting her. "Horses have hooves and he was just shooing away a fly when he moved his leg." Blake took a bite of his steak. "And for the record, Boomer didn't snort. Gently blowing through his nose like that is a horse's way of sighing. It signals that he's relaxed, curious or in some cases just saying hello. Boomer was just being friendly."

"His name doesn't exactly instill a lot of confidence," she said, shaking her head. "Boomer sounds rather...explosive."

Blake laughed out loud at her inaccurate assumption that the gentle gelding's name reflected his temperament. "Boomer is short for Boomerang and the reason he got that name is because he likes people so much he can't stay away from them. I can turn him out into a pasture with other horses and before I know it, he turns around and comes right back to me."

"That's great, but it doesn't mean he likes *me*," she said, looking doubtful.

Blake grinned. "I'll introduce you tomorrow morning when we go out to the barn to take care of the calves. You'll see. He's as gentle as a lapdog."

She looked skeptical, but didn't comment until

they had finished their meal. "I can help you feed
the babies, but I'm afraid riding a horse tomorrow is
out of the question. I didn't expect to be away from
home more than a couple of nights and I really don't
have anything to wear that would be suitable for a
horseback ride."

He smiled at the relief he heard in her soft voice.
He'd bet every dime he had that she'd spent the entire meal trying to think of a way to get out of riding.

"We'll remedy that tomorrow morning after I get
the feeding done," he said, smiling as he helped her
clear the table. "We'll make a trip down to Eagle
Fork's Western store and get everything you need."

"That sounds like a lot of time and trouble for a
pair of jeans," she said as she put containers of left-
overs into the refrigerator. "And besides, I don't want
to interfere with the work you need to get done."

"It won't be any trouble at all," Blake said, barely
able to keep from laughing at her attempts to escape his plans. He was not only determined to find
out what she wasn't telling him, he was also going
to give her a ranch experience she'd never forget. "I
need to get a new shirt for a Labor Day barbecue on
Monday anyway and you'll need something to wear
to that as well. In fact, it would probably be a good
idea to get you enough clothes for a few days since
there's no telling how long the strike will last."

"I can't crash your friend's party," she said as she
turned to wipe off the kitchen island.

"You won't be crashing the party." Blake wasn't

about to take no for an answer. "You'll go as my date."

"That would be rather awkward," she insisted.

"Only if you make it that way," he said, even though he knew she was right.

"How on earth would you even introduce me?" She gave him a pointed look. "We may be married right now, but we're little more than strangers on the way to a divorce. We wouldn't even be married if the papers had arrived as they should have. I'd just as soon avoid a lot of questions about our hasty marriage and the upcoming divorce."

"Easy. I'll just tell them that we met in Vegas and you came for a visit," Blake explained.

She stared at him before she frowned. "Do you really think it will take that long for the strike to be settled?"

He shrugged. "It's a holiday weekend. There's really no telling. Even if they come to an agreement over the weekend it's going to take at least a day or two for the airlines to get all of the schedules lined up and the passengers from the canceled flights who haven't found other means of transportation on their way again. And with Labor Day on Monday that's going to delay things even more."

"I suppose I could drive from here to Lincoln County," Karly said, looking thoughtful.

"I know you want to get this divorce over with, but do you really want to drive fifteen or sixteen hours in holiday traffic?" he asked. "You couldn't possibly get there tomorrow before the courthouse closes and it won't reopen again until Tuesday. By that time the strike might be settled and you'd be able to fly."

She didn't look happy about what he was saying, but she finally nodded. "You're probably right."

"I know I am." When she yawned, he pointed toward the hall. "I can finish cleaning the kitchen. Why don't you go ahead and turn in for the night? Mornings around here start early."

"How early are we talking about?" she asked, hiding another yawn with her delicate hand.

"I'll start feeding the livestock in the barns around dawn," he said as he loaded the dishwasher. "That will take about an hour. Since you don't really have suitable clothes for that yet, I'll wake you up after I get finished."

She looked horrified. "Good Lord, are the animals even awake at that time of day?"

"They're not only awake, they're usually making a lot of noise because they know it's time for breakfast," he said, laughing.

When she yawned again, she started toward the hall. "In that case, I think I'll follow your advice and go to bed." She stopped at the door and turned back. "Thank you, Blake."

"What for?" he asked, walking over to her.

"For giving me a place to stay until the strike is settled and for being so nice about all of this," she said quietly. "You really didn't have to be, considering how badly I handled filing for the divorce."

He barely resisted the urge to reach for her. As he stuffed his hands into the front pockets of his jeans to keep himself from doing something stupid like taking her in his arms and kissing her until they both gasped for air, he shook his head. "Don't be so hard on yourself. You had no control over what happened after you put the papers in the mail. And like I told you earlier, I'm old-fashioned. As long as we're married it's my job to provide you with a roof over your head and something to eat."

She stared at him for several long moments before she finally nodded. "Well, thank you anyway. Good night."

"Yeah, see you in the morning," he mumbled as he watched her walk down the hall to the stairs.

Taking a deep breath, he waited until he heard her close the door to her bedroom before he started the dishwasher and turned out the kitchen light. As he slowly climbed the stairs to his own guest room, he couldn't help but wonder how everything had become so damn complicated. Eight months ago, things had been simple. He'd found the woman he was going to spend the rest of his life with and she'd told him that he was the man she wanted to share hers with, too.

He had no idea what had changed from the time they left Vegas until she called him a few days later from Seattle to tell him she wasn't joining him at the ranch as planned. But one thing was sure—before she left this ranch to file for divorce and return to her life in the city, he had every intention of getting an explanation and settling the matter once and for all.

The following morning, as Karly sat on the passenger side of Blake's truck, she looked out over the side of the mountain. On her drive up the winding road the day before, she'd been so focused on getting Blake to sign the new set of divorce papers and returning to Cheyenne to make her connecting flight back to Denver that she hadn't taken the time to notice the scenery. Although the mountains surrounding Seattle were more lush—with tall, straight conifers, beds of ferns and thick moss carpeting the forest floor—the ruggedness of the Wyoming landscape was no less beautiful. The pine and aspen trees didn't seem to grow as thick as the forests of the Northwest, but the jagged, snow-capped peaks and vast valleys of thick prairie grass, with colorful late-summer wildflowers, were utterly breathtaking.

"It's really beautiful here," she murmured aloud.

"Imagine that." Grinning as he steered the truck around a tight switchback, Blake added, "It's amazing how different things turn out to be from our preconceived notions, isn't it?"

When she'd called to tell him she'd changed her mind about the marriage, she'd said some things about the land he so obviously loved that she deeply regretted. In hindsight, she'd been trying to convince herself that living in a remote area of Wyoming was unsuitable for her. She'd been trying to create enough distance between them to make divorce the best option. But that didn't change the fact that he'd taken offense at her comments. She'd hurt him unintentionally.

"I guess I might have been a bit hasty in my assumption that the area had nothing to offer," she finally admitted. "But you have to understand. I've lived most of my life in a city, where everything I want or need is close by."

"I understand that," he said, nodding. "But it's not the backwoods, off-the-grid type of living you envisioned, is it?"

"No," she admitted. "But you helped to create that misconception."

"How do you figure that?" he asked, frowning.

"You said the ranch was in a remote location and I naturally assumed…" She paused when she realized that with the closest neighbors at least ten miles away at the bottom of the mountain and only one way to get to the ranch, it really could be considered isolated. "I guess I thought that you meant it was without some of the modern conveniences."

"Tell the truth," he said, laughing. "You thought that a trip to the bathroom in the middle of the night would involve a flashlight and a little shed with a half-moon carved into the door."

She laughed. "Well, not quite. But I didn't expect it to have a main ranch house that looks like a log mansion, or the house you live in to have such a cozy feel to it. I guess I was thinking it would be more rustic."

"You've been watching too many old Westerns on television," he said, steering the truck onto the main road as they reached the bottom of the mountain. "Living on a ranch is like living anywhere else. We have modern appliances, satellite TV and high-speed internet. About the only difference is having to drive a few miles to get to a store instead of it being just down the street."

"Maybe I have been thinking it would be like the Old West," she admitted thoughtfully.

They fell silent for the rest of the drive and by the time they reached downtown Eagle Fork, Karly had come to a conclusion that she wasn't overly proud of. She wasn't going to tell Blake, but it wouldn't have mattered if the ranch was rustic and isolated or sat right in the middle of a town. Her choice to divorce him would have been the same. It wasn't the challenges of living on a ranch that had held her back. It had been the fear she would turn out to be like her mother and discover that a husband and family weren't enough for her—that her career was more important.

A few minutes later, when Blake parked his truck in front of the Blue Sage Western Emporium, Karly noticed that the store looked as if it had been in business since hitching posts were used instead of parking meters. Abandoning her disturbing thoughts, she focused on their shopping trip. She hoped the clothing wasn't going to be too expensive. She wasn't poor, but she did live on a budget and hadn't planned on buying clothes that she probably wouldn't wear past the few days she was stranded at the Wolf Creek Ranch.

Blake grinned as he opened the passenger door to help her out of the truck. "Are you ready to get your cowgirl on?"

"Whether I'm ready or not, it looks like I'm going to," she said, feeling breathless.

She was in real trouble if his smile alone was enough to take her breath away. But it was the feel of his hand pressed to the small of her back as he guided her into the store that caused her knees to wobble.

Stepping away from him, she took a deep breath and the rich scent of leather assailed her senses. It reminded her of the man at her side and sent a shiver of longing straight through her. It would definitely be in her best interest to forego the shopping and make plans to drive to Lincoln County.

But even as she thought it, she knew that probably wasn't going to happen.

"Pick out as many pairs as you think you'll need," he said, ushering her over to a wall with large cubbyholes filled with folded pairs of women's jeans. He pointed to a couple of racks holding T-shirts and blouses. "And don't forget to get some shirts and something special to wear to the barbecue."

Before she could tell him that she wouldn't be needing clothes because she was going to leave the next morning to drive back to Washington State, a middle-age woman walked over to them. "It's good to see you, Blake," she said, smiling. She shot a curious glance toward Karly, as if wondering who she was. "How are things going at the Wolf Creek?"

"I can't complain, Mary Ann," he answered. "The hay crop was good this year and we should have more than enough to make it through the winter."

"That's always a relief," she said, nodding. "Eli Laughlin was in the other day and said pretty much the same thing about the Rusty Spur."

While Blake and the woman discussed what was going on at some of the other ranches in the area, Karly gave up on the idea of driving back to file the divorce papers. For one thing, she wasn't all that fond of spending so many hours in the car. And for another, sitting in a hotel room for a couple of days with nothing to do while she waited for the courthouse to open wasn't her idea of a good time, either.

Just as Blake had said, she'd be better off waiting here and looking for a way home after the holiday weekend. Most likely the strike would be done, and the courthouse would definitely be open. She didn't want to consider why the decision to stay here, with Blake, made her feel so warm inside.

By the time she found jeans and a few shirts that weren't too pricey, Blake joined her. "Are you ready to try on boots?"

"I hadn't even thought about footwear," she said, wondering how long it would take for her budget to recover from all of her unplanned purchases. She glanced down at her feet. "I know I can't wear these heels and I don't suppose flip-flops are suitable for helping you feed the orphaned calves, are they?"

He shook his head as he led her toward the back of the store, where boxes of boots were stacked on shelves from the floor all the way to the ceiling. "Not unless you want to risk a nasty cut or broken toes when one of them steps on your foot."

"Not hardly," she said, deciding that a financial headache was preferable to physical pain. Since she'd decided to stay the long weekend at Blake's ranch, she supposed she had to go all in and as he so eloquently put it, "get her cowgirl on."

A half hour later as she and Blake walked out of the store, Karly frowned at all the bags and boxes he carried. She knew she couldn't really afford all the things she'd bought, but she hadn't expected Blake to pay for her shopping spree. This was probably another obligation for him, because he was her husband. And the only reason she'd said yes was because her bank account wouldn't let her reject his kind offer. But she seemed to be getting deeper into the role of a wife even though the whole point of this trip had been to finalize their divorce.

"You should have let me pay for all of this," Karly said. If he had, she would have definitely gone with fewer and more economical selections. "I doubt the owner of the ranch will be all that happy about you putting my clothes on his charge account."

"Don't worry about it. He doesn't mind me charging things on the ranch account. And, like I said, you're my wife. If you lived with me, you'd be charging things all the time." Grinning, he shrugged as he put the purchases onto the backseat of the club cab truck. "It's one of the perks of being the boss."

"There's a difference between charging one or two items and loading up the account." She pointed to the two boxes he added to the pile. "That hat was outrageously expensive and those boots alone cost more than I've ever paid for a pair of shoes in my entire life."

"A good hat and a comfortable pair of boots are worth whatever price you have to pay for them," he stated as he helped her up into the passenger seat.

"But I won't be here that long," she argued, trying to make him understand. "Something cheaper would have served the purpose just as well."

She'd tried to tell him when he insisted she put them on that they were far too expensive. But when he gently wrapped his hand around her calf as he took her high heel off to put one of the boots on, her brain had short-circuited. Somewhere between her vocal cords and opened mouth her objection had turn into a gasp of awareness. His smile and the twinkle in his sexy brown eyes indicated that he'd noticed, but he didn't comment as he worked the boot onto her foot and she couldn't get her voice to work long enough to protest further.

He closed the door, walked around the front of the

truck and got in behind the steering wheel. "Let's get something straight. As long as you're at the ranch and we're still married, I provide for you. That includes the clothes and hat you'll wear and the boots on your feet. There are some things that I won't skimp on, no matter how expensive they are, because in most cases, you get what you pay for. Hats and boots are two of those things." He surprised her when he reached over to cover her hand with his. "And don't worry about me charging all of this on the ranch account. When the bill comes in, I'll pay for it."

The feel of his calloused palm on her skin and the memory of how his hands had felt on her body when they made love sent a shiver of longing straight up her spine. She tried her best to dismiss the reaction as nothing more than nerves. But as they continued to stare at each other, she knew it was going to take everything in her to keep from falling under his charming spell again.

She quickly slid her hand from beneath his and concentrated on what he'd said. "Blake, I appreciate that you feel it's your responsibility to see that I have what I need," she said, choosing her words carefully. "But I don't feel right about you buying a whole wardrobe for me."

He gave her a cursory glance as he started the truck and steered it out of the parking lot onto the street. "Why not?"

"If I had handled the divorce differently, you wouldn't be in the awkward position of giving me a place to stay or feeling obligated to buy things for me," she said, feeling guilty. For that matter, if she hadn't been so impulsive and made promises she hadn't been able to keep when they were in Las Vegas, neither of them would have found themselves in their current situation.

"Don't beat yourself up over this," he said, surprising her. "You did what you thought was best and it didn't turn out the way you planned." He stared straight ahead as he added, "It happens to the best of us."

Her guilt increased when she realized he was talking about his own plans for them to live together as husband and wife. He had every right to be bitter about how she'd ended things, but instead he was treating her like the wife she'd never been to him. Suddenly, she was wishing things could have worked out differently—but she quickly squashed that traitorous thought. "I suppose you're right," she murmured.

They fell silent for several minutes as Blake drove out of town toward the ranch. "Why don't we start over?" he suggested, breaking the silence.

She frowned. "What do you mean?"

"There's no sense wasting time pointing fingers or feeling guilty about what went wrong between us," he said pragmatically. "We've both signed the papers already. So why don't we forget the real reason for your trip to the ranch and look at this holiday weekend as a friendly visit? I'll show you what ranch life is all about." He laughed. "And you can look on your time here as one of those vacations people take just to play cowboy."

Her chest tightened at his offer, at the consideration he was showing her. They both knew she was to blame for the entire fiasco and that he had been terribly disappointed with her decisions. But he was willing to put aside any hard feelings in order for her stay at the Wolf Creek Ranch to be more pleasant. If she hadn't been so afraid that quitting her job and moving so far away from the city would turn her into her mother, she would have loved having this man for her husband.

"Thank you, Blake," she said, blinking back tears. "I think I'd like that."

"Then it's settled." His grin caused her pulse to flutter. "Let's get back to the ranch so we can get started on giving you the ranching experience of your life."

Three

The lingering shadows of night were just giving way to the misty light of dawn when Karly followed Blake out of the house and across the ranch yard toward one of the barns. Wearing a new pair of jeans, a hot pink T-shirt, her hat and a flannel-lined denim jacket he had insisted on buying her the day before, she stepped around puddles left by the thunderstorm that had popped up yesterday afternoon to keep from getting her expensive new boots wet.

The rain had prevented her and Blake from riding up to check on the herd of cattle in the upper pasture when they returned from the store and that had been just fine with Karly. It had given her a day's reprieve from having to learn to ride a horse.

It was probably too much to hope for that it would rain again today.

"How long does it take to feed the animals?" she asked when they entered the barn.

"It takes longer right now than it usually does because of the bucket babies," Blake answered, opening the door to a room filled with large sacks of grain and assorted sizes of buckets. "But we're usually finished in about an hour."

She assumed the bucket babies he was talking about were the orphaned calves. When he set two pails with large nipples protruding from the bottom edge on a small table outside of the door, she understood why he called them bucket babies.

"Why don't you use big bottles?" she asked. "Wouldn't that be easier?"

He laughed. "Two reasons. One, we'd be stopping to refill the bottle every few minutes. And two, calves tend to be extremely enthusiastic when they eat. Holding a bucket can be hard enough when they get going. But holding a bottle would be damn near impossible."

"How old are they?" she asked, when he started scooping cream-colored powder into each bucket. "If they're still on baby formula, they must be quite young."

"They're almost four weeks old," he said, adding premeasured jugs of distilled water to the buckets. He handed her a smooth wooden paddle. "If you'll stir the formula, I'll measure up the grain starter."

"They're already eating solids?" she asked, frowning. "Aren't they a little young for that?"

He laughed. "You know what they say. Kids grow up real fast these days."

She rolled her eyes. "Will you be serious? It was a legitimate question."

"Sorry," he said, continuing to chuckle.

"No, you're not." She couldn't help but laugh with him.

"Not really. I just couldn't resist." As he shook his head, his charming grin sent goose bumps shimmering over her skin. "Calves usually start nibbling on grass out in the field when they're a day or two old. But that's when they have their mamas with them and are able to nurse whenever they want. Because these calves are orphaned and have to be fed on a schedule, we start them on a little bit of hay a few days after they're born and grain starter about a week after that. When they're up to eating about a pound or two of grain a day we start weaning them away from the milk replacer. That's when they are about six to eight weeks old."

"They really do grow up fast," she said, marveling at how quickly the animal babies progressed.

While she stirred the calf formula, he went back into the feed room and began scooping grain into shallow pails. Glancing through the doorway to watch him, Karly decided that Blake Hartwell was without a doubt the most handsome, charismatic man she'd ever met. She was going to have to be extremely careful not to fall for him all over again.

That thought should have sent her speeding down the mountain as fast as the red sports car she'd rented could take her. But she had told him she would stay until the strike was settled and she'd already broken enough of her promises to him. She wasn't going to add another, especially after he'd been so nice about everything that had happened between them.

When he rejoined her in the wide barn aisle, he handed her the lighter pails with small amounts of grain starter in them and picked up the heavier buckets with the formula she had finished mixing. "Are you ready for your first lesson in the fine art of feeding calves?"

She nodded. "I guess I'm as ready as I'll ever be."

Other than the pony she'd ridden at the grocery store grand opening when she was in kindergarten, she'd never been around an animal larger than a cat or a dog and she was definitely feeling a little intimidated. Did calves have a tendency to bite? She didn't remember hearing of anyone suffering a cow bite. But that didn't mean anything. She knew absolutely nothing about livestock. And other than Blake, she didn't know anyone else who did.

That was another reason that she'd gotten cold feet about their marriage. She'd not only feared quitting her job and finding herself feeling as displaced and resentful as her mother, she would have also been living on this ranch with animals large enough to squash her like a bug.

The first time she'd ever seen those animals in action had been in Las Vegas when she met Blake and he'd invited her to watch him ride in the rodeo events. After returning to Seattle and remembering what the huge animals were capable of doing and the injuries their actions caused, she'd known for certain that ranch life wasn't for her. Yet, here she was doing the very thing that she'd feared—interacting with the beasts.

But when they reached the stall where the calves were, Karly couldn't help but smile. The two bucket babies immediately started bawling and pushing at the gate as she and Blake approached, as if they knew their breakfast had arrived.

"They're so cute!" she said, looking over the top board at the black calves. They seemed too little to do much damage. "Do they bite?"

Blake laughed as he set the two buckets of milk on a bale of hay outside of the stall, then took the pails of grain starter from her. "Cattle would have to have upper front teeth before they could do that."

"They don't have teeth?" she asked, doubtfully. She thought most all animals needed teeth to eat.

He shook his head. "They only have bottom incisors and a tough, thickly padded top gum, so it's highly unlikely that one could bite you and cause an injury. And even if they tried it, which they aren't prone to do, it would be more of a pinch than a bite."

"That's good to know," she said when he opened the stall door.

"I'll take care of feeding them the grain starter and then we'll give them the milk together," he said, entering the enclosure.

He was immediately accosted by the calves and she was amazed at how quickly the pair finished off the grain in the pails Blake held. "You were right about them being enthusiastic eaters," she said, laughing. They reminded her of two rather large, clumsy puppies.

When he walked out of the stall to get the buckets of calf formula, he chuckled. "Just wait until they see these. They'll be like sharks in a feeding frenzy."

Karly opened the door to the stall for him and cautiously followed him inside. The calves nudged up against her as they looked for the buckets Blake held. One of them even took two of her fingers in its mouth and started sucking.

"Oh, my." The calf hadn't hurt her and she laughed as she pulled back her hand. "They really are in a feeding frenzy."

Grinning, he nodded. "Just wait."

He showed her how to hold the bucket and she immediately understood what he meant. The calf she was feeding started butting its mouth against the bucket as it sucked on the nipple.

"Why is it doing that?" she asked, frowning.

"It's instinctive," he explained. "Out in the pasture, calves butt their mother's udder to help bring down the milk."

The calves had the buckets drained in no time and Karly couldn't help but wonder if they had to be on a four-hour schedule like human babies. "When will they need to eat again?"

"One of the other guys will feed them again in about twelve hours." He put a couple of flakes of hay in the stall, then washed the buckets and put them into plastic bags. When he finished, he smiled. "So what do you think of your first ranch experience?"

"I can't believe I'm going to say this, but I actually liked taking care of the orphaned calves," she admitted as they walked out of the barn. "They were so cute and when they looked up at me with those big brown eyes, I couldn't help but fall in love with them."

"If I remember correctly, you said something similar to me when we were in Las Vegas," he said, his voice low and intimate.

Karly swallowed hard as she gazed up at him. When they'd met, she had told him how much she loved his eyes. Gazing into the fathomless depths now, she found it hard to look away. Just as in Las Vegas, she felt as if she saw her future in the sexy warmth of his dark brown eyes and it took monumental effort to look away.

Blinking to break the spell, she gave herself a mental shake. That way of thinking was the exact reason she found herself in her current predicament and why she was facing the dissolution of their brief marriage instead of just ending a whirlwind affair.

Forcing herself to remember all the reasons why she had to stand firm in her decisions, she took a deep fortifying breath and attempted to change the subject. "Will my next ranch experience be breakfast?"

He stared at her for several long moments before he pointed toward the foreman's cottage. "While you go inside and wash up, I'll walk over to the bunkhouse and get something for us from the cook." Without another word, he turned and walked toward a building on the other side of the barn.

As she watched him go, Karly knew she should leave the ranch as soon as she could load the car. But she also knew she wasn't going to do that. For reasons she didn't want to think about, she felt compelled to stay with Blake until the strike was settled. Maybe it was due to the fact that she really didn't relish the idea of driving such a long distance. But more likely, it was the fact that every time she looked into his warm brown eyes she lost every ounce of sense she possessed.

Turning, she slowly walked to the house. Staying with him wasn't smart and she anticipated more than a few awkward moments over the course of the next several days. But with few other options open to her and a budget that couldn't really withstand a long stay in a hotel, she really didn't have much choice.

Now all she had to do was be strong and resist

falling under his spell again. Unfortunately, that might prove to be a monumental challenge, considering that it only took a look from him for her to feel as if she would melt.

When Blake finished saddling the gentle buckskin mare, he glanced over at Karly, who was sitting on a bale of hay by the tack-room door. She looked about as nervous as a long-tailed cat in a room full of rocking chairs. All through breakfast, she had questioned him about riding a horse. She'd wanted to know what would happen in a number of situations—all of which were highly unlikely.

She'd looked so darned cute as she interrogated him about riding that it had been all he could do to keep his hands to himself. But as much as he'd like to take her in his arms and reacquaint himself with his wife's sweet taste, he resisted the temptation. Papers had been signed and it was just a matter of time before she went her way and he went his.

Besides, giving into his need for Karly wasn't going to get him any closer to finding out what had changed her mind about them. That's why he was going to do his best to ignore the fact that she still turned him on like no other woman ever had and concentrate on showing her the beauty of his ranch and the wonderful life they could have shared. In the bargain, he hoped to learn more about the woman he'd married and would soon let go.

"Karly, this is Suede," he said, forcing himself to

smile as he led the mare over to where she sat. "She'll be your horse for as long as you're here at the ranch."

"She's awfully tall," Karly said, slowly rising to her feet. He noticed she was careful to keep him between herself and the gentle mare.

Trying not to laugh, he handed Karly the reins. "While you two get acquainted, I'm going to saddle Boomer."

"You're going to leave me alone with her?" she asked, sounding alarmed.

"Trust me, Karly," he said, trying to make his tone as reassuring as possible. "If I thought there was even the slightest chance you would get hurt, I wouldn't let you get anywhere near this horse." Before he could stop himself, he reached out to cup her cheek with his palm. "I promise you'll be just fine, sweetheart."

As she continued to stare up at him, he felt the ever so slight sway of her body toward his. That was all it took to send his good intentions right out the window and before he could stop himself, he leaned forward to cover Karly's mouth with his. Soft and every bit as perfect as he remembered, her lips molded to his and when her mouth parted on a soft sigh, Blake's heart took off like a racehorse out of the starting gate. He couldn't have stopped himself from deepening the kiss if his life depended on it.

Tracing her lips with his tongue, he slipped inside to reacquaint himself with her silky inner recesses. Every one of his senses sharpened and his lower body came to full arousal faster than he thought was humanly possible. Her taste and the tiny moan that she couldn't quite stifle caused him to groan with frustration. They were in a barn holding a horse by the reins. Not exactly the ideal situation to start something he knew damn well he wouldn't finish anyway.

When he felt himself fighting the urge to pull her into his arms and kiss her until they were both utterly senseless, he dropped his hand and took a step back. "You trust me, don't you?"

Apparently as stunned by the intimate moment as he had been and just as reluctant to comment on that kiss, she stared at him for several long moments before she finally nodded. "Y-yes. But if you're wrong about me and this horse, I swear I'll come back and haunt you."

He laughed out loud as much to relieve the tension gripping him as at the humor of her threat. Her quick wit was one of the things that he'd found so damn attractive about her. And he took her humor now as a good sign; she was becoming more relaxed with him again.

"If you want to score points with Suede, scratch her forehead and talk to her," he said as he turned to go get Boomer out of his stall. When he returned, he was glad to see Karly had graduated to patting the mare's neck.

"I think we've come to an understanding," Karly announced as Blake saddled the gelding. "I'm not going to upset her."

When she paused, he smiled. "It sounds to me like you've worked things out."

Nodding, she added, "We're both going to blame you if I do make the mistake of doing something she finds offensive."

"Now, why doesn't that surprise me?" he asked, grinning as he led Boomer over to where she and the mare stood.

"Probably because you're the one insisting that I have to ride a horse," Karly retorted as he handed the gelding's reins for her to hold as well as the mare's.

"Wh-what are…you doing?" she asked, her voice filled with panic once again.

"Don't worry, Boomer is just as well behaved as Suede," he called over his shoulder as he entered the tack room to get a rifle. They didn't have a lot of trouble with predators, but it was always wise to take protection along on a ride just in case.

"Just remember—"

"I know," he interrupted, returning to where she and the horses stood. "If something happens it's all my fault and you're going to haunt me for the rest of my days." He couldn't help but chuckle as he slid the rifle into the tooled leather scabbard attached to Boomer's saddle, then took the reins from her to lead the horses out of the barn to the round pen. "I guess it's fortunate for all concerned that I'm a damn good teacher."

"It's nice that you're humble about it, as well," she said, grinning.

Tying Boomer's reins to the top rail of the round pen, Blake turned to face Karly. "No brag, sweetheart. It's just a fact." He nodded toward the mare. "Now let's get you up in the saddle so you can start learning how to ride."

Her apprehension was apparent when she put her boot in the stirrup. But her expression changed to relief when she shook her head and lowered her foot to the ground. "This isn't going to work."

"Why not?" he asked, wondering what excuse she was going to come up with this time.

"I can't possibly climb up into the saddle with my knee under my chin," she said, shaking her head. "I guess you'll have to ride up to the pasture alone."

"That's an easy fix," he said, moving to stand behind her. "While you pull yourself up by the saddle horn, I'll give you a boost."

The offer had been an innocent one, but when he placed his hand on her delightful bottom to help lift her, he felt like the world came to a screeching halt. The feel of her body nestled in his palm sent his hormones racing through his veins like the steel bearings in a pinball machine.

He quickly helped her up into the saddle, stepped back and took a deep breath. Had he lost what little sense he had left? He wasn't looking for anything more to come from her visit to the ranch than finding out what had changed in the few days after they parted in Las Vegas. He was still recovering from his first heartbreak. No way did he want to start something new with Karly. So, considering the effect she still had on him, he'd do well to keep any kind of physical contact between them to a minimum.

If he hadn't known that before, he sure as hell did after that kiss and that touch.

"Dear Lord, I'm a lot farther off the ground than I thought I'd be," Karly said, her voice a little shaky.

"A little taller than that pony at the grocery store opening?" Blake asked, thankful for the distraction from his wayward thoughts.

"That would be like comparing a two-story house to the Seattle Space Needle," she retorted.

He chuckled and handed her the reins, then, taking hold of the mare's bridle, he led the gentle animal through the round pen's gate. "Just relax and move with her," he instructed as he stroked the horse's tawny neck. He showed Karly how to rest her boots in the stirrups with the heels down and the toes pointed slightly outward. "And when you feel comfortable enough, loosen the death grip you have on the saddle horn."

She shook her head doubtfully. "That's easy for you to say. You have both feet firmly on the ground. You're not the one sitting up here looking down at how far you're going to fall."

Blake grinned as he started leading Suede around the perimeter of the round pen. "Do you honestly think I'd let you fall and not catch you?"

Karly nibbled on her lower lip, causing him to bite back a groan. "I believe you would try. But what if you couldn't react fast enough? Or I was too heavy for you to hold on to?"

He frowned as he glanced up at her. "Did you see anything slow about my reflexes when you watched me ride bulls in Vegas?"

"Well, no...but—"

"Then why do you think I'd miss doing something as important as catching you if you fell?" he asked. "And for the record, I've been tossing around bales of hay that weigh more than you do every day since I was fourteen or fifteen years old. The day you're too heavy for me to catch is the day they bury me."

"But what if—"

"You can't let all of the what-ifs in life hold you back, Karly," he interrupted. He let go of the mare's bridle and continued to walk beside her as they made another trip around the inside of the round pen. "If you don't take a chance once in a while, you're just marking time. You're not living."

It was something his grandfather had always told him and Blake firmly believed it was true. It was one of the reasons he'd been so quick to ask Karly to marry him. He'd known what he wanted and he'd made her his. It was also the reason behind him asking her to stay at the ranch while he tried to find out why she'd been hell-bent on divorcing him. He might not like what was behind her abrupt decision, but at least he'd know for sure why she'd decided he wasn't the one for her.

Karly stared at him for several long moments. They both knew he was talking about more than her riding a horse. But she didn't seem willing to talk about it and he wasn't going to press her on the issue just yet.

Smiling, she finally shrugged. "If I didn't step out of my comfort zone once in a while, I wouldn't be on this horse now, would I?"

"And you're doing a great job of riding her on your own, too," he commented, holding up both hands to show her she was riding the mare independently.

"Oh, dear Lord!" From the look on Karly's pretty face, he knew she was a hair's breadth away from all-out panic.

"Don't freak out," he said calmly. "I haven't been leading Suede since the first trip around the pen and you've done just fine." When they reached the gate, he opened it and stepped out to untie Boomer while the mare continued to walk slowly around the inside of the pen.

"B-Blake?"

"I'm just going to get Boomer so I can ride beside you," he reassured her. Swinging up into the saddle, he guided the gelding into the pen and caught up with Karly and Suede as they made another trip around the inside. "There are a few more things I want to show you, then we'll be ready to leave the round pen and start the ride up to the pasture."

"Are you sure that's a good idea?" Karly asked. "I'd hate to have to spend eternity haunting you."

"I'll take my chances on that, sweetheart," he said, laughing.

As he showed her how to guide Suede by doing nothing more than touching the reins to either side of the mare's neck, he noticed that Karly began to relax. She sat looser in the saddle and actually started moving with the mare instead of remaining as stiff as a ramrod.

On the third trip around the inside of the circular fence, Blake nodded toward the open gate ahead. "It's time we take this show on the road."

Karly looked doubtful. "I really don't think—"

"Good idea," he said, grinning. "Don't think. Just do it."

When they rode the horses out of the round pen, he could tell by the tightening around her mouth that Karly was anything but confident. But he admired her willingness to give riding a try. He just wished she had shown that kind of consideration to giving their marriage a chance.

By the time she and Blake reached the pasture where the herd of steers had spent the summer, Karly was feeling a little more sure of herself. Suede had proved to be as docile as Blake had promised and once Karly relaxed in the saddle, riding the mare wasn't bad at all.

"Are these mountains part of the Rockies?" she asked, gazing at the splendor of the high mountain meadow.

"Yup. The Laramie Mountain range is part of the eastern edge of the Rockies," he answered, stopping his horse to look at the black cattle on the other side of the river that wound through the valley.

When she looked over at him inspecting the animals, she realized that he'd been right not to give up his way of life to move to Seattle with her. Blake Hartwell wasn't a man who was meant to be a city dweller. She could tell he loved living on this ranch, loved watching over the animals in his care. He was as deliciously rugged as this beautiful land and she couldn't imagine him living anywhere else.

As she continued to admire the man who had swept her off her feet eight months ago, she spotted the butt of a gun attached to his saddle that she hadn't noticed before. A sudden thought had her looking cautiously at the tree line surrounding the vast clearing. "Are there grizzly bears in the region?"

Grinning, he shook his head. "Black bear, mountain lion and bobcat, but no grizzlies."

All three species were prominent in the mountains surrounding Seattle and normally black bears and bobcats weren't overly aggressive unless startled or if they were being protective of their young. Although she was extremely cautious when she was in an area where they were known to be, she wasn't as concerned by them as she was by the mention of mountain lions. They were an entirely different matter. They were more aggressive and so silent, one could be within a few feet and a person might never realize the animal was there until it pounced.

Blake must have realized she was worried about the predators that might be close by. "Don't worry, the big cats and bears in the area don't normally wander down from the higher elevations unless there's a drought or a shortage of the game they prey on."

"What keeps them from making these cattle their next meal?" Karly asked as she gazed at the herd of steers grazing on the thick prairie grasses.

"Unlike grizzlies, black bears are too opportunistic to bother with hunting larger game," he explained. "They'll eat whatever is available—roots, berries, bugs, carrion. They'll even eat garbage or whatever else they happen to find along the way."

Karly laughed as she nodded. "They really aren't very discerning when it comes to what they eat. Sometimes one will come down from the Cascade Mountains into one of the suburbs surrounding Seattle and everyone has to secure their trash cans. If they don't, they risk having the trash strewn all over their yards show up on the evening news as a warning to others to take precautions."

"Yeah, bears like an easy meal," he agreed. "But mountain lions are natural-born hunters. We do have a problem occasionally with one of them straying down here. If we see one or find tracks too close to the herds or ranch buildings, we try to call the Fish and Wildlife Service and they send one of the game wardens to deal with a nuisance cat."

"Do they kill the animal?" Even though the predators scared her outside the confines of a zoo, she hated that something might be killed because it had the misfortune to wander into the wrong place.

To her relief, he shook his head. "Not always. They first try to trap it for relocation to a more remote area. Exterminating the animal is a last resort unless it's known to be a threat to humans or livestock."

"Is that what the gun is for?" she asked, eyeing the hardwood stock sticking out of the leather holder. "For protection in case one of them becomes a threat to us?"

His expression changed to one of determination as he nodded. "It's always better to be safe than sorry. I told you I'd protect you no matter what and I meant it." He gave her a look that caused her insides to quiver. "I give you my word that as long as there's a breath left in my body, I won't let anything happen to you, Karly."

The intense promise in his dark brown eyes stole her breath and reminded her of the kiss they'd shared in the barn. Neither of them had seemed to want to acknowledge that the chemistry they'd discovered between them in Las Vegas was just as strong, if not stronger, than it had ever been. As she continued to gaze into the fathomless depths of his eyes, she'd never felt as safe and secure in her entire life as she felt at that moment.

They both remained silent for several more moments before they started across the pasture toward the trail that led back down to the ranch. There wasn't a doubt in her mind that he would do whatever it took to protect her from any and all dangers.

Her heart skipped a beat as she thought of how difficult it was becoming to keep him at arm's length. He'd acted just like the husband she'd always dreamed of, even though she'd presented him with divorce papers to end their union. And it was getting harder and harder to remember why it was the best for both of them to go through with the divorce.

She sighed when she glanced at him from the corner of her eye. He might be prepared to protect her from the four-legged predators that could hurt her. But who was going to protect her from the force of nature that was Blake Hartwell?

Four

"I told you riding isn't as hard as you thought it would be," Blake said, smiling as he helped Karly dismount the mare.

"I think I need to join a gym," she commented as she patted Suede's neck and moved away from the horse. Karly's wince and the way she walked told him that she'd spent too much time in the saddle for her first time riding.

His smile faded. He could have kicked himself for being an inconsiderate jerk. A new rider needed to condition their thigh and back muscles on shorter rides before they attempted long hours in the saddle. Otherwise they risked soreness much like what someone would expect after a strenuous workout. How could he have been so thoughtless?

He'd been so caught up in showing her the ranch and his way of life, he'd forgotten all about her being new to the experience of being on a horse. Now she was paying the price for his oversight.

"Why don't you go on up to the house and try to relax while I take care of the horses?" he suggested.

"I think I'll take you up on that offer," she said, nodding. She smiled. "I may be out of shape, but you're right about the riding. I can't believe I'm going to say this, but I actually enjoyed myself."

As he watched her turn and walk slowly toward the house, he knew what he would do if they were at the main house. He'd make sure she took a nice long soak in the hot tub, then give her a massage with a good soothing liniment. His body tightened at the thought of once again touching her satiny skin as he ran his hands over her thighs and back. Then he would turn her over and sink himself…

"You're one sorry son of a bitch, Hartwell," he muttered as he brushed down the horses. Karly was hurting from his insistence that she ride a horse and his carelessness about the hours she spent in the saddle. They'd both signed divorce papers that she was eager to file. But all he could do was think about what a pleasure it would be to make love to her again. If that didn't make him a prize jerk, he didn't know what did.

Blake took a deep breath to relieve some of his building tension. She obviously didn't want him touching her that way and if he wanted to preserve what little sanity he had left, he shouldn't want that, either. But as long as he kept his hands to himself, he could drive her over to the ranch house for some time in the hot tub to ease her discomfort.

Of course, that would require introducing her to Silas. Blake wasn't worried about the old guy telling her that Blake was the owner of the Wolf Creek Ranch. He knew that if he asked Silas to keep that information to himself, the old man would take it to his grave before he told a soul. But introducing his soon-to-be ex-wife and then keeping secrets from her was going to add a lot of fuel to the fire of the many lectures Blake would have to endure before Silas found something else he felt compelled to preach about.

With his mind made up, Blake took the saddles and bridles to the tack room, brushed down the horses, then led them back to their stalls. Giving them generous scoops of oats and flakes of hay, he reached for the cell phone clipped to his belt as he left the barn.

"I'm bringing Karly over for supper," Blake said when the old man answered.

"So you decided I'm decent enough to meet your bride after all?" Silas queried, his tone filled with sarcasm. "What changed your mind, boy? Did you finally fess up and tell her you own this spread?"

"You ask a lot of questions," Blake complained.

"Well, I would never find anything out if I didn't," Silas retorted. "So did you tell her?"

"No."

"Tarnation, boy! Why not?" The old man grunted his disgust. "The way I see it, that little gal's got a right to know just who she's hitched up to."

"I told you, I don't want my net worth influencing her decisions," Blake said, irritated that they were having the same argument they'd had every time he'd talked to Silas since Karly arrived on the Wolf Creek.

"Not every woman is as money-grubbin' as that heifer your daddy married or as connivin' as that little tart that tried to rope you into marryin' her by claimin' you were gonna be a daddy," Silas insisted. "All this gal did was take a trip down the aisle with you. And she did it so fast she must not have cared if you had millions or if you were flat broke."

Blake groaned at the mention of the fiasco with the buckle bunny that had taken place several years ago. He didn't like thinking about the hell he'd gone through proving that he wasn't Sara Jane Benson's baby daddy. Just the fact that he'd given the rodeo groupie a reason to accuse him had been bad enough. There were some women a man could have a good time with and then there were the ones that when they came toward him, a man would do well to turn around and run like hell. Sara Jane fell into the latter category.

But he'd been a little drunk that night and pissed off over his stepmother's latest refusal to sell him his family's ranch. He'd regretted his lapse in judgment the following morning, but he'd been fit to be tied when Sara Jane showed up a month later claiming that he'd made her pregnant. When he finally discovered that Sara Jane had lied—that there wasn't a baby and never had been—he didn't think he'd ever been more relieved in his entire life. After he confronted her, the woman had finally admitted it was all a ruse to try to get money from him after she discovered that he wasn't just a dust-covered rodeo rider. But aside from narrowly missing the trap she'd set, the incident had taught Blake a valuable lesson about letting anyone know that his family owned one of the largest private ranches in the state of Wyoming.

"She may have married me fast," Blake finally answered. "But she divorced me just as fast. I'll tell Karly when the time is right."

"When's that gonna be?" Silas persisted. "You know the longer you wait, the bigger the chance of somebody tellin' her for you."

"The chances of that happening are slim," Blake said confidently. "The men have been leaving before daylight to make sure the fences are ready for the herds when we bring them down from the summer pastures. And I know I can count on you not to say anything."

"It ain't my place to tell that little gal," Silas said, sounding affronted that Blake even mentioned the possibility. "But what are you gonna do when you take her over to the Rusty Spur for that barbecue day after tomorrow? What if one of the Laughlins says somethin' about it? What are you gonna do then?"

"I'm going to call Eli and fill him in before we go over there," Blake stated. "Neither Eli or Tori will say a word about it."

He'd given it some thought on his and Karly's ride back to the house and he knew he could trust his friends not to mention that Blake owned the ranch, or pass judgment on him for wanting to keep that fact from Karly. Eli Laughlin and his wife, Tori, had their own unorthodox tale of how they'd met and married, not to mention the obstacles due to secrets of Tori's past and Eli's trust issues that they'd had to work through.

Tired of arguing with the old cowboy, Blake decided it was time to bring the conversation to an end. "Go ahead and set the table. We'll be over in about fifteen minutes."

Ending the call before Silas could come up with more of his endless questions, Blake took a deep breath. He might be irritating as hell, but Silas was right. Karly had married him because she wanted to, not because she thought she could get something from him. And even though they were headed for a divorce, it was becoming more difficult to defend his stance on not telling her.

A sudden thought stopped him dead in his tracks. Could she have rejected him and their marriage because she thought just the opposite about him? When she got back to Seattle, had she decided that he didn't make enough money to support her and the kids he had hoped they would one day have?

Blake shook his head as he climbed the back steps and started into the house. Either way, he needed to find out what her reasoning had been for ending things with him. Once he knew that, he could put this marriage fiasco behind him. Until then, he'd simply wait and see what he could find out.

When Blake drove his truck up the asphalted driveway toward the huge log lodge, Karly caught her breath at the sheer size and beauty of it. "This is absolutely gorgeous," she said, falling in love with the way the home and the rugged landscape complemented each other so perfectly. No other style of house would have looked as natural with the vastness of the land surrounding it. "Can you imagine living in a place like this?"

"You like it?" he asked, staring straight ahead as he parked his truck in front of the porte cochere covering the entrance to the house. Made with the same huge logs as the main structure, it provided shelter from the weather as well as added to the grandeur of the home.

"Who wouldn't love this?" she asked, noticing a small waterfall cascading over boulders not far from the stacked stone steps. It emptied into a little pool by the bottom step and looked so natural that it took a moment for her to realize it was man-made.

"Everything about it is perfect." She frowned. "But shouldn't we be going through the back entrance?"

"Why would we do that?" he asked, sounding confused.

"It's not like we're invited guests," she said, shaking her head. "The owner—"

"He isn't staying here right now and even if he was, he wouldn't care." He grinned as if finding something humorous about her question. "He's a pretty easygoing guy."

She had a hard time believing anyone would want an employee and his guest taking advantage of their good nature. "And you're sure he won't mind us just walking in like we own the place?"

He laughed and shook his head as he got out of the truck and walked around to help her down from the cab. "Take my word for it, sweetheart. He doesn't have any problem at all with us making ourselves at home while we're visiting the main house."

When he lifted her from the truck seat and set her on her feet, he kept his hands resting at her waist as he gazed into her eyes. Her breath caught and her pulse sped up. He was going to kiss her again and heaven help her, she wanted him to do just that.

Mesmerized by the heated light in his incredible brown eyes, she could only watch as he slowly began to lower his head. But just when she thought his lips would cover hers, he took a step back and smiled down at her. "Silas is expecting us."

Not entirely certain whether she was disappointed

or relieved that he hadn't kissed her, she blinked. "Silas?"

He nodded. "I think I'd better warn you," he said as he put his arm around her and guided her toward the steps. "The housekeeper here is ornery, opinionated and downright disagreeable at times. But the old cuss has a heart of gold and if he thought you needed it, he'd give you the shirt off his back."

"Does he know…about us?" she asked hesitantly. She'd only told a couple of her friends at work about what had taken place on her Las Vegas vacation. But he hadn't mentioned telling anyone.

Blake nodded. "Keeping anything from Silas Burrows is damn near impossible. But don't worry. He's won't say a word to you about it, unless you bring it up."

She doubted that would happen, but she forgot all about her concerns or the housekeeper's opinion when they reached the entrance doors. Hand-carved images of black bears and pine trees overlaid the glass and added to the appeal of the lodge.

But when Blake opened the door and they stepped into the foyer, Karly couldn't believe the rustic beauty of the home. "This isn't just a log home, it's a mansion," she said as they walked into the great room.

With a vaulted ceiling and massive fireplace made of river rock, the room had a surprisingly cozy feel for such a large space. But when she noticed the panoramic view of the mountains through the wall of windows on the opposite side of the room, it felt as if the room opened up to the landscape beyond.

"Do you like it?" Blake asked.

She nodded in awe as she continued to look around the room. Even the interior walls were made of logs. "It's gorgeous."

"I'll give you the grand tour after supper," he said, smiling as if her approval pleased him.

"I'd like that." As an afterthought, she added, "As long as you don't think the owner would mind."

"Not at all." Blake's sexy grin sent a shiver up her spine. "Trust me, he'll be fine with it."

"Supper's ready and if you want it hot you two better get in here."

Turning, Karly spotted an older man who looked like every child's favorite jolly old elf. On the portly side, his thick hair and long, full beard were snow-white and although he wore jeans, his green suspenders and long-sleeved red shirt would have convinced young and old alike that he might very well be Santa Claus.

As they walked toward him, Blake made the introductions. "Karly, this is Silas Burrows."

"It's nice to meet you, Mr. Burrows," Karly said, extending her hand.

He stared at her for several moments before he gave her a wide grin as he shook her hand. "Just call me Silas or Si." He motioned for her and Blake to follow him. "I fixed beef stew and sourdough bread for supper. It ain't fancy, but it's hot and there's plenty of it."

"If it tastes half as good as it smells, I'm sure it's going to be delicious," she said when they entered the kitchen and the smell of baking bread and the rich aroma from the bubbling pot on the state-of-the-art range assailed her senses. "Is there anything I can do to help you finish getting it ready?"

Silas shook his head. "Not really much left to do. While I slice the bread, I'm gonna let Blake pour us all glasses of iced tea and we'll be ready to eat."

After Blake guided her over to the large oak table across the room and held her chair for her to sit down, he whispered close to her ear, "It looks like you've got a fan."

"What do you mean?" she asked, barely able to keep from shivering when his warm breath feathered over her sensitive skin.

"I haven't seen Silas grin this much since the former owner's second wife sold the ranch to his son," he said, nibbling a kiss along the column of her neck as if it was the most natural thing in the world for him to do.

Startled by his show of affection, her heart pounded against her ribs and she tried not to think about what it might mean as he crossed the kitchen to pour their drinks. To distract herself, she looked around. She loved to cook when she had the opportunity and someone to cook for. Unfortunately, that only happened a few times a year—usually when she and her coworkers had a potluck lunch at the office. But if she had a kitchen like this one, she might be tempted to cook more. All of the appliances were commercial grade and top-of-the-line. And she absolutely loved the spaciousness and convenience of the entire room's layout. Cooking, even if it was just for herself, would be a joy in a kitchen like this.

As the two men finished putting the food on the table, Karly suddenly realized just how hungry she was. She and Blake had had an early lunch before her riding lesson and trip to the upper pasture. Glancing at the digital display on the microwave, she was surprised to see that had been almost seven hours earlier.

When both men brought the food and iced tea to the table, Silas filled their plates with thick stew. Seating himself, he pointed to her plate with his fork. "You'd better eat up, gal. There's more where that come from." He grinned. "And I made a chocolate cake for dessert."

"I'll be sure to save room for a piece," Karly said, picking up her fork. "I love chocolate."

Smiling, Silas nodded. "Most women do."

"How would you know what women like?" Blake asked, frowning.

Silas grunted. "Just why do you think men give women chocolates on Valentine's Day, hotshot?"

"I don't ever remember you having a girlfriend," Blake said, sounding doubtful.

Silas shook his head. "Don't go thinkin' I didn't

have my pick of the women in my day, boy. I used to be quite the lady's man about forty years back."

Karly couldn't help but laugh as she listened to the good-natured banter. It was like a game of verbal one-upmanship and she could tell the two men thought the world of each other. Blake treated Silas like a favorite uncle or beloved grandfather and it was clear the old gentleman cared just as much for him.

By the time the meal was over and Silas served them all slices of the chocolate cake, Karly couldn't remember the last time she'd laughed as much. "You two are hilarious. How long have you known each other?"

"I've known him and his brother since the day they were born," Silas said, taking a bite of cake.

"You have a brother?" Karly asked, turning to Blake. He hadn't mentioned having a sibling. But then they hadn't really talked about family, or much of anything in their lives, when they were in Las Vegas.

He nodded. "Sean's a couple of years older than me."

"Does he live close by?" she asked, wondering what it would be like to have someone who shared the same memories of family and growing up. Being an only child, she'd never experienced that and she couldn't help but feel that she'd missed out on something meaningful.

"Sean has a ranch about twenty miles to the

north—on the other side of the mountain," he answered as he took their empty plates to the sink.

"That must have been nice, having someone to play with when you were little," she said, unable to keep from feeling wistful about it. "I always wanted a sister or brother, but I guess it wasn't meant to be."

While Silas loaded the dishwasher, Blake poured them each a cup of coffee and rejoined her at the table. "I take it you are an only child?"

"Back in December, we didn't get around to talking about family," she admitted, nodding.

He eyed her over the rim of his coffee cup for several long moments before he set it on the table and reached to cover her hand with his. "There were a lot of things we should have discussed, but didn't."

The feel of his warm calloused palm covering her hand made her feel heated all over and she found herself longing for the way things might have been between them. Before she could give in to that longing and do something she shouldn't, she pushed her chair back. "I…suppose I should help Silas with the dishes," she said, needing to put distance between her and Blake in order to regain her perspective.

She hadn't traveled all this way to rekindle what they'd shared in Vegas. She'd come to put an end to it once and for all. But unlike the certainty she'd felt in Seattle when she'd first made the decision, the thought of ending it after this lovely visit made her want to cry and she wasn't entirely certain why.

But when she started to rise from the chair, her

thigh muscles were so stiff and sore, her legs threatened to fail her. "I shouldn't have sat that long," she said, slowly getting to her feet.

"That's another reason I wanted to bring you over here," he said, starting to lead her into the great room. "You'll feel better after some time in the hot tub."

Karly stopped to stare at him. "Blake, are you out of your mind? I can't get in the hot tub."

He looked thoroughly confused. "Why not?"

"For one thing, I don't have anything to wear." She motioned toward the double glass doors leading from the great room to the stone patio beyond. "And for another, I know the owner of this place may be good-natured, but I'm sure he would draw the line at having someone he doesn't know taking a dip in his hot tub."

"Trust me, sweetheart, he won't care," Blake said, guiding her out of the house toward the in-ground pool and spa. "I have free rein here, which means you do, too. You can slip out of your clothes and soak for a while in the hot tub and no one will be the wiser."

"I'm not going to go skinny-dipping in a stranger's spa," she said, looking around as they walked outside. If the owner had a hot tub, she certainly couldn't find it.

The sun had already gone down and the lights around the stone patio and pool made it look as if they were standing on the edge of a tropical lagoon. At one end, a waterfall cascaded down a huge natural-looking rock formation into the pool. But when she looked closer, she realized that the hot tub was set behind the curtain of water, as if it was inside a hidden cave.

He pointed toward the waterfall. "It's completely private. And I promise it will help to soothe your aching muscles."

Relief from the stiffness in her thighs and lower back did sound like heaven. "The owner—"

"Won't mind at all," he interrupted. He grabbed a couple of bath sheets that were sitting on a lounge chair they passed on the way to the waterfall.

"Where did those come from?" she asked, beginning to realize he had this planned all along.

"I laid them out when we first got here," he answered, looking smug. "It was while you were surveying the kitchen."

"You had this planned when you invited me up here for dinner," she accused.

He nodded and grinned. "Now take your clothes off and hop in."

Five

When Karly continued to glare at him, Blake frowned. "What?"

"I'm not taking my clothes off in front of you," she said, stubbornly crossing her arms beneath her breasts.

He tried not to remember how perfectly those breasts fit in the palms of his hands or how responsive her nipples were when he teased them with the pads of his thumbs. Obviously, he hadn't considered the full effect of the temptation she'd present when he'd come up with this hot-tub idea.

"Why not?" he asked, grinning and putting aside thoughts of her lovely breasts. "We did a lot more than just take our clothes off in Vegas and I don't remember either one of us having a problem with that."

If looks could kill, she would have dropped him right there where he stood. "That was different," she insisted.

He raised one eyebrow. "How do you figure?"

"We were married."

He shook his head. "Not at first we weren't. If you'll remember I ran into you in the hotel lobby in Vegas on Monday morning just as you were arriving to check in." He smiled. "And I made love to you for the first time that night. We didn't get married until the following Saturday night."

"That was a long time ago," she said softly.

"Not really." Reaching out, he cupped her soft cheek with his palm. "Sweetheart, we're still married and I'm still your husband until a judge says I'm not. There's no reason for you to feel shy with me."

Her expression softened a little, but she was apparently going to stand her ground. "We haven't been together in over eight months, Blake." She shook her head. "And in three months we'll be divorced."

There was a sadness in her eyes that he hadn't expected. Was she regretting her decision?

The notion that she might be having second thoughts caused a hitch in his breathing and he didn't want to consider why. But he immediately abandoned the likelihood that she had changed her mind again. Just because she might be sorry for what had—or more accurately hadn't—taken place after they left Las Vegas, didn't mean anything. In light of the choices she'd made and the way things had turned out, he had his own doubts that it would have worked out between them, as well.

Fighting to keep from lowering his head to kiss her slightly parted lips, Blake dropped his hand to his side. "Follow me. There's an entrance at the side of the waterfall. Going in that way will keep you from getting your hair wet." Once they entered the secluded area, he flipped a switch, turning off the underwater lights in the custom-made, sunken tub. "You can put your clothes over there to keep them dry," he said, motioning toward a lounge chair a couple of feet away. Turning his back to her, he added, "Let me know when I can turn around."

"I still can't believe your boss won't have a problem with someone using his hot tub without permission," she said.

He started to tell her she was beginning to sound like a parrot, but the words lodged somewhere between his vocal cords and open mouth when he heard the rustle of clothing being removed a moment before her jeans and T-shirt landed on the end of the lounge chair. Blake swallowed hard. Then he took a deep breath when her lacy panties and bra landed on top of the pile. Just knowing she was as naked as the day she was born and standing right behind him was enough to send his blood pressure sky-high.

The sound of her stepping into the spa caused sweat to pop out on his forehead. He hadn't anticipated remembering how he'd sipped water droplets from her satiny skin when they'd showered together. He gritted his teeth and tried desperately to think of anything but how her lithe wet body had felt against his.

"Oh, dear heavens that feels good," Karly said, her tone appreciative. As if it was an afterthought, she added, "You can turn around now."

Thankful that he had switched off the submerged lights to keep her from seeing the obvious evidence of how she still affected him, Blake sat down on the side of the lounge chair and took his time pulling off his boots and socks. Maybe if he gave himself a few minutes before he got into the water with her, he could get a grip on his suddenly nonexistent control.

When he stood up to unbuckle his belt and release the button at the waistband of his jeans, he thought he heard her moan softly. "Are you all right?" he asked, unzipping his fly to shove his jeans and boxer briefs down his legs.

He couldn't help but chuckle when Karly sent a little wave of water over the rock edge of the tub as she quickly whirled around to look away from where he was undressing. "I-I'm just…amazed at how wonderful this warm water feels."

"I think you'll have to agree, the hot tub was a good idea," he said, knowing that wasn't the real reason behind her moan.

But he kept that knowledge to himself. Pointing out that she was no more immune to him now than she had been in Las Vegas would only put her on the defensive and prevent him from learning why she had changed her mind about them.

By the time he had removed his clothes, he felt a little more in control of his body. So he walked over to the side of the heated spa and stepped into the bubbling water. Lowering himself to the stone seat beside her, he closed his eyes and took a deep breath as the soothing, heated water swirled around them. Just knowing that her nude body was only inches away from his was playing hell with his good intentions.

"This is an unusual hot tub," she commented. "I don't think I've ever seen one made out of stones. It looks so natural."

Nodding, he opened his eyes. "The owner told some pool designer what he wanted and the guy made it happen."

"Well, whoever the designer was, he did a wonderful job." She looked toward the curtain of water separating the hidden room from the pool. "This feels like we're in a tropical paradise."

"I'm pretty sure that was the plan," Blake said, smiling.

Her appreciation for his home and for the attention to detail that he'd put into it pleased him more than he would have thought. The fact that he had wanted to share it with her for the rest of their lives made her approval bittersweet.

Deciding it was a good time to get a few answers

about why she'd changed her mind about them, he asked, "Have you always lived in Seattle?"

She turned her head to give him a puzzled look. "Where did that question come from?"

"Just wondering," he said, shrugging. He didn't want to give her the impression she was being interrogated. And asking her the questions he hadn't asked in Vegas would be a good way to keep his mind away from thoughts of her nude body.

"To satisfy your curiosity, I was born in New York City and with the exception of living in a small town in the Midwest for a few years, I was raised there," she said, answering his question. "From what you said about going to school in Eagle Fork, I assume you've always lived around here?"

He nodded. "Yup. And I take it the pony ride happened while you lived in the small town."

"Yes." She laughed. "I don't think I've ever heard of a market in Manhattan that has pony rides during their grand opening."

"Why did your family move from the city?" he asked, making sure to keep his tone from sounding too interested.

"My father was an industrial engineer and the company he worked for sent him to study and improve the productivity of one of their manufacturing plants." She stared at the waterfall. "He loved it in the Midwest, but my mother hated it."

"What about you?" he asked. "How did you feel about it?"

"To tell you the truth, I was really too young to have much of an opinion one way or the other," she commented. "And when my mother decided she'd had enough of small-town life, she took me back to New York and that was that."

"Your parents divorced?" he asked gently.

She nodded. "Unfortunately, I only saw my father a couple of times after we moved. He was killed in a car accident within a year after the divorce."

Without a second thought, Blake put his arm around her bare shoulders and pulled her to his side. "I'm sorry, Karly. I know how hard that is on a kid. I lost my mom when I was ten."

"I was only six when he died and all I really remember about him was that he worked a lot and he took me for ice cream more than my mother wanted him to," she said, her voice somber. He could tell it bothered her that she couldn't remember the man who helped to give her life.

"Dads have a tendency to do things moms would rather they didn't," he said, chuckling. "I remember one time my mom gave my dad a hard time for taking my brother and me to Cheyenne Frontier Days and letting us eat so many corn dogs and so much cotton candy that we were sick for two days."

"My mother wasn't as afraid that I'd get sick as she was that I would gain weight," she explained. "Martina Ewing was an editor for one of the premier fashion magazines before we moved to the Midwest and she was determined that I would be in the industry, as well." She shook her head. "It never occurred to her that I might want to do something else with my life."

"Did your mother resume her career when you returned to New York?" he asked when she fell silent. He sensed there might be something about her parents splitting up that was relevant to their marriage situation. He just couldn't put his finger on what it was.

"She tried going back, but she'd been out of the loop long enough that she'd lost her place in the industry," Karly answered. "She blamed my dad for the loss of her career and never forgave him for it."

They both fell silent for a few minutes and Blake knew beyond a shadow of a doubt that her parents' marital problems had been a big influence on Karly. He wasn't sure exactly how it had factored into her decision to pursue a divorce, but he had every intention of finding out.

As he sat there pondering her reasoning, one thing became very apparent. He was sitting in a bubbling hot tub with her soft, nude body pressed closely to his. The lighted waterfall cast a dim glow into the tiny room, which only added to the intimacy of the moment. His reaction was not only predictable, but it was also inevitable.

With only a fleeting thought to the consequences, Blake pulled Karly closer and lowered his head. The feel of her water-slickened body rubbing against his was enough to send him into orbit, but the moment their mouths touched, a smoldering heat filled his lower belly and quickly sent liquid fire streaking through his veins. He briefly wondered how he could burn to a cinder while sitting in a tub of water.

When she sighed and brought her arms up to encircle his neck, it didn't even occur to him to resist deepening the kiss, and as he stroked her tongue with his, her sweet taste and eager response only heightened the need building inside of him. It was like nothing had changed since they were in Vegas. He was as hot for her now as he had been then. And he could tell she wanted him just as much.

Unfortunately, his timing was lousy. Making love to her right now could very well scare her into leaving the ranch without him getting to the bottom of what went wrong between them. Besides, he wasn't prepared to protect her. He hadn't come to the hot tub with seduction on his mind. And an unplanned pregnancy now would only add another wrinkle to an already complicated situation.

Easing away from the kiss, Blake held her close as he took several deep breaths. His hormones were racing through him like a herd of mustangs at a wild horse roundup and knowing there were no barriers between his body and hers wasn't making his decision to pull away any easier.

"It's probably time we got out of the hot tub and headed back to the foreman's cottage," he said half-heartedly.

"I—I think...you're right," she said, sounding just as reluctant as he felt.

Leaning back, he stared into her incredible blue eyes. "Karly, what..." He stopped and cleared his throat to keep from asking her what went wrong with them. Instead he declared, "I'll get out and get dressed first. Then I'll wait for you out by the pool."

"That's a good idea," she agreed. "Thank you."

Damning his nobility, Blake got out of the hot tub before he could change his mind, quickly toweled himself dry and got dressed. Picking up his boots and socks, he made it a point not to look back at Karly, who was still sitting in the spa as he left the man-made cave. If he had looked back, he wasn't sure he would have been able to walk away.

As he sat down on the foot of one of the lounge chairs by the pool to pull on his socks and boots, Blake told himself he was doing the right thing—that making love to Karly again would only make things worse when he watched her drive away in a few days. But that reasoning didn't do a thing to lessen the need for her that still burned in his gut.

Rising to his feet, he took a deep breath. He might as well face facts. He wanted her—had never stopped wanting her. If he hadn't known that before, he sure as hell did now.

He rubbed the tension at the back of his neck. He could see a lot of cold showers in his near future and the first one would be tonight—as soon as they returned to the foreman's cottage.

* * *

"Blake, I think I'll leave to make the drive to Lincoln County after we have breakfast tomorrow morning," Karly said as he drove the truck away from the log mansion.

"I thought we had that settled," he said, staring straight ahead. "You were going to wait until the strike was done and fly to Spokane."

"I just think it would be for the best," she said, unwilling to admit out loud that she was in real danger of falling under his spell once again.

Sitting in the hot tub next to him, having him put his arm around her and feeling his naked body against hers had almost been her undoing. Even though she hadn't been able to see much in the dim light of the little cave housing the hot tub, her memory had filled in the blanks. In her mind, she had seen every well-defined muscle, every plane and valley of his impressive physique. Remembering how his strong arms had held her so securely and how gently he made love to her was overwhelming, and she shivered as a wave of desire coursed through every part of her.

"I know I shouldn't have kissed you." He took a deep breath and added, "Either in the barn or tonight in the hot tub. But it felt right and I'll be damned if I'm going to apologize for it."

She couldn't in good conscience allow him to shoulder all of the blame. "You wouldn't have kissed me if I hadn't let you."

His deep chuckle sent heat pulsing through her veins. "Yeah, I noticed you weren't protesting."

"That's the problem." She sighed. "I should have."

He glanced over at her. "Why didn't you?"

"I…wanted you to kiss me," she admitted.

"But you didn't want to want me kissing you." It wasn't a question.

"No."

"Sweetheart, a wife wanting her husband to kiss her is allowed," he said, reaching over to take her hand in his. The moment their palms touched a delightful tingling sensation streaked up her arm.

She did her best to ignore it and tried to focus on what he'd said. "That's the problem, Blake. Three months from now we'll be divorced. I shouldn't want you kissing me, not anymore."

He gave her hand a gentle squeeze. "Have you asked yourself why you do?"

His question took her by surprise. But as she tried to think of an answer, she decided it probably wasn't wise to delve too deeply into the reason behind her wanting his affection. If she did, she was certain she wouldn't be all that comfortable with the answer.

"You're only going to be here a few more days, Karly," he said pragmatically. "And I give you my word that nothing is going to happen between us unless that's what you want. But I'm not going to lie to you and tell you it isn't what I want."

As he drove the truck up the lane to the foreman's

cottage, Karly thought about what Blake had said. What *did* she want?

Eight months ago, she'd been confident she was making the right decision when she'd said yes to his marriage proposal. She had been certain at the time she married him that she loved Blake and wanted them to spend the rest of their lives together. But when she'd returned to Seattle her practical side had taken over. That's when she'd known ending things was the right call—for both of them.

She'd questioned falling in love with him so quickly and feared that their feelings for each other might not last. Then she'd thought about her parents. Her mother had been in love with her father, but in the end it hadn't been enough for her. She'd become bitter and resentful, and Karly had borne the brunt of that bitterness.

Karly loved her own career as an import buyer— loved the travel to foreign countries—and feared that love might not be enough for her, either, if she had to give up all of that. Had she been wrong about her feelings for her job? Could she have been happy being the wife of a ranch foreman in a remote part of Wyoming when all she'd ever known was living in a city with conveniences just steps from her apartment door?

She'd been so sure of everything when she left Seattle to come to the ranch for him to sign the new set of divorce papers. But then she'd seen him—

stayed with him, had him treat her like his wife—
and the doubts about her decision had set in.

She might have been able to keep things in perspective if she hadn't been stranded on the ranch by
the airport workers' strike. She'd have gone back to
Washington, filed the papers for the dissolution of
their marriage and resumed her career with the confidence she was doing the right thing.

The trouble had come from seeing him again,
being in his arms and experiencing the magic of his
kiss. It all reminded her of what she'd wanted when
she'd walked down that aisle in Vegas—what she
was giving up—and had her questioning herself at
every turn.

Had there been serious flaws in her reasoning?
By insisting they continue with the divorce was she
making the biggest mistake of her life? Would he
even give her a second chance if she did want for
them to try to make their marriage work?

Karly glanced over at Blake when he parked the
truck beside the foreman's cottage. The way he held
her—kissed her—he seemed open to rekindling what
they'd found together in Las Vegas. But he hadn't
once mentioned wanting her to change her mind.
He'd even signed the divorce papers without a word
of protest or even the slightest hesitation.

She sighed when he got out of the truck and she
waited for him to walk around to open the passenger door. She wasn't nearly as sure of everything as

she'd been when she arrived here. And the only way she was going to determine what was best would be to stay with Blake on the ranch and give herself the time to sort it all out.

Six

On Sunday morning when Blake walked back into the foreman's cottage after getting their breakfast from the bunkhouse cook, Karly was seated at the table waiting for him. "I thought you'd still be asleep," he said as he set the containers of food on the kitchen island.

"My phone woke me," she said, her tone pensive. He noticed her tightly clasped hands resting on the table in front of her. Her knuckles were white and she looked like she had something pretty heavy on her mind.

Without giving it a second thought, he walked over to where she sat, took her hands in his and pulled her to her feet. "What's wrong?" he asked, loosely

holding her to him. He wasn't sure why, but it bothered him to think she might be worried about anything at all.

Instead of her backing away as he thought she
might, she wrapped her arms around his waist and
laid her head against his chest. "The strike at the
Denver airport is over. The airline can get me on a
flight out of Cheyenne tomorrow morning."

She didn't sound overly happy about it and he took
that as a sign that despite what she'd said last night
on the way home from the main house, she wanted
to stay with him a little longer. And that was just fine
with him. He told himself that he was okay with it
because he hadn't yet discovered what had originally
changed her mind about them. But if he was perfectly
honest with himself, he would have to admit that he
wanted to spend more time with her before he had
to say goodbye and watch her drive out of his life
for good. The way he saw it, having one more day
with her was worth whatever hell he would have to
face of a lifetime without her.

"You don't have to leave." He put his index finger
beneath her chin to tilt her head up until their eyes
met. "Why don't you stay a few more days?"

"I can't afford to miss work," she said, shaking her
head. "I only have a couple of vacation days left and
I'll need to use those for the stop in Lincoln County
to file the…d-divorce."

She stumbled over the word and he would bet

nearly every dime he had that she was starting to second-guess her decision. "Can you work from here?"

She looked thoughtful. "You mean telecommute?"

He nodded. "The signal here is good, but it's a lot better over at the main house. You could work from there."

"As nice as your boss is, I'm sure he'll draw the line at some stranger using up all of his bandwidth," she stated.

Blake shrugged. "Like I said, he's not staying there right now. When he had the Wi-Fi installed, he made sure it was unlimited usage with no slowdowns." He purposely omitted that Blake himself was one of the internet company's principal shareholders.

She looked thoughtful a moment before she shook her head. "I didn't bring my laptop."

"Not a problem," he said, smiling. He knew she was giving it serious consideration and he was determined to convince her to stay on the Wolf Creek Ranch a little longer. "You can use mine."

"Are you sure?" she asked. "You might have something on it that's private."

He shook his head. "I only use it for breeding records and to keep track of the cattle we'll be sending to market. There's more than enough room on the hard drive for anything you'll be doing and if you need a special program we can always download it."

"I'll have to call the office on Tuesday morning and explain that I'm going to be working from here for a few days," she said, her expression thoughtful. "I've telecommuted in the past, so it shouldn't be a problem to set it up. And I'll need to email one of my coworkers to have her send me a couple of files I'll need."

"Then it's settled," he said, refusing to acknowledge just how important it had become to him that she extended her stay. "After breakfast we'll go over to the mansion and get everything arranged in the office."

She frowned. "Blake, I know you say your boss is easygoing and won't mind, but I'm sure he'd have a big problem with me using his office."

"There's a writing desk in one of the upstairs bedrooms," he said, thinking quickly. "We'll just move over to the mansion and you can work out of that bedroom."

"That's even worse, Blake," she said, shaking her head. "We can't just move into your boss's home." She stared at him. "Who is this man and why do you insist on taking advantage of his good nature so often?"

He took a deep breath. He should tell her the truth. He'd boxed himself into a corner and he had nobody to blame but himself. If he told her now that he was the owner of the Wolf Creek Ranch she thought he was taking advantage of, she'd think he had been playing her for a fool or, worse yet, that he had been trying to hide his assets from her because of the divorce. But the longer he waited, the worse it was going to be when she did find out.

Deciding he needed to dial things back a little while he tried to figure out the best time and way to tell Karly he was the man in question, Blake backtracked. "You're right. We don't want to take advantage while he's away from the mansion. But there's one place that I know he won't mind you using."

"Where's that?" she asked, seemingly distracted from finding out who the owner was—at least for the time being.

"There's a table in the library just off the family room that would be the perfect place for you to work," he said, bringing his hand up to twine his fingers in her silky blond hair. "It's quiet in there and you won't have to worry about anyone interrupting you or you using a room the boss would find objectionable." He lowered his head to brush her perfect lips with his. "And when you take a break for lunch all you'll have to do is walk down the hall to the kitchen and Silas will make you something to eat."

Unable to resist, he gave in to temptation and settled his mouth over hers. He knew he was playing with fire and would most likely get burned by his weakness for her. But he couldn't seem to control himself when he was around Karly. It had been that way in Vegas and it was that way now. Whenever he was with her, all he could think about was holding her close, kissing her until she sagged against him and making love to her until they both collapsed from the sheer pleasure of being together.

As he deepened the kiss, she put her arms around his neck and melted against him. Her soft curves pressed against his rapidly hardening body and the sweetness that was uniquely Karly caused his heart to thump against his chest like a jungle drum. No other woman had ever fit against him so perfectly or responded to his kiss as readily.

When she moaned softly and snuggled even closer, he realized that she felt his arousal straining against his fly. The fact that she was as hot for him as he was for her sent adrenaline pumping through his veins at the speed of light. Whatever caused her to want out of their brief marriage apparently had nothing to do with her desire for him. That was as strong, if not stronger, than it had been when they'd taken that trip down the aisle at that little chapel on the Vegas strip.

Barely able to resist the urge to take off both of their clothes and make love to her right there in the kitchen, he forced himself to ease away from the kiss. "Sweetheart, as much as I'd like to take this all the way to a satisfying conclusion for both of us, I think we'd better take a time-out."

Her smooth porcelain cheeks wore the blush of passion and he sensed that if he hadn't called a halt to things, she probably wouldn't have, either. That's when he knew beyond a shadow of doubt that there was every likelihood they would be making love before she left. And soon.

"I, uh, y-yes." She looked a little dazed. "I'll get flatware and coffee mugs."

While she walked over to get the items from the cabinets, Blake took a deep breath and set the two plates of bacon, scrambled eggs and hash browns on the table, along with a thermos of coffee. How the hell could a man feel like he'd done the right thing and, at the same time, regret doing it?

He wasn't sure. But he knew now that he needed to come clean with Karly and tell her that he owned the ranch before things progressed any further between them. Karly was intelligent and she'd already started questioning why he kept taking advantage of the mysteriously absent ranch owner. It was just a matter of time before she figured it out or someone unwittingly told her.

And the worst part of all, his reasons for keeping it from her were making less sense, even to him, with each passing day.

Karly sat at the library table in the log mansion and looked around at the volumes of books on the shelves lining the room. The owner's tastes were eclectic and included ranching manuals, nonfiction, autobiographies and novels by some of the most popular, bestselling authors of the past one hundred years.

As she continued to look around, she couldn't help

but smile. Unlike a lot of home libraries, which felt gloomy and heavy with the knowledge of the ages, the room felt cozy and extremely inviting. So much so that she could imagine herself spending endless hours on a rainy or snowy day curled up with a good book and a warm, comfy afghan on the big leather sofa in front of a crackling fire in the stone fireplace.

She rose to her feet and walked over to look out one of the windows at the surrounding mountains. Now that she'd visited the ranch, she could understand why Blake had told her he couldn't leave Wyoming for life in a bustling city. The land was beautiful and although she loved the green beauty of both the Cascade and Olympic Mountains, she couldn't look out any of the windows in her apartment and see them. If she wanted to enjoy the lush scenery, she had to take a ferry across Puget Sound or drive out of the city to the thick forests beyond.

But here on the Wolf Creek Ranch, every window had a spectacular view of the Laramie Mountains and experiencing nature took little more than walking out the door.

She sighed. When she had returned to Seattle after their whirlwind courtship and wedding, she had reasoned that living so far from a city would eventually end her and Blake's marriage the way it had with her parents'. She'd even convinced herself that she was doing what was best for both of them—that there would be less emotional pain by ending it so early in the union than there would be a few years down the line.

But she had to admit that although most of her conclusions made sense, they weren't her only motivation for insisting on a divorce. The main, most compelling reason that she'd refused to move to Wyoming with her new husband had been due to fear—not that he would fail her, but that she would fail him.

She had been afraid she would eventually feel about Blake the way her mother had felt about her father. And that was something she wasn't going to let happen. She cared too much for him to blame him for things he had no control over.

Martina Ewing had become a bitter, resentful woman once she returned to New York and learned she had lost her place in the world of high fashion. Until her death just a few years ago, Karly's mother had blamed Karly's father for the loss of her career, her unhappiness and just about everything else unpleasant that happened in her life. She still managed to find fault with him, even though he'd passed away not long after they divorced. Karly sometimes wondered if her mother had even blamed him for leaving her saddled with a child to raise.

But in Karly's attempt to protect Blake from the possibility that she would turn out to be as unreasonable as her mother, had she allowed her fear to deprive them of a real chance at happiness?

"It's beautiful, isn't it?" Blake asked, wrapping his

arms around her waist and pulling her back against his solid chest.

Startled, she jumped. "I didn't know you had returned to the house."

After they'd finished breakfast, he had given her his laptop and driven them over to the mansion to set up her workspace in the library. Once he'd made sure the internet connection was the speed she needed, he'd told her he was going out to see that the indoor arena's floor had been properly prepared for the training of a new stallion and left her to familiarize herself with his computer and to download a couple of programs she would need to do her job. But she suspected that had been an excuse to give her the time and space to think about the direction her visit had taken and what she wanted to do about it.

They were both aware that the chemistry between them was as strong as ever and that it wouldn't take much to send it spiraling out of control. It had almost happened last night in the hot tub and then again this morning when he kissed her.

"Did you get everything ready to start to work?" he asked, sending a wave of goose bumps shimmering over her arms.

She nodded. "And I went ahead and sent the email to my coworker so it's waiting for her when she arrives at the office Tuesday morning."

"I'm glad you'll be here at the mansion." He brushed her long hair out of the way to nibble kisses down the column of her neck. "I have to start working in the arena with the new stallion and I'd hate for you to spend the day alone over at the foreman's cottage."

"I was going to ask you about that," she said, attempting to get her mind off how good he was making her feel. "Why are the barns and corrals at the foreman's cottage instead of here at the main ranch house?"

His low chuckle caused her knees to wobble. "Sweetheart, in the warmer months, having the barns and livestock a quarter of a mile away makes entertaining guests out on the patio a lot more pleasant."

"Oh, I hadn't thought about the dust and the noise the animals make," she commented.

"Along with Essence of Barnyard floating on the breeze. It doesn't inspire people to attend a cookout or pool party," he said, laughing.

Smiling, she nodded. "It makes perfect sense now." She frowned suddenly and turned in his arms to face him. "But the barn is no more than fifty yards from the cottage and I haven't noticed a lot of dust or barnyard odors at the foreman's cottage."

"When the owner's family established the Wolf Creek Ranch back in the late 1800s, they made sure to build the barns and outbuildings downwind of the house." He shrugged. "I think that held true for most ranches back then. They figured out which way the wind usually blows and planned their layout accordingly."

"So the foreman's cottage was the original ranch

house?" she asked. She hadn't really thought about it before, but he had mentioned the owner building the mansion after he bought the ranch a couple of years ago.

He nodded. "I think every generation has remodeled and built onto it, but the original homestead is in the foreman's cottage somewhere."

"How do you know so much about the ranch?" she asked, puzzled by his knowledge of its history.

He looked a little taken aback by her question. "My family has lived here…as long as the owners have." Although not overly common anymore, she'd heard that in years past it wasn't all that unusual for generations of cowboys to work for the same ranch.

"By the way, I don't recall hearing you mention the name of the man who owns the ranch," she said, frowning.

She hadn't much more than gotten the words out than Blake lowered his head and pulled her to him. With his mouth moving so masterfully over hers, it suddenly didn't matter who owned the ranch. All she cared about was having him continue to hold her to his broad chest, kiss her until she was breathless and so much more.

That thought should have had her pushing away from his secure embrace. Wanting to make love and wanting their marriage to work out were two entirely different things. Or were they?

But when Blake deepened the kiss, Karly abandoned all thought in favor of losing herself in the way he was making her feel. A delicious warmth flowed throughout her body the moment his tongue touched hers and as he explored her with such tender care, her knees failed her completely. He caught her to him and the feel of his rock-hard body sent waves of longing all the way to her core.

Lost in the overwhelming need he was creating, her heart skipped a beat when he brought his hand up along her side to gently cup her breast. The feel of his thumb teasing her through the layers of her T-shirt and bra only intensified her desire, making her restless and impatient to feel his calloused hands touching her bare skin.

When he broke the kiss to nibble his way along her jaw, then down her neck to the hollow below her ear, Karly couldn't stop herself from vocalizing what she wanted. "Blake, please."

"What do you want, Karly?" he asked as he continued to tease her.

"You. I…want you."

"And I want you, sweetheart," he said, leaning back to look at her. His brown gaze held hers as a slow smile curved his lips. "Let's go back to the foreman's cottage."

Needing him more than she needed her next breath, Karly let him lead her through the mansion and out the front door to his truck. On the ride back to the foreman's cottage, reality began to intrude and by the time Blake parked the truck at the side of the house, she had begun to question her sanity. She longed for him to make love to her—and, to her own surprise, she longed for him to *love* her again—but she needed him to understand the depth of the fears and insecurities that had held her back for the past eight months. Before they could move forward into a future together, she had to explain about her past.

When he got out and walked around to help her down from the passenger side of the truck, she had to let him know about her apprehension. She had to try to make him understand so he could forgive her for not believing in them. "Blake, we need to talk before we do anything impulsive."

He stared at her for several long moments and the heated look in his dark brown eyes stole her breath. "Karly, do you want me?"

"Y-yes. B-but—"

"I give you my word that we'll talk later," he said, putting his arm around her waist and tucking her to his side as he walked them into the house. "But not now. I haven't made love to my wife in over eight months and I've needed you every second of every day since we left Vegas."

His words sent a fresh wave of longing from the top of her head to the soles of her feet. She hadn't re-alized it before she came to Wyoming, before she'd spent this time on the land he loved so much, but she felt the same way.

She needed him with every fiber of her being. She didn't know how she'd gone these long eight months without him. And after they made love they could discuss why she had refused to join him here, why she'd insisted a divorce was the right decision. They could figure out where they were headed in the future after they made love. Right now, she craved the magic of his touch and the overwhelming pleasure of being one with him.

She could hardly believe what she was about to say. But as she stared up at him, she knew that from the moment she'd decided to bring him the divorce papers in person, she'd never really had a choice.

"Blake, please take me upstairs and make me forget how long it's been."

Seven

When Blake opened the door to the room she'd been using since her arrival at the ranch, memories of the first time they'd made love caused Karly's stomach to flutter with anticipation. It had been so long since he'd touched her and for the past eight months she'd lain in bed every night missing the feel of his skin pressed to hers, their bodies entwined in an embrace as old as time. A shiver slid up her spine and her heart skipped a beat at the thought.

When he closed the door behind them, he reached for her. Neither of them said a word as they stood with their arms around each other and simply enjoyed the moment.

As he drew back to look at her, he placed her

hands on his shoulders for support before he removed her boots and socks, then pulled off his.

"Karly, I want you to know there hasn't been anyone since we left Vegas," he said, his brown eyes reflecting the truth in his words as he straightened to his full height and took her back into his arms. He brought his hand up to gently caress her cheek. "When we got married, I vowed that I would be faithful to you. And as far as I'm concerned, I'm still your husband until I receive papers telling me otherwise."

She nodded. "That's the way I felt about it, as well."

Leaning forward, he brushed her lips with his. "I promised you we would talk about all that later, and I meant it. But right now, I intend to get reacquainted with my wife's beautiful body." Her pulse sped up when he reached for the hem of her T-shirt and slowly pulled it up and over her head.

"I can't let you be the only one having all the fun," she said, tugging his chambray shirt from the waistband of his jeans. She unfastened the top snap and slowly, methodically released the closures. She placed her hands beneath each side of his open shirt to brush it from his shoulders and her breath caught. She'd always found the hard ridges and valleys of his well-developed chest and abdomen fascinating. "Your body is perfect."

"If you want to talk about perfection—" he paused and reached behind her, releasing the clasp of her bra "—you're the one who's stunning."

The appreciation in his dark eyes stole her breath. But when he cupped her breasts with both hands, then kissed each hardened tip, her knees wobbled and she had to place her palms on his chest to steady herself.

The moment her fingers came into contact with the thick pads of his pectoral muscles, he shuddered and she knew he loved having her touch him as much as she loved having him touch her. Inspired to give him as much pleasure as he was giving her, she continued her exploration of his body and let her hands drift down to his belt buckle.

When she paused to glance up at him, he grinned. "Don't stop now, sweetheart. This is just starting to get interesting."

"That's one of the things that I've always found amazing about you," she said, unbuckling the tooled leather strap of his belt.

"What's that?" he asked, his breathing sounding a bit labored.

"You openly encourage me to do the same things to you that you're doing to me," she said, releasing the button at the top of his jeans.

"That's a big part of making love, sweetheart" he said, teasing her nipples with the pads of his thumbs. "It's about trust and the freedom to learn what we like and how to bring the most pleasure to each other."

She wasn't all that experienced, but she had a feeling not all men were willing to be vulnerable with their partner. Her heart swelled with emotion at the thought that Blake was secure enough in his manhood to trust her that much when they made love.

When she smiled and took hold of the tab at the top of his fly, he drew in a deep breath. "Don't get me wrong. I love what you intend to do," he said, his smile so sexy it sent her pulse racing. "But an excited man and a metal zipper can be a real bad combination."

She gazed up at him as she eased one hand inside his jeans between his cotton underwear and the zipper. "Maybe this will keep you safe," she said, delighting in the heat she detected in his eyes as she eased the offending zipper down over his insistent erection.

But she hadn't anticipated the effect his arousal would have on her. The feel of the hard ridge against the backs of her fingers caused heat to flow through her veins and her insides to feel as if they had turned to warm pudding.

By the time she finished the task of unzipping him, she felt as if she might go up in a puff of smoke. But when she looked up at Blake's handsome face, his eyes were closed and a muscle worked along his lean jaw as if he might be in pain.

"Are you all right?" she asked, concerned.

He opened his eyes and his slow, sexy grin sent a shiver up her spine. "Sweetheart, do you have any idea what it does to a man when a woman touches him like that?"

"Even through your underwear?" she asked playfully.

Laughing, he nodded. "It's a thin barrier and a real sensitive area. I'd have to be a eunuch not to react."

Moving her hands to his sides, she carefully pushed his jeans and boxer briefs down his lean hips and muscular thighs. When she lowered them to his ankles, she caressed the backs of his knees and strong calves. Rewarded with his deep groan, she realized that something as simple as skimming her hands down the backs of his legs could bring him pleasure.

When he stepped out of the denim and cotton, then kicked his clothing to the side, she bit her lower lip to keep a tiny moan from escaping. "You're absolutely beautiful. I've always thought so."

Shaking his head, he pulled her to him. "Women are all gentle curves and soft, smooth skin. That's beautiful. But men are too angular, hard and hairy to be anything but passable at best."

"Don't sell yourself short," she said, gazing up at him.

He surprised her when he raised one dark eyebrow. "Really? I'm standing here without a stitch of clothes on and you had to mention the word *short*?"

In truth, he was a man who had nothing whatsoever to be insecure about and the humor in his eyes told her he knew it. She couldn't help but giggle as she placed her hands on his wide chest.

"I suppose that was a poor choice of words. But do

you really want to talk about my word choices now?" she asked, running her index finger down the shallow valley between his chest and navel.

"No." He kissed his way from her cheek down her neck to her collarbone. "I fully intend to take the rest of your clothes off, lay you on that bed over there and spend the rest of today and tonight loving every inch of you."

When he lifted his head, his gaze caught and held hers as he reached to release the button at her waist, then lowered the zipper. His smile held so much promise as he ran his index finger along the elastic waistband of her bikini panties, Karly thought she might melt right then and there.

As he began to ease her jeans and underwear over her hips and down her legs, the tantalizing abrasion of his calloused hands on her skin caused her heart to skip several beats and a delicious shiver to run through her. When she stepped out of the garments, the heated appreciation in his dark eyes took her breath away.

"Gorgeous," he said, stepping forward to wrap his arms around her.

The feel of her breasts pressed to his hard, hair-roughened chest caused her knees to give way. But when he caught her and pulled her more fully against him, his strong arousal nestled against her soft lower belly. The feel of it made Karly's head spin.

Without a word he led her over to the bed and pulled back the comforter. "I'll be right back," he said, walking over to where their discarded clothing lay on the floor.

As she watched, he picked up his jeans to get something from his wallet. When he returned, he placed a foil packet on the bedside table and stretched out on the mattress beside her.

Gathering her into his arms, he smiled. "I'm assuming you still aren't on any kind of birth control."

"There hasn't been a reason for it," she said honestly. She'd intended to talk with her doctor about it once she returned from Las Vegas, but when it seemed that their marriage had ended she hadn't bothered.

"It's not a problem," he said, kissing her forehead. "It's my job to take care of you and protect you, even if that protection is from me."

"Thank you," she said, touching his lean cheek. She'd been so caught up in the moment, she hadn't given protection a second thought.

He stared at her and the look in his eyes was breathtaking before a slow smile curved his lips. He lowered his head to kiss her with a tenderness that brought tears to her eyes. No other man had ever shown her so much reverence or been as devoted to bringing her pleasure as Blake. And in that moment, she knew that no other man ever would.

When he deepened the kiss, he brought his hand up to cup her breast and tease her nipple with gentle care. Her pulse sped up as ribbons of desire coursed through every part of her and an ache began to form deep inside. A mixture of impatience and anticipation filled her as he moved his hand to caress his way down her side to her hip then her knee.

As he continued to stroke her tongue with his, he slowly moved his calloused palm along the inside of her thigh. When he touched her, it felt as if an electric current skipped over every nerve in her body and she couldn't stop a tiny moan from escaping.

Needing to touch him as he was touching her, she moved her hands from his wide chest down his abdomen to his lean flanks. She felt him shudder against her and, encouraged by his reaction, she moved her hands lower. When she found him, she stroked his length and tested the heaviness below. He suddenly went perfectly still a moment before a deep groan rumbled up from his chest. He broke away from the kiss to take several deep breaths.

"Sweetheart, as much as I hate to say it, I think you'd better stop…and let me catch my breath," he said haltingly. He trapped her hands in his and placed them back on his chest. "If you don't, you're going to be disappointed and I'm going to be real embarrassed."

"It's been so long," she said, knowing that if they didn't make love soon she was going to go out of her mind with longing. "I need you, Blake."

"And I need you, Karly," he said, reaching for the foil packet he'd placed on the bedside table earlier. Arranging their protection, he nudged her knees apart and rose over her. "I promise next time it won't be as rushed."

If she could have found her voice she would have told him that she couldn't have waited any longer. But words were impossible when he guided himself to her and she felt him slowly begin to fill her.

As her body stretched to accommodate his, her chest tightened with emotion. She had never felt as complete as she did when Blake made them one. It had been that way in Las Vegas—it was that way now. And she knew in her heart that's the way it would always be. He was her man—her other half— and no amount of time or distance or fear or insecurity would ever change that.

Her heart stalled as she realized she'd fallen in love with him all over again. But as she stared up at his handsome face, she knew that wasn't true. If she was honest with herself, she'd have to admit she'd never fallen out of love with him.

"You feel so damned good," Blake said, oblivious to her realization.

Deciding to think about her sudden insight later, Karly noticed his clenched jaw and the strained expression on his handsome face. It reflected his struggle for control and his determination to bring her pleasure before he found his own.

"Please make love to me, Blake," she said, wrapping her arms around him as she arched her body into his.

Groaning, he lowered his lips to hers and to her

delight, he began to rock against her. Slow and gentle, she was certain his movements were calculated to bring her the most pleasure he possibly could. He made her feel as if she was the most cherished woman on earth and that it was his privilege to be with her.

But all too soon the tension he was building within her gathered into a coil of longing in her most feminine parts. Blake must have sensed her readiness because he increased the depth and strength of his strokes. Just when she thought her body would shatter from the exquisite tightening inside of her, she was suddenly set free. Pleasure flowed through every cell in her body and she felt as if she might faint from the beautiful sensations that seemed to go on forever.

As she slowly began to drift back to reality, Karly felt Blake's body surge into her one final time. He tightened his arms around her as if she was his lifeline and held her to him as he found his own shuddering release.

When he buried his head in the pillow beside her, she stroked the dark brown hair at the nape of his neck and reveled in their differences. His weight felt absolutely wonderful pressed against her and she felt surrounded by his much bigger body.

"I'm too heavy for you, sweetheart," he said, levering himself up on his forearms. He brushed a strand of hair from her cheek as he smiled down at her. "Are you all right?"

"I'm wonderful," she said, nodding.

"You can add *amazing* to that, as well as *exciting* and *beautiful*," he stated, brushing her lips with his. When he moved to her side, he pulled her to him and covered them both with the comforter. "It's been so long since I made love to you, I'm afraid my control wasn't what it should have been. I give you my word that the next time I'll make sure to give you more pleasure."

She shivered with anticipation at the thought of having him make love to her again. "As much as I love that idea, I think it would be best if we discussed a few things first," she said, knowing that even though this had been wonderful, everything had become a lot more complicated.

When he failed to respond, she moved her head from where it was pillowed on his shoulder to look up at him. His eyes were closed and she could tell by the movement of his broad chest that he had fallen asleep.

Karly kissed his chin and closed her eyes. He was probably exhausted from working with the stallion he had been training most of the day.

She yawned and snuggled closer to him. It might be for the best that he'd fallen asleep before they could talk. She needed to come to terms with the newfound knowledge that she was still in love with her husband, as well as decide what she wanted to do about that insight.

Did she have the courage to ask him to put the

divorce on hold for a while to see if they could make their marriage work? Was that what she really wanted? Could he forgive her for the mistake she'd made in thinking their marriage would lead to her resenting him as her mother had resented her father? What would she do if she asked him for another chance and he decided that wasn't what he wanted?

She yawned again and felt the shadows of sleep begin to tug at her. Maybe if she rested for a while, she'd be able to think more clearly and the answers would come to her. They had to. Happiness for the rest of her life might very well depend on it.

The following evening, Blake took a swig of his beer as he watched his wife chatting and laughing with Tori Laughlin across the patio at the Rusty Spur Ranch house. Karly seemed to be having a good time, and he couldn't help but wonder if she would be around for the next get-together with his friends and their guests.

They hadn't talked about the future beyond agreeing that she would stay a few more days and she hadn't seemed any more ready to discuss what would happen after that than he was. Before they made love, he had promised her they would talk afterward. But they'd both fallen asleep and when they woke up together in bed, nature had taken its course once again. They'd spent the rest of the night reacquainting themselves with each other's bodies and that morning they had awakened just in time to get ready to leave for the late-afternoon barbecue.

"You've really got it bad for her, don't you?" Eli Laughlin asked, walking up to stand next to Blake.

"Yeah, I guess I do," he admitted.

"She seems real nice," Eli commented. "When did the two of you meet?"

"During the Nationals Finals in Vegas before Christmas," he said, never taking his eyes off Karly. He took another swig of his beer. "That's when we got married."

When he'd called Eli a few days before to tell his friend he would be bringing a guest to the get-together, Blake had explained that she wasn't aware he owned the Wolf Creek Ranch and that he'd like to keep it that way. As he expected, Eli had immediately agreed. But Blake had known that at some point he'd need to explain his strange request and tell Eli that he and Karly were married.

In the middle of taking a drink of his beer, Eli choked and Blake reached over to pound him on the back. When his friend stopped coughing, he stared at Blake like he'd sprouted another head.

"You got married," Eli repeated as if he couldn't quite believe what Blake had just said.

Blake nodded and explained the events leading up to the current situation he and Karly found themselves in. "But filing for the divorce is on hold—at least until the end of the week."

Eli nodded. "That gives you a little time to figure

out how you're going to ask her to stay—and how to tell her you own the Wolf Creek. You're also going to have to tell her why you kept that from her in the first place."

Watching his wife play with the Laughlin's two-year-old son, Aaron, Blake tried to imagine having a family with Karly. If her interaction with the toddler was any indication, she loved kids and would be everything he could possibly want for the mother of his children.

"Any suggestions about how I should go about handling all of that?" he asked, grinning.

Blake had known his friend would be the last to pass judgment on the way Blake and Karly met and married. Eli and Tori hadn't gotten together in the usual way, either. And Blake had been confident that Eli wouldn't question his reasoning for keeping his wealth out of the equation. Before he met Tori, Eli had dealt with his own share of unscrupulous women going after his bank account.

Eli laughed. "You know better than to ask me for advice when it comes to women. I'm sure you remember what a stubborn jackass I was when Tori and I got married. I just thank the good Lord above that she loved me enough to give me a second chance."

"And look at you now," Blake agreed, laughing with his friend. "You're still a jackass, just a little less stubborn than you used to be."

"It takes one to know one," Eli retorted.

"What are you two laughing about this time?" Tori asked.

Looking up, Blake grinned as he watched the women and the toddler walking toward them. "I was just agreeing with your husband that he's a jackass."

"I was telling him that it takes a jackass to know one," Eli explained.

Tori laughed. "Well, it's nice to know some things never change. But right now, I need to steal Eli for a few minutes. The band has arrived and he needs to let them know where to set up while I take Aaron inside for a few minutes to change him into his pajamas."

"She said he'd be asleep before the band finished their first song," Karly commented as Tori carried the little boy inside the house.

Putting his arm around her shoulders, Blake pulled Karly to his side. "Are you having a good time?"

When she smiled up at him, it caused a hitch in his breathing. He suddenly wished they were back at the foreman's cottage, where he could spend the rest of the evening making love to her.

"I'm having a wonderful time," she said, sounding happy and relaxed. "I really like your friends. I'm just sorry I didn't get to meet your brother. Tori said he was supposed to be here, but was called away on business."

"Sean used to be a special agent with the FBI," Blake said, nodding. "They still get in touch with him sometimes to act as an independent consultant on certain types of cases."

"That sounds fascinating," she said, sounding genuinely interested. "Is your brother still involved in law enforcement?"

"Yes and no," he answered, setting his empty beer bottle on one of the patio tables to take her in his arms. "He's a private investigator now. But when he was with the Bureau he was a crisis negotiator. He gets calls from law enforcement agencies all over Wyoming and the surrounding states when they have a situation that requires his expertise." He leaned close to nibble kisses along the side of her neck. "But I don't want to talk about Sean right now. I want to discuss when you think it would be acceptable for us to leave for home."

She shivered against him and he knew she was anticipating the night ahead of them the same as he was. "I think we could leave after a couple of dances, since we have an hour-and-a-half drive to get back to the ranch."

"I'll be right back," he said suddenly as he released her and started across the patio to where the band was getting ready to start playing. When he reached the frontman, Blake pulled his wallet from the hip pocket of his jeans and took out a couple of hundred dollars. He handed the money to the man. "I'd really appreciate it if you could make the first couple of songs slow ones."

"Hey, for two hundred dollars we'll make the

whole first set slow ones," the man answered as he pocketed the money.

"After the first two, you can play whatever you want," Blake said, grinning. "Just make sure what you play is slow and good to dance to."

The man nodded. "You got it."

Blake walked back to where Karly stood and draped his arm across her shoulders. "Two slow dances and we're out of here."

"You didn't," she said, her voice filled with laughter.

"Yup, I sure did." He brushed his lips over hers. "I wasn't leaving anything to chance."

When she rose up on tiptoes, she whispered, "Don't tell anyone, but I'm not the least bit sorry."

Ten minutes later, when the band broke into a popular slow country love song, Blake led Karly out to the section of the patio that had been designated as the dance floor. Taking her into his arms, he swayed her back and forth in time with the music. The feel of her body aligned with his and the sensual brushing of her lower stomach against his steadily growing arousal had him wishing it had been one and done, instead of the two dances they'd decided were socially acceptable.

His heart stalled when she put her arms around his neck and pressed herself closer. "You're making me a little crazy, sweetheart," he warned.

"Only a little?" Her sexy smile sent his blood

pressure sky-high. "I guess I'll just have to try a bit harder to make you a lot crazy."

Blake swallowed around the cotton clogging his throat in order to get his vocal cords to work as he looked around to find the Laughlins. When he spotted them talking to some of their guests, he took her by the hand and started toward the couple.

"Where are we going?" Karly asked, sounding like she already knew.

"To thank Eli and Tori for having us over." Giving her a quick kiss, Blake grinned. "Social conventions be damned, sweetheart. We're heading back home where we can both be as crazy as we want to be."

Eight

The moment he closed the door to the master bedroom in the foreman's cottage, Blake took Karly into his arms and captured her mouth with his. The hour-and-a-half drive from the Rusty Spur Ranch had taken its toll and he was wound up tighter than a two-dollar watch. Every nerve in his body was on high alert and he ached with the need to once again claim her as his wife.

His wife. Even the words felt right and if he'd had any doubts about marrying her before, they had been erased this evening. Watching her with his friends—seeing her play with little Aaron—had been enough to convince him that Karly was the woman for him. She fit in perfectly and he could tell that she and Tori would end up becoming best friends.

If this was even a glimpse of what their lives would be like as husband and wife, he'd be the happiest man alive for the rest of his days. And he fully intended to make sure she was the happiest woman.

Deepening the kiss, he gently stroked her tongue and explored her soft, sweet recesses. Her taste and eager response to the caress were all he could have hoped for. Reaching down, he tugged the tail of her T-shirt from the waistband of her jeans.

Her warm, satiny skin was like a fine piece of silk beneath his calloused palms. Easing away from the kiss, he skimmed his lips along her jawline and down her neck to the fluttering pulse at the base of her throat. "Sweetheart, I'd like to go slow and love every inch of you. But I need you so much right now, I'm not sure that's going to be possible."

She caught his face with her delicate hands and lifted his head until their gazes met. "You can go slow the next time, Blake. I need you now."

"Thank God," he said, burying his face in her silky blond hair. "I don't think I could wait much longer, even if my life depended on it."

"I feel the same way. I thought I would burst into flames when we were on the dance floor and I felt how much you needed me." She shivered and he knew it had nothing to do with being chilled. "But I want you to do something for me."

Without a second thought, he nodded. "Anything for you, Karly."

"Let *me* make love to *you*," she said, giving him a look that sent his hormones racing through his veins at the speed of light. "Do you mind?"

What man in his right mind would turn down a beautiful woman doing incredibly sexy things to his body?

"I need you to promise me something, Karly," he said, pulling her close for a quick kiss.

"Wh-what's that?" she asked, sounding a little short of breath.

"If I tell you to stop whatever you're doing, can you give me your word that you will?"

She looked confused. "All right. But I don't un-derstand—"

"I want us to finish this race together," he said, grinning.

He could tell she understood his meaning when she smiled. "I want that, too. I promise."

"Good." Stepping back, he held his arms wide. "I'm all yours, sweetheart."

Karly wasted no time in pointing to the side of the bed. "If you'll sit down, I'll take your boots off."

Looking forward to seeing what she had in mind, he did as she requested. He swallowed hard when she turned her back to him, straddled one of his legs and bent over. But when she started tugging on his boot and her delightful little bottom bobbed mere inches in front of his face, Blake was pretty sure he was going to have a coronary. By the time his boots and socks lay on the floor beside the bed, sweat had popped out on his forehead and his upper lip, and he felt like he just might need CPR.

"Sweetheart, why don't we take off our clothes and get into bed," he said, forcing himself to breathe as he stood up to unbuckle his belt. "Otherwise, I'm not going to last long enough to get to the main event."

"I think that would be a good idea," she said, sounding a little winded herself.

"I give you my word that I'll let you take my clothes off me another time when I'm not so revved up," he said, making quick work of his clothing.

He made it a point to keep his gaze averted while she removed hers. If he hadn't, he wasn't sure he wouldn't have gone up in a blaze of glory.

As Karly got into bed, he reached into his jeans for one of the condoms he'd remembered to get from his medicine cabinet when they were over at the mansion the day before. Placing it on the bedside table, he stretched out beside her.

When he started to pull her to him, she shook her head. "Remember, this is all about me giving you pleasure," she said, her smile causing another wave of heat to course from the top of his head to the soles of his feet.

"Just keep in mind that I'm only human and I do…have my limits," he said, feeling like he had been branded when she placed her hand on his chest.

When he cupped one of her perfect breasts, she closed her eyes and nodded. "I've almost reached mine, as well."

Just knowing that she was as turned on as he was had him clenching his teeth in an effort to slow down his overly active libido. But when she reached over to take the packet from the bedside table and carefully opened it, Blake closed his eyes and held his breath. He'd never had a woman do what Karly was planning to do and he could only hope that he had enough strength to hold on to what little control he had left.

At the first touch of her fingers to the most sensitive part of his body, Blake felt like he'd been treated to the business end of a cattle prod. He groaned and tried to think of something—anything—to take his mind off what the woman of his dreams was doing for him.

"Are you all right?" she asked when he let loose with a deep groan.

He nodded as he reached to take her hands in his. "I think you'd better give me…a minute."

"You need to catch your breath?" she asked.

"Yeah, we can…call it that," he said, breathing deeply in an effort to release some of the tension gripping him. When he felt like he had regained a degree of control, he warned, "I'm not going to be able to take much more, sweetheart."

"I can't, either," she said, rising to her knees.

His heart stopped completely when she straddled his hips and guided him into her. As he watched, she lowered herself onto him and just the sight of her body taking him in was mind-blowing. But the feel of her warmth surrounding him caused his body to respond with a tightening that left him feeling light-headed.

He watched her close her eyes as if she savored being one with him. Humbled that a woman as loving and beautiful as Karly would even want to be with him, he knew beyond a shadow of doubt that he still loved her.

It made him more determined than ever to find out what happened after she returned to Seattle. Whatever it was they'd find a way to work through it. And he could only hope she'd be able to forgive him for not telling her about himself sooner and give him a chance to make it up to her.

But he didn't have time to dwell on what he was going to do about his self-discovery and whatever obstacles they still faced. As he watched the woman who owned his heart, she opened her eyes, gave him a smile that caused his chest to tighten with emotion and slowly began to move against him.

He placed his hands on her hips and held on as the friction of their bodies increased the pressure building inside of him. He could tell Karly was experiencing the same sensations from the blush of passion on her porcelain cheeks and the rapt light in her big blue eyes.

As he felt himself reaching the point where his satisfaction was inevitable, Karly's tiny feminine muscles tightened around him a moment before her head fell back and she gasped from the intense sensations flowing through her. That's when Blake took control of the pace and did his best to give her as much pleasure as he possibly could before his own release set him free. Groaning, he shuddered as he gave up his essence to the woman he loved.

When Karly collapsed on his chest, he wrapped his arms around her and held her to him as their bodies cooled and their breathing returned to normal. "Are you doing okay?" he whispered close to her ear.

"That was incredible," she said, raising her head to kiss his chin.

"You're incredible." He enjoyed the feel of her lying on top of him and the connection they still shared. "Next time I promise you can take my clothes off and have your wicked way with me," he said, chuckling. "But I was so turned on, I wouldn't have lasted five minutes if you'd taken your time."

When she remained silent, he realized that she had fallen fast asleep. Kissing her cheek, he rolled them to their sides, pulled the comforter around them and held her close. He wasn't sure how he was going to explain why he hadn't been entirely honest with her about owning the ranch or the fact that neither of them would ever have to work another day in their lives if they didn't want to.

But it was past time he told her everything about himself and the reasons he'd felt compelled to keep the information from her. He hoped she'd understand his past experience with his gold-digging stepmother and the years she'd held his family's ranch hostage in her attempt to get the most money she could out of it. He also hoped Karly would be able to do the same when he told her about that buckle bunny, the one claiming he had made her pregnant in an effort to extort money from him, and how it had left him deeply suspicious of women's motives, as well.

When she murmured his name and snuggled into his embrace, he kissed her forehead. He wasn't sure how she would react to his revelations. But tomorrow he was going to tell her everything, pray that she understood and ask her to stay with him for the rest of his life.

The morning after the barbecue at the Laughlins', Karly sat at the table in the mansion's library, staring at the screen on Blake's laptop. She was supposed to be finishing up a purchase order for novelty items from one of the import companies in Hong Kong. But she couldn't have cared less about cases of rubber ducks, plush finger puppets and inflatable plastic beach balls. Her mind was on what would happen at the end of the week when it was time for her to leave the Wolf Creek Ranch. Blake hadn't mentioned anything about wanting them to stay married and have her remain in Wyoming with him. And she hadn't told him that she would like to stay and be his wife.

Nibbling on her lower lip, she thought about her reasons for refusing to join him at the ranch after they left Las Vegas and how she felt about that now. After she and Blake parted eight months ago, she had returned to pack up her apartment and quit her job. And that had been when her doubts set in. She had worried that she might move to the ranch and discover that she couldn't stand the quiet remoteness or that she would miss having a productive career. She had been so afraid of being unhappy that she'd convinced herself not to even take the chance.

But now that she'd spent time on the ranch, she found that she loved the peace and quiet. And it came as no small surprise that she found feeding a couple of orphaned calves much more rewarding than keeping a warehouse stocked with rubber ducks and plastic beach balls.

She sighed. She'd watched her mother sink into a deep depression after they returned to New York from the Midwest, especially after Martina hadn't been able to resume her career in the fashion industry. Her mother's misery had left a lasting impression on Karly and one of her biggest fears had always been that she would turn out to be as dissatisfied and resentful as her mother.

But looking at things objectively, Karly could never remember a time when her mother had been truly happy—not before they'd moved to the Midwest or after. Martina Ewing had been dissatisfied before her husband moved them away from New York. She'd been unhappy living in a small town in Middle America and when she and Karly returned to New York, she hadn't been content there, either. It was a hard truth to face, but her mother had been one of those people who always searched for something to make her happy and when she couldn't find it, blamed someone else. She had never discovered that true happiness comes from within and that just being with the people she loved was a real blessing.

But this time with Blake had convinced Karly of that truth. No matter where they lived or whatever job she needed to work to help with their finances, she knew she would be truly fulfilled as long as they were together. And she finally felt ready to create a life of happiness with him. She hoped he was ready for that, too.

"You wouldn't happen to know where Blake is, would you?" a man's voice asked from just inside the door.

Unaware there was anyone else around, Karly jumped and placed her hand on her chest as if that would slow down her racing heart. "Oh, dear heavens!"

"I'm sorry," the man said, stepping forward with his hands outstretched in front of him as if to stop her from panicking. "I didn't mean to frighten you." He looked contrite as he hooked his thumb over his shoulder toward the hall. "I would have asked Silas, but he's taking his afternoon nap and it's easier to wake the dead than to try to rouse him once he's asleep."

"Silas does seem to be able to sleep through anything." She'd noticed that fact while working to set up her workspace in the library a couple of days ago. Feeling calmer, Karly smiled. "Blake is out in the arena working with a new stallion."

The man nodded. "Thanks." He turned to leave, then turned back. "By the way, I'm Sean Hartwell, Blake's brother."

Once he'd introduced himself, she could immediately see the resemblance between the two men. About the same height, Sean had the same dark brown hair and brown eyes as Blake.

"I'm Karly Ewing," she said, not sure if Blake had mentioned he had a wife.

"Are you his new secretary or assistant?" Sean asked.

She wondered why Blake would need an assistant. It suddenly dawned on her that Sean must have meant to ask if she was the ranch owner's new secretary.

Smiling, she shook her head. "No, I'm staying with Blake for a few days over at the foreman's cottage."

Sean surprised her when he frowned. "Why are the two of you staying over there? He hasn't lived there since he built this place and moved in almost two years ago."

Karly stared at Sean for several long moments as reality began to sink in. "I-I'm not sure," she said slowly. "I suppose you'll have to ask him."

"You can count on it," he said, nodding.

"Do you and Blake own the ranch together?" she asked, feeling as if she had a knot the size of her fist in her stomach.

"No. My ranch is about forty-five minutes away on the other side of the ridge," he said, apparently unaware of his brother's ruse. He pointed toward the laptop on the library table. "I'll let you get back to whatever it is you're doing. It was nice to meet you, Karly. I hope you enjoy the rest of your visit to the Wolf Creek."

"It was nice to meet you, too, Sean," she murmured when he turned toward the door.

As she watched him leave, her chest tightened and it was extremely difficult to draw air into her lungs. Why would Blake lie to her? Why hadn't he told her he owned the Wolf Creek Ranch when they were in Las Vegas?

Of course they hadn't talked about much of anything personal. But that didn't explain why he had failed to tell her when she arrived to have him sign the new set of divorce papers.

A cold wave of sadness suddenly swept over her. He hadn't asked her to sign a prenuptial agreement. When she told him it would be best for them to end their marriage, Blake had obviously been afraid she would try to get part of his ranch.

She looked around the library and it became crystal clear that Blake had to be extremely wealthy. Log homes were some of the most expensive types of houses to build and one the size of this mansion would cost several millions of dollars just for the construction. The custom-built furnishings for a place this size would cost at least that much more. Then there was the pool area, with its waterfalls and tropical oasis hot tub. No telling how much that cost. Factor in a huge indoor arena and heated stable, the house and barns down the road and thousands of acres of land…

"Oh, my God," she said, sinking back down onto the chair at the table. "He thought I would try to take…" She covered her mouth with her hand to hold back a sob. His assets and hanging on to them was obviously more important to him than telling her the truth. He hadn't even given her the opportunity to assure him she had no interest in taking anything away from him.

Yes, she'd broken her promise to him when she'd asked for a divorce, but never once had she deliberately lied to him.

Standing up, she hurried into the foyer, threw open the massive front door, ran out to the ranch truck Blake had been using and got into the driver's seat. He made a habit of leaving the keys in the ignition whenever they were on ranch land and she was thankful he did.

When she started the truck and drove down the lane to the road, she didn't look back in the rearview mirror. Blake had made it crystal clear there was nothing back there for her.

She'd made her own mistakes by giving into her

fears and not telling him the real reason behind her asking for a divorce. But what he'd done had been far worse. He had deliberately misled her and had no intention of asking her to stay with him to see if they could work things out. He'd probably been relieved when she called to tell him she wouldn't be moving to Wyoming with him. That would certainly explain why he hadn't been more insistent that she give their marriage a chance.

Tears streamed down her cheeks as she drove the short distance to the foreman's cottage, she went inside to retrieve the things she'd brought with her from Seattle and loaded the rental car. It was just as well that she'd found out about his ruse. Even if he had finally come clean about what he'd been trying so hard to hide, she didn't think she would ever be able to trust him.

Sobbing, she drove down the mountain road toward Eagle Fork. She hadn't been after his ranch, his money or anything material. Whether Blake was as rich as sin or as poor as a pauper, all she'd ever wanted, all she'd ever cared about, was having him love her.

"Hey there, bro," Blake said, riding the stallion over to where Sean stood just inside the arena doors. "You missed a great party last night over at the Rusty Spur."

His brother nodded. "I was on my way back from a situation up in Sheridan."

"Anything you can talk about?" Blake asked.

"Some guy is robbing banks all over the state and I was asked to review the details of his latest robbery," Sean answered.

"If he's been at this a while, I'm surprised they haven't called you in before now," Blake commented.

"This was the first time somebody got killed," Sean answered.

When his brother fell silent, Blake knew that was all Sean would say on the matter. Blake wasn't surprised that Sean didn't go into more detail about the case. He never talked about the work he did for the FBI and Blake never pressed for more than his brother was willing to tell.

"So what are you up to this afternoon?" Blake asked, dismounting the horse.

"I came by to see if you want to go fishing with me tomorrow." His brother shrugged. "But after I met your houseguest, I decided you probably wouldn't be interested."

"You met Karly?" Blake asked, hoping the subject of who owned the ranch hadn't been a topic of conversation.

"Yeah, she seems real nice," Sean commented. "But why are you two staying over at the homestead?"

"It's…complicated." A knot began to form in his gut as he realized Karly must have mentioned where they were staying. He asked, "Did you mention that I own the ranch?"

Sean stared at him for what seemed like forever before he finally nodded. "She asked and I wasn't going to lie to her." When Blake cut loose with a string of cusswords that had his brother raising his eyebrows, Sean asked, "Care to explain what brought on that little display of profanity?"

"Have one of the men take care of Blaze," Blake said, handing Sean the stallion's reins.

"What's going on?" Sean demanded when Blake took off across the yard toward the house.

"I'll tell you later," he called over his shoulder. "I have to go talk to my wife."

Blake knew he would face an interrogation from Sean later on but he'd worry about that when the time came. Right now, he needed to talk to Karly and explain why he hadn't told her everything months ago.

Running across the patio, Blake started calling her name as soon as he entered the house. When his calls went unanswered an icy dread began to settle in the pit of his stomach.

His heart stalled when he went into the foyer and found the front door ajar. Looking out, he really couldn't say he was surprised to see the ranch truck gone and along with it, his wife.

By the time he went back inside to get the keys for one of the vehicles in the garage, his brother met him in the kitchen. "What the hell's going on?" Sean demanded.

"I don't have time to get into it," Blake said, heading over to the key rack. "I have to get over to the foreman's cottage to stop Karly."

"My truck's out front," Sean said, starting for the door. "Come on, I'll drive you over there. And on the way you can explain when you got a wife and why she didn't have a clue that you own this spread."

As they drove away, Blake explained about their marriage in Vegas, Karly showing up with the new set of divorce papers and his reasoning behind not telling her up front that he was more than a ranch foreman and part-time rodeo rider. "I had planned on telling her when she moved here, right after Vegas. Then there seemed to be no real reason to share the truth, when we were headed for divorce. After the past few days…I had planned to tell her everything this evening after supper and ask her to stay with me."

His brother nodded. "Sorry I spoiled your reveal."

Blake shook his head. "Not your fault. I knew I was running out of time." He groaned as Sean parked beside the ranch truck. The little red sports car was gone. "She's headed back to Washington." He paused as he tried to think. "I'm just not sure if she's headed for Seattle or Lincoln County."

"What's in Lincoln County?" Sean asked.

"The divorce court," Blake answered, explaining the reason Karly intended to file there instead of in Seattle.

"Let me make a couple of phone calls," Sean said, reaching for his cell phone.

Blake knew if there was any chance of finding Karly, Sean had the connections to do it. But finding her was only half the battle. Getting her to listen to him was an entirely different matter.

While his brother tried to track down where Karly was headed, Blake went into the foreman's cottage to see if Karly had taken her luggage. He wasn't surprised to see that she'd taken the things she'd brought with her, but left the clothing, hat and boots he'd bought for her on their shopping trip to the Blue Sage Western Emporium.

Blake walked back downstairs and met Sean on the back porch. "She just called Cheyenne and made reservations for a flight to Denver. From there she's headed to Seattle."

Blake took a deep breath. He'd caught a break. "What time does her flight leave Denver?"

"Not until around six this evening," Sean said, grinning. "She's going to miss the earlier afternoon flight by about an hour."

Blake checked his watch. "Can you get me down there to catch that early flight?"

His brother snorted. "If I can't, I'll turn in my license to fly helicopters." Sean had earned his pilot's license during his stint in the marines and because of his work with the FBI, regularly flew himself into Denver to catch flights to wherever there was a situation in need of his expertise.

Without another word, they both headed for Sean's truck. As his brother drove toward his ranch on the other side of the western ridge surrounding the Wolf Creek Ranch, Blake called to reserve a seat on the earlier flight to Seattle.

He didn't have a clear-cut plan, but he wasn't overly concerned. He had several hours before Karly's flight arrived and by then, he had no doubt he'd have something in mind.

When Karly called eight months ago, he'd told himself he was doing the right thing when he let her go without putting up a fight. It was what she wanted and he'd reasoned that pushing her would have done nothing to change her mind. But he wasn't going to make that mistake again. This time he was going to pull out all the stops.

He had no idea how long it would take to convince her, but one thing was certain. Blake wasn't returning to the Wolf Creek Ranch without her.

Nine

As Karly walked through the terminal toward the baggage claim area, she watched people as they met up with their loved ones and friends. It seemed that everyone else had someone there waiting to greet them. As usual, she had no one.

Tears threatened and she blinked several times to chase them away. It had never bothered her that she didn't have anyone to welcome her home after a trip. She had always collected her luggage, caught a cab and hadn't thought twice about being alone.

But that had changed with her trip to Wyoming. She'd never felt more alone in her entire life than she did at the moment.

Picking up her bag, she had to admit that wasn't

quite true. The only other time she had felt such a keen sense of loneliness had been eight months ago when she'd returned from her vacation in Las Vegas and she was facing the night alone without Blake to hold her.

Her breath caught on a sob and she hurried out of the exit to the line of yellow cabs, waiting to take travelers to their destinations. While the driver stored her bag in the trunk, she settled into the backseat and prayed that the man wasn't overly chatty. She really didn't think she could talk to anyone without making a fool of herself. All she wanted to do was go home to her apartment away from the prying eyes of strangers and cry herself into oblivion. Thankfully it was dark enough that even if she did lose control, chances were the man wouldn't notice.

When they reached her apartment complex, she paid the cabdriver and pulled her travel bag along behind her as she slowly walked the short distance to her ground-floor apartment. But once she approached the door, she spotted a man sitting in the shadows on her porch step. Unsure whether to proceed and demand that he leave or turn around and run for help, she stopped dead in her tracks. That's when he looked up.

Her heart pounded and drawing a breath was all but impossible. "Blake?"

"This isn't safe," he said, shaking his head. "There should be lights along these sidewalks and dusk-to-dawn security lights on every building."

"I left the front-door light on," she said defensively. "It must have burned out."

"I don't like you living in a place where the security is this lax," he said, rising to his feet as he looked around.

"Oh, really?" She shook her head as she reached inside her handbag for her key. "How safe it is where I live isn't any of your concern anymore."

"Like hell!" When she pulled the key from her bag, he took it from her trembling fingers and unlocked and opened the door for her. "You're my wife. Your safety is of the utmost importance to me."

His attitude and his reference to her as his wife infuriated and broke her heart at the same time. How could he claim to want the best for her when he hadn't trusted her with the truth?

"Get real, Blake." She brushed past him to enter her apartment and turn on one of the lamps at the end of the couch. "The most important things in your life are your precious ranch and your bank account. I doubt that I even make the top ten on your list of things you value."

"That's not true," he said, following her into her small living room. "You're more important to me than my next breath."

"Whatever," she said, dropping her purse on the coffee table. She turned to face him. "I don't know why you're here or what you think you're going to accomplish by following me to Seattle, but—"

"I came to talk to my wife," he said, closing the door behind him.

"I don't see that there's anything left to say." She shook her head. "You had ample opportunity to talk to me while I was at the Wolf Creek Ranch and you chose not to. And stop calling me your wife."

"I'm here now to set things straight," he said stubbornly crossing his arms. He stood like a stone statue and she realized he had every intention of making her listen to what he had to say. "And why shouldn't I call you my wife?" he asked. "We're still married."

She rubbed at the tension, causing her temples to pound unmercifully. "Please leave, Blake. I'm exhausted and you're not helping my developing headache."

He took a step toward her. "Sweetheart, I'm—"

"Don't call me that," she said, shaking her head as she backed away from him. "That's an endearment and one that you obviously don't mean and never have." She took a deep breath. "Now, will you please leave and go back to Wyoming, where you belong."

"I belong where you are." He walked over and sat down on the couch. "And I'm not leaving until we work this out."

Frustrated with his persistence to the point of tears she absolutely refused to let him see, she pulled her travel bag to the bedroom door. "I'm not going to argue with you any longer. I'm going to bed and I would prefer that you're gone when I get up in the morning. Please lock the door on your way out."

Without looking back, she walked into the bedroom, closed and locked the door, then leaned back against it. She couldn't imagine what Blake thought he could say to explain his actions or why he even cared to try. On the flight back to Seattle, she'd faced the brutal reality of the situation. No matter what he'd told her, Blake had never intended for their marriage to work. He'd never even told her what his life in Wyoming was really like! For that matter, she couldn't imagine why he'd married her to begin with. He'd probably been immensely relieved when she'd refused to join him on the ranch eight months ago.

It suddenly occurred to her that he might be here now to make sure she wasn't going to go after his money or try to take part of his ranch. The divorce wasn't final yet, after all.

"He doesn't need to worry," she murmured as she walked into the adjoining bathroom to brush her teeth. Even if he offered her a settlement, she would tell him what he could do with it. She had never wanted anything from him but his love, his respect and his honesty.

But even though he hadn't given her any of that, her heart had stalled and she'd barely resisted the urge to run into his arms when she first saw him sitting on her step. Nothing would have made her happier than to have him hold her close and tell her that it would all be all right and they could work things out.

As she looked in the mirror at the miserable woman staring back at her, Karly couldn't help but wonder if she'd lost her mind. How could Blake possibly look so darned good to her when he was the last person in the world she should want to see? Or trust?

Sitting at the small table in Karly's breakfast nook, Blake shifted in his chair in an effort to relieve the kinks in his back from sleeping on her couch. Sometime around midnight, he'd decided the damn thing should be certified as an instrument of torture. Not only had both of his feet gone to sleep from hanging over the end of it, but there was also a definite sag in the middle that had his back feeling like it had been broken in several places.

But as uncomfortable as it had been, there was no way he was going to leave this apartment until she heard what he had to say—even if he had to sleep on that damn couch all week. After he'd laid it all on the line, then if she still wanted to kick him to the curb, he'd somehow find the strength to bow out of the picture—even if it killed him—and let her go. The bottom line was and always had been that he loved her and wanted nothing but her happiness. He could only hope that happiness included him.

"I thought you'd be gone by now," she said when she walked into the tiny kitchen carrying a box of tissues. Her eyes were red and puffy and he knew she'd spent most of the night crying. Just knowing he was the cause of her distress nearly killed him.

But as he continued to look at her, his heart stalled. With her long blond hair slightly mussed from sleep and wearing a nightshirt that was at least two sizes too large and about as shapeless as a tow sack, he didn't think he'd ever seen her look sexier.

He took a sip of his coffee and shook his head as he tried to focus on what he needed to say to get her to listen. "I'm not going anywhere until we talk."

"I have to go to work," she said, placing the box on the table and walking over to pour herself a cup of the coffee he'd made earlier.

"I'll be here when you get home." He shrugged. "Whether it's now or later, we are going to discuss this, Karly."

She stared at him for several long seconds before she closed her eyes as if trying to find patience. When she opened them, the emotional pain he detected in the blue depths just about tore him apart. The thought that he was the cause of that sadness was more than he could bear.

"Blake, I don't know what you could possibly say that's going to make a difference," she said, sinking into the chair across the table from him. "You obviously didn't want me to know that you own the Wolf Creek Ranch or that you're quite wealthy."

Guilt settled across his shoulders. "Karly, there were a couple of reasons I didn't tell you about my assets when we first met."

"I remember you telling me about the owner's stepmother being a gold digger and how hard it was to get the ranch back," she said, sounding defeated. "I just wasn't aware you were talking about yourself and the difficulties you had with her. But I had nothing to do with that."

"I know." He slowly set his coffee cup on the table. "Sean and I had hints of the way she was after Dad married her, but when he passed away she took the gloves off and made it clear she was going to do everything she could to cut us out and keep us from inheriting anything she thought she could turn into cash."

"It's unfortunate that she turned out to be so ruthless and I can understand you becoming suspicious of other women's motives." Karly shook her head. "But I didn't know anything about you having money and you had no right to blame me for crimes I didn't commit. And for that matter, never would commit."

"I know, sweetheart, and I can't tell you how sorry I am for that."

He stared down at his loosely clasped hands resting on the table a moment before he took a deep breath and met her accusing gaze head-on. She needed to know all of the reasons behind his caution, even if those reasons were something he was less than proud of.

"I also had my own run-in with a woman several years back who tried to extort money from me," he said, cursing himself for being such a fool.

"Once again, I had nothing to do with that," she reminded him. He hadn't expected her to make his confession easy on him and he deserved nothing less than her condemnation.

"I realize that, but I owe you an explanation and an apology." He took a deep breath. "About six years ago, I was at a rodeo in San Antonio and won the bull-riding event. Instead of celebrating with a can of beer and a good night's sleep like I should have, I went out on the town."

"You got drunk," she said, cutting right to the heart of the matter.

Blake nodded. "Yeah. And I should have stopped with that and gone back to the hotel."

"But you didn't," she mused.

"No. I went back to a cheap motel close to the bar." He hesitated. "I was with one of the buckle bunnies."

"What are those?" Karly asked, taking a sip from her coffee cup. Her doubtful expression hadn't changed, but she was at least showing an interest in his explanation.

"Rodeo groupies," he answered, wishing he'd never heard of them, either. "Some of them are harmless, but others want to sleep with rough stock riders who win."

"Why?" she asked, frowning.

"For the bragging rights," he said, disgusted with himself for falling into that trap. "It's like a feather in their cap to say they've slept with this or that rider." He shook his head at his foolishness. "Anyway, I spent the night with one of them and a month later she showed up claiming I had made her pregnant."

Karly's eyes widened. "You have a child?"

"Good God, no," he said hurriedly. "It turned out that she wasn't pregnant at all. She had asked around and found out that I had money and was in line to inherit at least part of the Wolf Creek Ranch. She decided I was an easy mark for a big payoff."

"She thought you would pay her to end the pregnancy?" Karly asked, looking affronted.

He nodded. "Just about the time I offered to raise the baby on my own, I learned she wasn't pregnant and never had been."

Karly looked thoughtful for a moment as if she was processing what he had told her. "I suppose something like that would leave you with an over-abundance of caution."

"It had been my experience not to let people know that I was more than just another dust-covered cowboy trying to make a living off riding bulls and herding cattle," he said, nodding. "Then I met you and before I found a way to tell you about myself, we got married and started making plans for you to move to the ranch."

"Why didn't you tell me then?" she asked, her tone accusing. "Was it because you failed to get me to sign a prenuptial agreement before the wedding ceremony?"

"Not at all." He had to make her understand. "I had plans to tell you when you joined me at the ranch. I thought it would be a nice surprise learning that we'd never have to worry about finances the way other couples do when they first start out. You'd have the option of continuing with your career, work part-time or quit and be a full-time ranch wife. Whatever you wanted to do."

"Only I called and told you that if we stayed married, you'd have to move to Seattle," she said slowly.

"Yeah." He stared down at his empty cup. When he looked up, he added, "But I wasn't the only one with a secret, was I?"

"What do you mean?" she asked, frowning. "I've always been honest with you."

"Sweetheart, from what you've told me about your parents and their divorce, I think that carried a lot of weight in your decision not to come to Wyoming eight months ago." He reached across the table to cover her delicate hand with his. "The only thing I don't know is how it influenced you and why."

She had opened up about her parents during their conversation in the hot tub and he was positive their divorce had somehow played into her choices about them. But he needed to know how their problems had become her problems. How were they holding her back?

When Karly remained silent, he got up to round the table. He picked her up and sat down with her on his lap. "I know I screwed up by not telling you everything about myself and the reasons I felt I had to be cautious. But you've left out some important information about yourself, too. What we've got is good and worth fighting for, Karly. Talk to me. Tell me what held you back and why you were so frightened—why you're still frightened."

"You won't understand," she said quietly. She shook her head. "I'm not even sure it makes sense."

"Why don't you tell me and maybe we can make sense of it together?" he suggested, loving that she was in his arms again and wasn't pushing away from him.

She remained silent for a minute before she finally spoke. "From the moment we moved to the Midwest my mother hated it and before it was over with, she despised my father as well." She turned her head to give him a pointed look. "After she and I moved back to New York she blamed him for everything that went wrong in her life—the loss of her career, her unhappiness. Sometimes I even think she didn't like me because I was part of him."

When she fell silent, Blake kissed her cheek and hugged her close. "I'm sure she loved you, sweetheart."

She shrugged one slender shoulder. "Whether she did or not, I was afraid that if I discovered I didn't like living outside of a city the same thing would happen to us." Tears filled her blue eyes when she looked at him. "I care too much for you to let that happen, Blake. You deserved better than to be resented and blamed for something you had no control over."

Giving her a kiss that left them both breathless, he raised his head to smile at her. "I love you, too, sweetheart. I always have and I always will."

That was all it took for the floodgates to open and when she lay her head on his shoulder, Blake held her while her tears ran their course. He hated seeing a woman cry, but Karly's tears were especially gut-wrenching. She was crying for the child who had doubted her mother's love, as well as what her parents' mistakes had almost cost the two of them.

When she raised her head he handed her a tissue from the box on the table. "Feel better now?" he asked, smiling at the only woman he had ever loved.

Her cheeks turned a rosy pink. "I'm sorry. I hate being so emotional."

"You don't have to apologize to me, Karly," he said, kissing her forehead. "It's my job to be here for you during the bad times, as well as the good."

"I love you so much, Blake," she said, throwing her arms around his neck.

"And I love you, Karly," he said, hugging her tightly against him.

They sat that way for some time, content just to be in each other's arms.

"So where are we going to live?" he finally asked.

She sat back to give him a strange look. "I...assume we'll live in Wyoming at your ranch."

"Only if that's where you want to live," he assured her. "As long as I have you, I'll live anywhere and make a trip back to the ranch periodically."

"Blake, I was wrong," she said, placing her soft palms on his cheeks to gaze into his eyes. "I love your ranch."

"Our ranch," he amended. "It's yours now, as much as it is mine."

She shook her head. "All I want is you."

"Do you really want to argue about this now?" he asked, laughing.

Smiling, she shook her head. "I want to live with you on the Wolf Creek Ranch. That's where I want to ride Suede and help you feed bucket babies and raise our own babies." Her smile faded. "I know we haven't talked about it, but you do want a family, don't you?"

"There are a lot of things we haven't talked about," he said, nodding. "But now that you're coming home with me, we have plenty of time to share our hopes and dreams." When she continued to look at him, he grinned. "Yes, Karly. I want a family and I'll be more than happy to give you all the babies you want."

"I love you so much," she said, snuggling against him. "I can't wait to go back home."

His chest tightened with emotion at her reference to the ranch as home. "There's something else I intended to do for you after we got married in Vegas."

"What's that?" she asked, kissing his neck.

Her lips sent a flash fire blazing through his veins and he had to take a deep breath in order to answer her. "The ceremony we had in Vegas wasn't very fancy and I want to see that you have the wedding of your dreams."

"Oh, Blake, I would love that," she said, tears filling her eyes once again. "But we'll have to wait until spring."

He frowned. "Why would we have to do that?"

"I'd really like to renew our vows out on the patio by the waterfall," she said, looking hopeful. "I think it would be beautiful if we could have a sunset wedding."

"We can make that happen," he said, nodding. "It's warm enough right now. How about this coming weekend?"

"We don't have time to arrange everything," she said, looking doubtful.

"Sweetheart, you'd be surprised how quickly things can be arranged when you have the money to do it," he said, laughing.

"How about the following weekend?" she asked. "I really need time to think about what I want."

"That sounds good to me," he said, standing up with her in his arms.

"Where are we going?" she asked as he carried her across the living room.

"I'm going to take my wife into her bedroom and make love to her," he said, kissing her soundly. "Then while you go to work, I'm going to try to get some sleep. Do you know how uncomfortable that damned couch is?"

Her laughter was one of the sweetest sounds he'd ever heard. "After we make love, I'm going to call and tell my boss that I won't be coming back. Then I'm going to stay in bed and take a nap because I didn't get much sleep last night, either."

As he placed her on the bed and stretched out beside her, Blake kissed her soft, perfect lips. "Are you sure you want to quit your job, Karly? I don't want you doing anything you might regret."

"I'm positive." She reached for the snaps on his chambray shirt. "Now, will my husband please make love to me?"

They could plan their wedding and discuss her decision to quit her job later. Right now, he had his beautiful wife asking him to make love to her and she wasn't going to have to ask him twice.

"I love you, Karly Ewing Hartwell. You own me, heart and soul."

"And I love you, Blake. More than you'll ever know."

Epilogue

Two weeks later, as Karly stood in front of the mirror in the bedroom she'd used at the foreman's cottage, she waited for Tori Laughlin to work the tiny buttons through the decorative loops at the back of her long, white satin and lace strapless wedding gown. "Is Eli here with the carriage?" she asked.

"He just arrived," Tori answered, finishing with the buttons on Karly's dress. She walked over and picked up the veil they'd laid out on the bed earlier. "Thank heavens Blake got the road asphalted these past two weeks. I'd hate to see your beautiful dress covered in Wyoming dust."

Karly nodded. "I couldn't believe how quickly the

crew from the construction company finished surfacing the road from here to the main house."

"It doesn't take long," Tori said as she pinned the tulle and lace to the back of Karly's loosely upswept hair. When Karly's new best friend stepped back, she smiled. "You're going to knock the socks off Blake when he sees you in this."

"That's the plan," Karly said, smiling as she looked at herself in the full length mirror.

After she and Blake returned to the ranch from Seattle, Karly had gone into full wedding mode and, with Tori's recommendation, hired a wedding planner from Cheyenne. The woman had been nothing short of a miracle worker and once Karly had told her what she wanted and the date, all that had been left for Karly to do was decide on the perfect dress. Fortunately, she found what she wanted at the first bridal shop she and Tori visited and once the alterations were completed there really hadn't been all that much for her to do.

A knock on the door signaled that it was time for Eli to drive them over to the main house for the ceremony that would renew Karly and Blake's wedding vows. When Tori opened the door he grinned. "You ladies look beautiful." Eli kissed his wife. "Blake and I are the two luckiest guys this side of the Great Divide."

"And don't you forget it," Tori said, kissing her husband's cheek. Turning to Karly, she asked, "Are you ready?"

"I'm more than ready," Karly said, picking up the bouquet the wedding planner had delivered earlier.

As they made their way downstairs and out to the white horse-drawn carriage that would take them over to the main house for the ceremony, Karly couldn't stop smiling. She felt a little like Cinderella and knowing that her very own Prince Charming would be waiting to help her down from the carriage once they arrived at the ranch house made her impatient to get there. She hadn't seen Blake since earlier in the day when Tori arrived to take them to get their hair and nails done down in Eagle Fork and she'd missed him terribly.

When Eli drove the carriage up the drive to the log mansion, Karly's breath caught at the sight of Blake waiting for them at the end of the sidewalk leading to the patio. Dressed in a Western cut tuxedo, black snake-skin boots and a wide brimmed black hat, he truly was the man of her dreams.

"You're gorgeous," he whispered close to her ear as he lifted her down from the carriage.

"You clean up real nice yourself, cowboy," Karly said, rising on tiptoes to kiss his lean cheek.

"Are you ready to become Mrs. Hartwell?" he asked as he tucked her hand in the crook of his arm and started walking toward the waterfall where the minister and his brother Sean were waiting on them.

"I'm already Mrs. Hartwell," she said, loving her new last name.

He nodded. "But this time it's permanent, sweetheart."

As she glanced toward the Western sky, the sun was just beginning to sink behind the mountain peaks and it was time for her sunset wedding to begin. "I've never been more ready for anything in my entire life," she said as they walked past over a hundred guests assembled on the patio.

As the last of their wedding guests drove away from the ranch house, Blake took Karly in his arms and kissed her until she sagged against him. "I've got a surprise for you," he said, taking her by the hand to lead her around to the other side of the pool.

When he stopped by the fire pit where he'd lain a small amount of kindling, the woman he loved more than life itself looked up at him like he'd lost every ounce of sense he possessed. "Seriously? Do you really want to build a fire now?"

Happier than he'd ever been, he grinned. "Trust me. I think you'll like this."

"I was looking forward to going upstairs to give you a wedding surprise of my own," she said as she continued to stare at him.

"I promise this won't take long," he said, lighting the dry wood. When the fire began to crackle, Blake reached into the inside pocket of his tuxedo and pulled out an envelope. "I thought we could get rid of these together."

A look of understanding sparkled in her pretty

blue eyes and a smile curved her lips. "The divorce papers. I had forgotten all about them."

"I hadn't," he said, removing the documents from the envelope. He gave them to her, then just as they'd done when they cut their wedding cake, he covered her hand with his and they tossed them onto the fire together.

As they watched the papers curl and turn black as they burned, Blake held Karly close. "Now that we have that taken care of, what's this about you having a gift for me?"

Her lovely smile sent his blood pressure sky-high. "You'll have to wait until early summer for the actual gift. But I can tell you about it."

He leaned forward to press his lips to hers. "I'm listening."

"It's going to be small and loud at times," she said, grinning. "And you're probably going to lose a lot of sleep because of it."

Blake had no idea where she was going with this, but she definitely had his full attention. "Okay," he said cautiously. "Would you like to tell me what *it* is?"

"I don't know yet." Something about the look in her eyes caused the air to lodge in his lungs a moment before she grinned. "But as soon as we find out, we'll be redecorating the room across the hall from the master suite in either pink or blue."

"You're pregnant."

"No, we're pregnant," she said, laughing. "*We* got

me into this together and *we're* going to get me out of it. Together."

He suddenly couldn't stop grinning and he was pretty sure he looked like a damned fool. He couldn't have cared less. They were going to have a baby.

Pulling her in his arms, he kissed her until they both gasped for breath. "It happened the morning we worked things out."

She nodded. "We were so caught up in the moment, that's the only time we forgot about protection."

"I love you, Karly Hartwell," he said around the lump clogging his throat.

When he swung her up into his arms and started toward the house, she cupped his face with her soft palm. "And I love you, Blake. Now, please take me upstairs so I can show you just how much."

* * * * *

Maureen Burke danced with abandon.

Throwing herself into this pocket of time, matching the steps of this leanly athletic man with charismatic blue eyes and a sexual intensity as potent as his handsome face.

Brains. Brilliance. A body to die for and a loyal love of family.

Xander Lourdes was a good man.

But not her man. Only her boss.

And too soon, her work visa was due to expire. And officials had thus far denied her requests to extend it. She would have to go home to Ireland. To face all she'd run from, to leave this amazing place.

So Maureen breathed in the salty air mixed with the scent of burning wood from the bonfire and allowed herself to be swept away by the dance. By the look of this man with coal-black hair that spiked with the sea breeze and a hint of sweat. His square jaw was peppered with a five-o'clock shadow, his shoulders broad in his tuxedo, broad enough to carry the weight of the world.

Shivering with warm tingles that had nothing to do with any bonfire or humid night, she felt the attraction radiating off him the same way it heated her. She'd sensed the draw before, but his grief was so well-known she hadn't wanted to wade into those complicated waters.

Maureen wasn't interested in a relationship, but maybe if she was leaving she could indulge…

* * *

The Boss's Baby Arrangement
is part of Mills & Boon Desire's No.1 bestselling series,
Billionaires and Babies: Powerful men…
wrapped around their babies' little fingers.

THE BOSS'S BABY ARRANGEMENT

BY
CATHERINE MANN

First Published in Great Britain 2016
By Mills & Boon, an imprint of HarperCollins*Publishers*
1 London Bridge Street, London, SE1 9GF

© 2016 Catherine Mann

ISBN: 978-0-263-91875-5

51-0916

Printed and bound in Spain
by CPI, Barcelona

USA TODAY bestseller and RITA® Award winner **Catherine Mann** has penned over fifty novels, released in more than twenty countries. After years as a military spouse bringing up four children, Catherine is now a snowbird—sorta—splitting time between the Florida beach and somewhat chillier beach in her home state of South Carolina. The nest didn't stay empty long, though, as Catherine is an active board member for the Sunshine State Animal Rescue. www.CatherineMann.com

To Jeanette Vigliotti, a brilliant professor
and a dear friend. So happy you are
an unofficial part of our family!

One

Xander Lourdes had loved and lost his soul mate.

Parked in an Adirondack chair by the Gulf waters, he knew deep in his gut he wouldn't find that again. Even after a year, his wife's death from an aneurysm cut Xander to the core, but he'd been working like hell to find solace as best he could in honoring her memory every way possible.

By parenting their baby girl.

And by revitalizing a wildlife refuge in his dead wife's beloved Florida Keys. He'd invested half of his personal fortune to revitalize this place. No great hardship as far as the executive angle went. He thrived on that part.

Although the fundraising parties? Like tonight? The endless schmoozing? A real stick in the eye. His preferred way to spend an evening was with his daughter, Rose, or in the office. These social gatherings tried his patience. For a moment his mind wandered back to how his wife had always stabilized and smoothed functions like this for him. She'd been a natural complement for him.

For his wife's memory, he endured the beachside gala.

Xander drank tonic water, half listening to the state politician rambling beside him about a childhood pet parakeet. Small talk had never been Xander's thing.

Waves crashed on the shore and a bonfire crackled at the high-end outdoor fundraiser. Tiki torch flames flickered, reaching toward the starlit sky as a steel-drum band played. Marshes *swooshed* with softer sounds in the distance, grasses and nocturnal creatures creating a night ensemble all their own.

A lengthy buffet table and bar kept the partygoers well stocked by the waitstaff currently weaving through the crowd of partiers talking or dancing barefoot on the sand, silk and diamonds glinting in the moonlight, tuxedo ties loosened. His brother—the head veterinarian—and his sexy-as-hell lady assistant led the dancing. The redheaded zoologist was just the sort to keep the party going.

Xander's wife, Terri, hadn't been much for dancing, but she'd loved music. When they'd found out she was pregnant, her first reaction was to track down a special device to play classical music for their baby in the womb. Music, she believed, could change a person's life—convey emotions stronger than any other type of language. This belief had also prompted her to find compilations for the animals at the refuge to soothe them. Terri had been his calm and support since they were in first grade, when Xander had been labeled an outcast for already performing three grade levels above the others.

They'd been inseparable since she approached him on

the playground that first day and he'd missed her every minute since she'd died.

His daughter—Terri's legacy—meant everything to him.

Washing down the lump in his throat with another swallow of tonic water, he nodded at something or other the politician said about expanding the bird care portion of the refuge's clinic. Xander tucked the info away for later. At least he had the executive power and the portfolio to make that happen, to control something in a world that had denied him control over so damn much.

There was no space tonight for thinking about that now. It wouldn't help the cause his wife had devoted so much time and energy to.

Her volunteer work here had been important to her. When Xander's brother had started at the refuge, Terri's interest ignited. And then she'd discovered her passion, starting foundations to try to channel more funds into reviving the place.

His brother, Easton, oversaw the medical aspect of the refuge as an exotic animal veterinarian with a staff of techs and zoologists. Easton had worked here back in the early days, more concerned with animals than with the money he could make at a bigger, tourist-trap outfit. Xander had supported the refuge's efforts with donations, but now his interest was more personal and yet also more professional. He'd been elected chairman of the board of directors. Terri had wanted him to take that role for years and now she would never know he'd fulfilled her hope that he could grow the refuge.

Damn.

He'd had enough of small talk.

Xander shoved out of his chair. "I appreciate your taking the time to chat and attend. If you'll excuse me,

I need to attend to some business, but my brother would thoroughly enjoy talking to you about those clinic additions. I'll get Easton off the dance floor for you."

Making a beeline for his brother who was still dancing with the fire-headed zoologist, Xander shouldered through the partiers, nodding and waving without stopping until he reached the throng of dancers. He tapped Easton on the shoulder.

"Mind if I cut in, brother?"

His eccentric younger brother turned on his heel, his forehead creased, a trickle of sweat beading on his brow. "What's up?"

Easton wore the Prada suit Xander had made sure was delivered for the occasion, but his brother hadn't bothered with a tie. No surprise. Dr. Easton Lourdes had always been more comfortable in khakis and T-shirts.

Xander tipped his head toward the politician still knocking back mixed drinks. "Donor at your nine o'clock. Needs your expertise on possible additions to the aviary in the clinic."

His brother's forehead smoothed and his face folded in a smile, all charm. "Can do." He clapped Xander on the shoulder. "Thanks again for this shindig. It's going to pay off big for the place."

Easton charged past like a man on a mission, leaving his dance partner on the floor alone.

Maureen Burke.

An auburn-haired bombshell, full of brains and energy. She was an Irish native who'd spent much of her life in the States, so her brogue was light. Her degree in zoology along with her rescue experience made her the perfect second-in-command for his brother. Lucky for them she'd received her work visa at exactly the right time. She was extroverted, but also all business. And a woman Xander didn't have to worry was out to take advantage of the Lourdes family fortune passed down for generations. A portfolio Xander had doubled and that women were attracted to when it came to dating Easton.

Maureen was an individual guaranteed not to mistake Easton's attention as interest and an invitation to leave ten voice mails. Maureen was much like Xander when it came to romance.

Not interested.

He'd learned she was divorced and, from her standoffish demeanor just beneath that plush-lipped smile, he got the impression it hadn't been a pleasant split. No doubt the man had been an idiot to let such a gorgeous, intelligent woman walk out of his life.

Xander extended his hand. "Sorry to have stolen your dance partner. I had to send my brother off. Dance with me."

"Dance? With you?" She swept her long red curls back over her shoulder, her face flushed from heat and exertion.

"Is that such a strange request?"

"I didn't expect you to know how to dance, much less to know an Irish jig."

He winced. "An Irish jig?"

She grinned impishly, gesturing to the stage with elegant hands, nails short but painted a glittering gold for the party. "Next up on the band's request list. Your brother double-dog dared me."

Double-dog dare? No wonder Easton had left the dance floor so easily and with a grin on his face. He'd set Xander up.

And Xander wasn't one to back down from a challenge. "I'm a man of many talents. Our mother insisted we boys attend dance classes as teens." He braced his shoulders. "Whatever I don't know, you can teach me."

"Good for your mama."

"And that dance?"

She propped a hand on her hip, her whispery yellow gown hitching along curves as she eyed him with emerald-green eyes. Finally she shrugged. "Sure. Why not? I would like to see the big boss give it a try."

"Remember, you'll have to help me brush up on the steps."

"We'll keep the moves simple." She extended an elbow. "Steel drums playing Irish tunes is a first, not too intricate but still fun."

He bowed before hooking elbows with her. Damn. He'd forgotten how soft a woman's skin felt. Clearing his throat, he mimicked her steps, mixed with a periodic spin. Her hair fanned across his chest as she whipped around.

His body reacted to the simple contact.

Had to be lack of sex messing with his brain.

But holy hell, the dance seemed to go on forever with his blood pressure ramping by the second until, thank God, the band segued to a slower tune. And still he didn't step away. In spite of the twinge of guilt he felt over the surprise attraction, he extended his hands and took her into his arms for a more traditional dance. The scent of citrus—lemons and grapefruit—teased his nose like an aphrodisiac.

Maybe the Irish dance hadn't been such a good idea after all.

He searched for something to say to distract himself from the gentle give of her under his touch, the occasional skim of her body against his. "I'm glad you're enjoying yourself."

"I enjoy anything that makes money for the refuge."
Her eyes glimmered in the starlight, loose curls feathering over the top of his hand along her waist. "I love my work here."

"Your devotion is admirable."

"Thank you." Her face flashed with indecision.

"You don't believe me?"

"It's not that. But let's not talk shop right now and spoil the moment. We can talk tomorrow." She chewed her bottom lip. "I have an appointment to see you."

"You do? I don't recall seeing your name on my calendar."

"Not all of us have a personal assistant to keep track of our schedules."

"Am I being insulted?" He had a secretary, but not a personal assistant who followed him around all day like his brother did. Although his brother was known to be an absentminded-professor type.

"No insult meant at all. You've made a great future for yourself and for Rose. It's clear you didn't ride off your family fortune, but increased it. That's commendable." She shook her head, sending her curls prancing along his hand again. "I'm just frustrated. Ignore me. Dance."

Her order came just as the band picked up with a sultry Latin beat.

Maureen Burke danced with abandon.

Throwing herself into this pocket of time, matching the steps of this leanly athletic man with charismatic blue eyes and a sexual intensity as potent as his handsome face.

Brains. Brilliance. A body to die for and a loyal love of family.

Xander Lourdes was a good man.

But not her man.

So Maureen allowed herself to dance with the abandon she never would have dared otherwise. Not now. Not after all she'd been through.

She breathed in the salty air mixed with the scent of fresh burning wood from the bonfire. What a multifaceted word. *Abandon.* She danced with freedom. But she'd also been abandoned and that hadn't felt like freedom at all. The pain. The grief. Being given up on for no good reason other than the fact she wasn't a good fit for her ex-husband's life after all she had put up with. After she'd ignored the urgings of so many friends to leave him and his emotional abuse.

Rejection.

She'd known they had problems. Maureen was always willing to work at broken things. Hell, her never-say-die nature made her compatible and adept in a wildlife refuge. Vows meant something to her. She'd always expected if she ever got divorced it would be because of a major event—physical abuse or drugs. But for nothing more than "I love you but I can't live with you"? Like she'd filled their home with some toxic substance.

More of that negative thinking born of years of his tearing her down until finally—thank God, finally—she'd wised up and realized he was, in fact, the toxin.

So she'd let him go and left their home full of insults and negativity. Hell, she'd left County Cork to get as far away from him and the ache as possible. It wasn't like she had family or anything else holding her back. Her parents were dead and her marriage was a disaster. There'd been nowhere else for her to go except to the US and accept the job in a field of work she loved so much.

She allowed herself to be swept away by the dance,

the music and the pulse of the drums pushing through her veins with every heartbeat, faster and faster. Arching timbres of the steel drums urged her to absorb every fiber of this moment.

Too soon, her work visa was due to expire, and officials had thus far denied her requests to extend it. She would have to go home. To face all she'd run from, to leave this amazing place where *abandon* meant beauty and exuberance. Freedom.

The freedom to dance with a handsome man and not to worry that her husband would accuse her of flirting. As if she would run off with any man who looked her way. How long had it taken her to realize his remarks were born of his own insecurities, not her behavior?

She was free to look now, though, at this man with coal-black hair that spiked with the sea breeze and a hint of sweat. His square jaw was peppered with a five-o'clock shadow, his shoulders broad in his tuxedo, broad enough to carry the weight of the world.

Shivering with warm tingles that had nothing to do with any bonfire or humid night, she could feel the attraction radiating off him the same way it heated in her. She'd sensed the draw before but his grief was so well known she hadn't wanted to wade into those complicated waters. But with her return to home looming…

Maureen wasn't interested in a relationship, but maybe if she was leaving she could indulge in—

Suddenly his attention was yanked from her. He reached into his tuxedo pocket and pulled out his cell phone and read the text.

Tension pulsed through his jaw, the once-relaxed, half-cocked smile replaced instantly with a serious expression. "It's the nanny. My daughter's running a fever. I have to go."

And without another word, he was gone and she knew she was gone from his thoughts. That little girl was the world to him. Everyone knew that, as well as how deeply he grieved for his dead wife.

All of which merely made him more attractive.

More dangerous to her peace of mind.

As the morning sun started to spray rays through the night, Xander rubbed the grit from the corners of his eyes, stifling a yawn from the lack of sleep after staying up all night to keep watch over Rose. He'd taken her straight to the emergency room and learned she had an ear infection. Even with the doctor's reassurance, antibiotics and fever-reducing meds, he couldn't take his eyes off her. Still wearing his tuxedo, he sat in a rocker by her bed. Light brown curls that were slightly sticky with sweat framed her face, her cherubic mouth in a little cupid's bow as she puffed baby breaths. Each rise and fall of her chest reassured him she was okay, a fundamentally healthy sixteen-month-old child who had a basic, treatable ear infection.

A vaporizer pumped moisture into the nursery, which was decorated in white, green and pink, with flowers Terri had called cabbage roses, in honor of their daughter's name. A matching daybed had been included in the room for those nights they just enjoyed watching her breathe. Or for the nanny—Elenora—to rest when needed. A glider was set up in the corner and his mind flooded with memories of Terri nursing their baby in the chair, her face so full of maternal love and hope, all of which had been poured into putting this room together. A week before Rose was born, he and Terri had sat on the daybed, his arms wrapped around her swollen belly, as they'd dreamed of what their child would look like. What she would grow up to accomplish. So many dreams.

Now his brother catnapped in that same space, as he so often did these days, quirky as hell and a never-ending source of support. An image of his brother dancing with Maureen Burke flash through Xander's mind. His brother hadn't had much of a social life lately, either, and even knowing Xander would help Easton if the roles were reversed didn't make it fair to steal so much of his brother's time.

Xander pushed up from the rocker and shook his brother lightly by the shoulder. "Hey, Easton," he said softly. "Wake up, dude. You should head on back to your room."

His brother's eyes blinked open slowly. "Rose?"

"Much better. Her fever's down. I'll still take her to her regular pediatrician for a follow-up, but I think she's going to be fine. She's past needing both of us to keep watch."

"I was sleeping fine, ya know." His lanky brother swung his legs off the bed.

"Folded up like pretzel. Your neck would have been in knots. But thank you. Really. You don't have to stick around. I know you have to work."

"So do you," Easton said pointedly, raking his fingers through his hair.

"She's my kid."

"And you're my brother." His eyes fixed on Xander's. Steady and loyal. They'd always been different but close since their parents traveled the world with little thought of any permanent home or the consistency their kids needed to build friendships. They relied on each other. Even more so after their father died and their mother continued her world traveling ways, always looking for the next adventure in the next country rather than connecting with her children.

And, thank God, Xander's brother could work at any wildlife refuge around the world and he'd chosen to stay on here and help him. That meant the world to him. Easton had done special projects here for Terri, but this place wasn't on the scale of the other places where he could work.

Hell, it wasn't on Xander's scale. But for Terri, for Rose, too, he would put this place on the map. Whatever it took. This was his wife's legacy to their child.

"Thank you."

"No thanks needed other than getting this little one better." Easton smoothed an affectionate hand over his niece's head. "Well…and a bottle of top-shelf tequila to drink at sunset."

"Put it on the list." A long list, all he owed his brother. But he would find a way to pay him back someday. A kick of guilt pushed him to say, "If you need to move on to a larger job—"

"I wouldn't be needed. Being needed, making a difference—" he shrugged, eyes flicking to Rose "—that's what life's all about."

Xander swallowed hard. Terri had said that to him more than once. God, he missed her. "Fair enough." And before he even realized the thought had crossed his mind, he stopped his brother at the door. "Might you really be sticking around because of a certain red-haired zoologist?"

"Maureen?" Easton said with such incredulity there was no doubting the truthfulness of his statement. "No. Absolutely not. There's nothing going on between the two of us. We're too much alike."

Laughing lightly, he shook his head, scratched the

back of his neck and chuckled again on his way out the door, leaving Xander more confused than ever. Not because of his brother's denial.

But because of his own relief.

Two

Maureen listened for the familiar *click-click* of her key in her beach cabana door. The double click meant that the teal-colored cabana was, indeed, actually locked. One click meant a well-targeted gust of wind would knock the door in. She would miss these sorts of quirks when she moved out of the brightly painted cabana and tropical Key Largo.

But that wasn't happening yet. Shoving the thought aside, Maureen adjusted her satchel filled with notebooks and began her commute to work. A leisurely five-minute walk.

And today, with the sunshine warming her fair skin, she was content to take in her surroundings as she made her way to the Lourdeses' home residence, built on property they'd bought at the edge of the refuge. Sauntering to the main house—a white beach mansion that always reminded her of the crest of a wave in a storm—she let her mind wander.

Absently, she watched volunteers from town and from farther away gather and disperse on the dock on-site. Even from here, she could hear the bustle of their excitement as the crowd moved toward the fenced and screened areas beneath the white beach mansion on signature Florida Keys stilts.

Eyeing more volunteers who were gathering by the screened areas where recovering animals were kept, she scanned the zone for Easton. Not a trace of him.

Or Xander. After last night, her thoughts tilted back to the dance. To his warm touch, the way he looked after his daughter. The kind of person he was. And those damn blue eyes that cut her to the quick, pierced right through her.

She'd spent most of the night attempting to navigate her sudden attraction to Xander. Not that it really mattered. Instead of admitting that the dance echoed in her dreams last night, she attempted to turn her attention to more practical matters like the school group that was due at the refuge shortly.

Though located on Key Largo, the refuge's secluded location meant tourists didn't wander in haphazardly. The public could access the refuge only through a prearranged guided tour. This policy was one Maureen loved. It made the wildlife refuge into her own kind of sanctuary, one that often felt independent of the tourist traps and straw-hat community of the main part of town. The limited public interaction allowed her to enjoy the mingled scent of salt and animals. There was truly a wildness here that called to some latent part of Maureen's soul.

Surveying her watch, she noted the time. The school children would be here soon. That meant she had to find Easton quickly.

And if she happened to see Xander…well, that'd be just fine by her.

Though, if she were being honest, the thought of accidently on purpose running into him made her giddy. Flashes of last night's dance pulsed in her mind's eye again.

What would she do if she actually ran into him anyway? Running a hand through her ringlet hair, Maureen stifled a sigh as Xander came into view.

Well, she certainly was committed now. At least, committed to some harmless small talk with a man who had pushed her sense of wild abandon into the realm worthy of Irish bards.

Biting the inside of her lip, she dropped her hands to her sides. Xander's smooth walk was uninterrupted as he pulled on his suit coat.

He'd built an office extension onto the refuge when Terri, his wife, had started to volunteer. Terri had fallen in love with Key Largo and her volunteer work. Three years ago, when Maureen had just started with the refuge, Xander had commuted back and forth to Miami for work, using the office at the refuge as a satellite. After Terri passed away, he'd moved here full-time.

Maureen's thoughts lingered for a moment on her memories of Terri. She had been a quiet, gentle woman. It hadn't taken Maureen very long to figure out Terri's heart was bigger than most, and that her kindness and empathy were genuine. Wounded creatures were comforted by Terri's presence. When Terri had become pregnant, she'd begrudgingly performed office work, though Maureen could tell she'd rather have been among the animals.

After she'd passed away, Xander had poured himself into the refuge. In the beginning, Maureen felt like Xander was trying to find some other piece of Terri here.

Now she felt like the refuge had woven its charm for him, too.

Shrugging his suit coat into place, Xander jogged down the long wooden stairway leading from the home on stilts. "Maureen?"

He said it as if he didn't recognize her. But, um, well, maybe she had taken more time with her appearance today. Jeans with a loose-fitting T-shirt was her go-to outfit. Minimal makeup—maybe a wave of a mascara wand over her lashes, a pale lip gloss, her wavy hair confined in a high ponytail. But today she looked considerably...nicer. Her fitted shirt revealed curves, and she'd deepened her lip color, daring a deeper nude that made her seem a bit more put-together, a bit more...well, sultry.

"Of course. Do I look that different?" Maureen's tongue skimmed the back of her teeth, causing her to smile awkwardly, hands flying to a stray strand of her hair that fell in a gentle wave against her chest. So much for nonchalance.

His eyes flicked over her. Slowly—as if he was trying to work something out.

"From last night at the party? Yes."

"We have a group of schoolchildren coming in for a tour this morning," she explained quickly. "They're due any minute and we're shorthanded. Shouldn't you be at work?"

Tilting her head to the side, she squinted at him. His top lip curled up, a smile playing at the corner of his mouth. Raising his eyebrows, he took a step closer, winking at her, more lighthearted than she could remember him being in the past. "Shouldn't you, Maureen?"

The smell of pine drifted into the space between them. Xander's lip was still playfully curled up and she felt a thrill run down her spine as she stared back at him, noticing the way his hair was still damp from a recent shower. Her thoughts stopped there. It felt like ages before she responded.

"I'm looking for your brother." How did Xander manage to keep from perspiring out here in a suit when she already felt like she was melting in a sauna?

Or melting from a different kind of heat.

"Easton's running late. We were both up late last night with Rose."

"You two took care of her?"

"Why is that a surprise?"

"I just assumed someone of your means would lean more on the nanny or call her grandparents."

"My father has passed away and my mother, uh, travels a lot. As for my former in-laws, they can be rather... overpowering. And Elenora needs her rest to be on the top of her game watching Rose while I'm at work. I'm her father. And my brother worried, as well. He also pitched in early this morning when I needed to snag a shower for work. He should be down soon." Xander gestured toward the pathway leading to the offices. "Shall we go?"

She stepped forward, aware of him in step beside her, his shoulder almost brushing hers on the narrow, sandy path. "That's admirable of both of you to take care of Rose. How is she doing?"

"Ear infection, according to the emergency room doctor. I'll be taking her to her pediatrician to follow up today."

"Is there anything I can do to help?" Maureen's thoughts drifted to Rose—the kind of child that adults fawned over. She was sweet, affectionate and filled with life. Maureen had seen testament to that sprinkled all over his office in the form of finger paintings and photographs. A shrine to childhood and a dedicated father.

Maureen's own interaction with Rose always left a smile on her face. With tiny fingers, Rose would reach up to play with Maureen's leather bracelet, touching it carefully as if it was a magical totem. Out of habit, Maureen's own hand flew to her leather bracelet. Feeling the worn leather, she felt assured. This bracelet had been everywhere with her. A certifying stamp of endurance. "Thanks. But I think we've got it covered. Although I have to admit, it's ironic that it took me and my brother to do one woman's job."

"And somewhere women are sighing."

He laughed.

In the pit of her stomach her nerves became bramble-twisted, much like the palm fronds blowing and tangled by the wind. Those damn blue eyes—they disarmed her senses, unsettling her more than any sounds from wild creatures chattering. Especially today as his gaze darted from her eyes to her lips.

A faint tautness pulled at his cheeks.

Warmth crept up her neck, threatening to flood her cheeks with a schoolgirl blush. *Get it together*, her inner voice scolded. Taking the cue from her sensibility, she drew in a deep breath and straightened her blouse.

"You're needed here to take care of animals." Dropping his gaze, he nodded his head. The momentary flicker of attraction melted off his expression. Xander's tone and eyes returned to their normal bulldog, business-man-slate stare.

"Of course. She's your child and doesn't really know me well." She held up her hands. "I've overstepped and I apologize."

He sighed. "I apologize. You're being helpful and I'm being an ass. I have a reputation for that."

She stayed silent.

"Not going to deny it?" His lip twitched upward.

"I wouldn't dare call the big boss anything so insulting."

He laughed. Hard. "You are surprising me left and right. Not at all how I've perceived you in the past."

"You thought about me?" Words tumbled out of her mouth before she thought better of them.

"As your employer."

"That makes things tricky. And you've had…a difficult year."

"Fourteen months. It's been fourteen months and three days." His voice lost an octave, felt like a whisper on a breeze.

"I'm so very sorry for your loss." An ache of deep empathy pushed hard against her chest. She'd seen the love Xander and Terri had for each other, a love she'd hoped to have in her own marriage.

"Me, too." His eyes met hers as a gust of island breeze carried the scent of flowers and the sound of distant motors. "Rose means everything to me. She's all I have left of Terri. I would do anything for my daughter but sometimes—" he thrust a hand through his tousled hair, his head tipping back as he looked up toward the sky "—I just feel like I'm short-changing her."

She touched his arm lightly. "You're tired, like any parent. And you're an amazing father, here for her, along with your brother. And Rose truly has a wonderful nanny. Elenora genuinely cares about her."

"Of course she does. I can see the affection they share." Was this the kind of thing she was supposed to say to a man baring his heart and acknowledging his pain? Maureen found the familiar spot in her bottom lip and chewed, wishing she could say something—anything—to take the hurt out of his voice.

"I spend time with her every day."

"I know that, too." She hadn't realized how much she'd noticed about his routine before. "You don't have to explain yourself to me. It's clear you love her."

"I do. She's everything to me."

"She's a lucky little girl."

The space between them thinned and now, shoulder to shoulder, she noticed how the pine soap pushed against a symphony of coffee beans and mint.

Turning to face her, his blue eyes sparked. He took half a step toward her, his own lips parted slightly as he searched her expression.

She stopped chewing her lip and tilted her head to the side to stare back at him, stomach fluttering the longer his gaze held hers.

"Thank you for your help last night organizing the gala."

"Thank you for the dance last night."

They stayed like that for a few moments until the buses were pulling up and pulling them back into reality. Away from whatever had electrified the air between them.

A full day in the office left Xander desperate for some salt air and sunshine. He'd worked, taken Rose to the pediatrician and had just settled her down for a nap. He'd read her a story before she drifted off to sleep. With the nanny on-call, he'd decided to take his brother up on his invitation to check the water samples from the nearby swamp.

He tried to convince himself he was only going out on the boat to become better acquainted with the procedures so he'd be of more use at the next fund-raiser. The fact that Maureen also was on the boat was pure coincidence. Xander tried to tell himself that was an accurate representation of reality.

His attempt to delude himself, however, was a hard sell, it turned out. He couldn't deny he wanted to be there. He'd looked forward to seeing Maureen and finding out if this attraction to her was just an anomaly.

Easton, his assistant, Portia, Maureen and Xander were all in swimsuits as the low-slung boat putted its way through the water. He tried not to notice Maureen's toned legs and the way her lavender one-piece swimsuit hugged her curves. Even her messy wind-whipped ponytail was sexy as hell.

Maureen was also a stark contrast to Portia Soto, his brother's assistant. Portia was also in a one-piece bathing suit, but a long patterned sarong swaddled her body. Portia embodied prim and proper. No detail was too minute to escape her notice. Portia adjusted her oversize hat and sunglasses, though she looked anxious.

So far, Xander couldn't understand why Portia had taken the job as his brother's assistant. She was efficient and talented. Of that, there was no doubt. But she seemed to be timid the majority of the time, not necessarily the sort that came immediately to mind when thinking of staff for a wild animal refuge.

Easton sat beside his assistant, who'd plastered herself in the seat with her back pressed against it, her fingers gripping the edge. Poor thing. She looked absolutely miserable and terrified. And while Xander's first instinct was to talk to the trembling woman, he couldn't help how his eyes seemed to always find their way back to Maureen.

"Would you like to return to the shore? You don't have to come with us every time," Maureen said gently, touching Portia's arm.

"The doctor relies on my notes." She nodded to the

bag in her hand, though Portia's eyes darted nervously to the brackish water and swamp animals outside. Clearly this job pushed her limits and yet here she was, anyway.

"They are helpful," he said absently while leaning over the edge. Wind tore through the boat, pressing Easton's blue swim trunks and white T-shirt hard against his body.

Maureen clucked her tongue. "A gator's going to bite your arm off one day."

Portia turned green.

Maureen's brogue lilted like the waves. "I'm only teasing."

Portia looked down and eased one hand free to pull her recorder from her waterproof bag. She began mumbling notes into the mike.

Maureen angled down to Easton. "I think she's plotting your demise."

"Possibly. But we have an understanding. We both need each other."

"It just seems strange she would take a job that scares her silly."

"I pay well. Not many enjoy this. I trust her and that counts for a helluva lot. Besides, I'm convinced she has an adventurous spirit buried underneath all that starch." His grin was wicked as he turned to face Maureen. That was his brother all right—always pushing people's comfort levels and making them laugh.

"If she doesn't have a heart attack first."

Portia chimed in, hands once again finding the edge of the seat cushions for stability. "Or die from some flesh-eating bacteria."

Easton laughed, his chuckles echoing over the water before he returned to his work again.

Xander caught his brother's eye before Easton turned to face Maureen. Something sly passed over Easton's expression and he quickly raised his brow to Xander before fully focusing on Maureen. "I'm damn sorry you're going to be leaving us."

"Me, too. This is a dream job." Her lithe arm extended out to the impossible shade of green water that surrounded them. Her attention seemed fixed on an imaginary spot on the horizon and Xander followed her gaze, trying to imagine what she was thinking about. Did she want to go home? It certainly didn't seem so from her crestfallen face, and she had asked him to look into extending the visa to complete her work here. He hadn't heard back, but then, that news would have gone to her and apparently the answer hadn't been positive.

Still, her face showed such distress, Xander couldn't help but wonder if it was about more than work.

Easton let out a low whistle. "And you're sure there's no way to extend the work visa?"

"It's been denied. Your brother even had the company lawyers review my paperwork to help, but with things tightening down regarding immigration, my request has been denied…" Maureen glanced back at Xander, her eyes as green as the crystal waters.

Did she know he could hear them?

He did his best to seem disinterested and aloof, channeling years of cutthroat business meetings to school his features into a mask of neutrality.

Easton's eyes momentarily flicked back to Xander. For a brief moment he swore Easton's head nodded slightly. Was that a sign to pay attention? What did his brother have planned?

"Xander has a lot of his time and energy—and heart—invested in this place."

"That, he does. I was surprised to see him dance last night."

"Who would have thought he could dance a jig?" Easton winked over his shoulder at his brother, making it clear he knew full well his brother could hear every word. "Who would have thought he would dance at all? That has certainly been in question since Terri died."

"She was a lovely lady." Maureen's voice meshed into the sounds of the nearby birds.

Xander tried not to look desperate as he strained to hear the rest of the conversation.

"She was. We all miss her. Her parents do, too, obviously. We always will. But I can't help hoping my brother will find a way to move on." Easton's lips had thinned into a smile and he stuck her with a knowing glance.

Maureen shook her head and tendrils of red hair fell out of her loose ponytail. "You're reading too much into a dance."

"I didn't say a thing. You did." A taunting, brotherly tone entered Easton's voice. He lifted up his hands to her, palms out in an exaggeration of placation.

"I'm definitely not making a move on your brother." The words were jagged on her tongue. Even from his seat, Xander could see pain jutting into Maureen's normally fair, bubbly features.

"Again, I didn't say that. You did."

"I'm divorced."

"I know."

Shrugging her shoulder, she leaned against the rail of the boat. "It was ugly."

"So very sorry to hear that."

"The past is past. I'm focused on my present and my job."

"Is that the reason you're so determined to stay here? Because your ex is back home?" Easton's eyes flicked back to Xander who pretended not to notice. But the truth was that his heart pulsated in his chest as he continued to listen to their conversation. A bad divorce? He couldn't help but wonder what had happened.

"Staying here is certainly easier. Fresh starts often are."

"It's not over yet."

"I appreciate your optimism."

"Um, hello?" Portia's voice rang out, urgency coloring every syllable. "Um, Doctor?"

"Yes, Ms. Soto?" Easton turned to face her.

"I'm getting seasick." And with that, Portia pulled herself up to the railing, turned a particularly sunset shade of scarlet and hurled the contents of her stomach overboard.

Xander reacted, setting their course back to the dock. Portia needed land, and fast.

They weren't too far away. Within minutes the dock was in sight.

And so were Xander's in-laws. It was never a good sign when they showed up from Miami unannounced. A pit knotted in his stomach and he felt his jaw tighten and clench.

Xander leaped off the boat as soon as it stabilized and helped Portia out. She'd gone ghost-pale and her hands were clammy—clearly she was much more seasick than she'd let on. Once Portia's feet were on solid ground, she covered her mouth, nodded politely at Xander's in-laws and dashed up to the house, probably stifling the urge to hurl the whole way.

His in-laws surveyed the landscape with eyes that revealed complete disgust. His mother-in-law's gaze followed Portia up the slope to the house. Delilah's brow arched, a silent conversation seemed to unfold between her and Jake, Xander's father-in-law.

So the verdict was out on this place. They'd hated it and did little to try to disguise that.

Jake looked at Portia's disappearing form and then back at Xander. Disapproval danced in his gaze.

Xander stifled the urge to grind his teeth. Did they actually think he was interested in Portia? And was that really any of their business to pass judgment on his dating life? Of course they all missed Terri, but she was gone, for over a year, and that was the tragic reality.

Besides, he wanted to tell them they had it all wrong, anyway. Portia wasn't his type. Xander didn't know why they'd assumed she'd be the kind of woman he was interested in, and he didn't want them to believe he hadn't loved their daughter with his whole soul. Xander certainly didn't want them to think she'd been so easily replaced.

The protest nearly formed against his tongue when reality jabbed him. Portia was polished, quiet, reserved… As far as types went, she shared a lot of Terri's qualities.

But Portia had never crossed his mind. Not once. Not in passing. There was no draw to her. Not like there was to the fiery Maureen. Xander's eyes flicked quickly to Maureen. She was helping Easton dock the boat.

Turning his attention back to his in-laws, he surveyed them, trying to anticipate the reason for this unannounced visit.

Jake and Delilah Goodwin were good people, if intrusive. They were what the news media deemed helicopter parents.

Xander had always imagined their hovering had everything to do with the circumstances of Terri's birth. For years Delilah and Jake had tried to conceive but never could. The doctors had told them it was practically impossible for them to become pregnant. But somehow

Delilah had been able to conceive and carry Terri to full term. The miracle child. Their only child.

Terri had been pampered and sheltered her whole life. They'd treated Terri like spun glass, like a fragile thing that needed protection from everything and everyone. Now having a daughter of his own, he understood the motivation and desire, but Jake and Delilah had taken hovering to its extreme.

Xander watched as Jake gave Delilah's hand a quick squeeze. His business instincts told him the gesture was one of support. He understood that. Terri's death had changed everything.

Delilah straightened her heirloom pearls on her neck, the only piece of jewelry that spoke to their enormous wealth. They were kind people, but they were used to dictating orders. They weren't the compromising type.

"We heard our grandchild is ill and you're out here. Who's watching her?" Jack said, his voice even but stern.

"She's napping while Elenora watches over her. Rose has an ear infection. We went to the emergency room last night and the pediatrician today."

Laying a manicured hand to her chest, Delilah stiffened. "She could have a relative watching her."

"She does. Her father and her uncle." Xander kept his tone neutral, doing his best to remember that they didn't mean to be insulting or accusatory.

"Both of whom are out partying on a boat," Delilah continued, her voice shrill and unforgiving.

The correction was gentle but necessary. He wished Terri was here to help him navigate this. "Working."

"Okay, then. Working. She could have her grandmother all day."

"I'm appreciative of your offer to help. Who told you about the ear infection?"

Delilah waved her hand dismissively. "Someone on the staff when I phoned to say hello."

To check up, more likely. His in-laws made no secret of the fact that they wanted custody of Rose. He would feel a lot more comfortable welcoming them for visits if they weren't taking notes and plotting the whole damn time.

He ground his teeth and tried to be as reasonable as possible. He didn't want to upset his daughter's world by having her taken from her own father. "Rose will be awake in about an hour. If you would like to stay for lunch, you can play with her when she wakes."

He glanced over his shoulder, checking on his brother and Maureen. Easton was tying the boat off along the dock while Maureen gathered up the samples. But that wasn't what caught Xander's eye. A massive gator swam in the dock area and bumped into the boat. The low-slung boat was tipped off balance and his eyes darted to Maureen, who was leaning over the railing.

Three

Water swirled around Maureen as she plummeted into the murky bay off the side of the boat.

Swimming had never been an issue for her. In Ireland, her childhood adventures had often unfolded in rivers and lakes. The water called to her. When she was young, she'd hold her breath and dive in undaunted. She'd even told her parents she was searching for kelpie— mythical Irish water horses. They were dangerous creatures of legend—sometimes drowning mortals for sport. At eight, Maureen was convinced that she could find kelpie and clear up the misconception. Her inclination to help and heal ran deep, to her core.

But here, in the swampy waters of Key Largo, there was no mythical creature that might whisk her to the bottom and drown her. No, in this water, an alligator slinked by. An animal that actually had the capacity to knock life from her lungs.

She tread water, schooling her breathing into calm

inhales and exhales. Or at least, this was the attempt she was making. Boggy, slimy weeds locked around her ankle, twisting her into underwater shackles.

Adrenaline pushed into her veins, her heart palpitating as she tried to force a degree of rigidity into her so-far-erratic movements.

From her memory depths, she recalled a time not unlike this one. She'd been swimming in Lake Michigan after her parents had relocated to Michigan. She'd been caught in weeds then, too, but her father had been there to untangle her. And that lake had lacked primitive dinosaur-like predators, which had made the Lake Michigan moment decidedly less dramatic.

Eyes flashing upward, she caught the panic flooding Xander's face.

Ready to help her.

The weeds encircling her ankle pulled against her. *Damn.* How'd she managed to become so ensnared so quickly? The pulse of the tide slashed into her ears, pushing her against the boat.

A loss of control kicked into her stomach. She heard vague shouting. Easton? Maybe. His voice seemed far away.

The grip on her ankle pulled taut, forcing her below the surface. The more she tried to tread water, to grab hold of the boat, the more she was pulled down. A new sort of tightness tap-danced on her chest. A mouthful of salt water belabored her breathing.

A vague sense of sound broke through her disorientation. Xander's voice. That steadying baritone. "Maureen, I'm coming!"

Words drifted to her like stray pieces of wood. Her salt-stung vision revealed Xander's muscled form coming toward her. She made out the people behind him—

his in-laws. Even from here, blurry vision and all, she read the concern in their clasped forms.

In an instant Xander was there, face contorted in worry. With an arm, he stabilized her against the boat. Air flooded her lungs again.

"I'm okay. I can swim. I just need to get my foot untangled from the undergrowth."

"Roger." He started to dive.

She grasped his arm. "Be careful of the—"

His gaze moved off to the side where the gator lingered with scaly skin and beady eyes. "I see. And the sooner we get out of here the better."

He disappeared underwater, a trail of small bubbles the only trace of him. Sinking fear rendered a palatable thrum in her chest—a war drum of anxiety. The gator disappeared under water.

Time stood on a knife-edge.

Suddenly she felt a palm wrap around her ankle and release her from the weeds. On instinct, she drew her knee to chest.

Xander followed. The edge of worry ebbed but refused to fade.

"I'm sure you can swim. But humor me. You may not know you're injured."

"I don't want to slow you—"

"And I don't want to hang out here in the swamp with gators and God only knows what else in addition to the leaking gas. Quit arguing." No room for negotiation in that tone. It must be the same voice Xander used in boardroom meetings.

"Okay, then. Swim."

His arms around her, she felt warmth leap from his body to hers. Feeling small and protected for the first time in ages. The muscles in his arm grew taught and retracted as he moved them through the water. Steadying her breathing, pushing her fear far away.

The water gave way to mucky sand and he helped her wade through that all the way to the shoreline.

Her body shook of its own accord. As if by reflex, he wrapped her into a tight hug and her head fit snugly beneath his chin.

The world, which a moment ago was filled with panic and fear, stilled. His breath on her cheek warmed her bones with more intensity than the tropical sun.

In that space, adrenaline fell back into her bloodstream. But fear didn't motivate that move this time. Awareness did as he held her close, breathing faster, somehow keeping time with her ragged heart. His body felt like steel against hers as she pulled away from him, her eyes catching his, watching as they fell away to her lips.

She hadn't imagined it, then, noting his desire.

"Maureen?" Her name sent the world crashing back into place. Willing her eyes away from his, she looked over her shoulder to see his in-laws and Easton standing a short distance away.

Knowing he needed coverage, even if just for a moment, she turned to face them, careful to stay angled in front of Xander. As if he'd done it a thousand times before, his hands fell to her shoulders. A mild but welcome distraction.

Xander's in-laws were visibly distraught.

"Are you okay?" Xander's father-in-law asked, face crumpled like he smelled something rotting. Maureen nodded dully, afraid her words might betray something private and real about this moment.

The man shifted focus from Maureen to Xander. "And you?"

"Yes. Thankfully. More of a scare than any real harm." His hands squeezed Maureen's shoulder blades before dropping. Immediately she felt the echo of his absence from her skin.

His mother-in-law sniffed in response. "Honestly. What if that had been Rose? I'm just glad she wasn't out here. A nature refuge is lovely, of course—" ice entered her words "—but such a dangerous, unpredictable place isn't so well suited for *our* grandchild."

Maureen squinted at the woman's response, which felt more like a warning than anything else.

Hours separated him from the gator run-in and he still couldn't think straight.

He'd always been a pro at compartmentalizing events, locking his personal life away so he could focus on whatever task at hand. That proved infinitely difficult with this afternoon's events.

As if his mind was a film loop, he kept revisiting Maureen falling in the water, a gator just a few feet away. The moment she looked like she was struggling sent him tumbling into action—a reflex and urge so primal, he couldn't ignore it.

Nor could he ignore the way she'd looked, soaked to the bone in her swimsuit. The feel of her shuddering with relief when they were on solid ground. How that relief reverberated in his own gut as he'd looked at her full lips.

There was no denying how turned on he was. The connection he'd felt to her in that beachside embrace had made him so damn aware of her. Sure, she'd always been attractive. He knew that, but there was something so sexy about the way she'd endured the gator run-in.

He wanted her, down to his core. All day, his thoughts drifted to her.

Did life ever get easy?

Watching his in-laws with his daughter provided a quick answer to that question. Delilah and Jake weren't mean—they were matter-of-fact. Particular. Things had to be just so.

Reflecting back on Terri's perfect makeup and clothes, he saw what a lifetime of being scrutinized could do. How that constant second-guessing had sometimes wrought Terri up with anxiety. Especially when her parents came for a visit. She'd agonize on the arrangement of pillows and the tenderness of the pasta. Her mother and father always had a critique, a method of alleged perfection. Deep down, he knew they meant well.

Seeing Delilah straighten Rose's bow and quietly comment on staying proper rubbed him the wrong way. He wanted his daughter to grow up confident in her own worth.

He wanted to bring up his child.

"You know, Xander, we could help you with Rose. Keep her until school starts. We're retired now and we can devote all of our attention to her." Delilah's polished voice trilled. She had been hunched over Rose, examining the little girl's drawing.

"Ah, well, I know she looks forward to seeing you both. I think that helps enough," he said sympathetically. The pain of loss seemed to form a permanent line on her brow.

"Barry, our family friend and lawyer, you remember him? He mentioned that the court might see an arrangement with us to suit Rose better. We know how hard you work. We have the time to devote to her that you may not right now." Jake stood behind Xander, resting a hand on his shoulder.

The blood beneath his skin fumed, turned molten. He

had to keep his cool. "Well, I know how much you love Rose. But it's time for her to nap. She's still not feeling well."

Smoothing her dress, Delilah nodded. "Yes, she does need rest."

"I'm sure you feel similarly. You both should probably get settled in your hotel." His even tone held a challenge in it. He needed separation from them. Boundaries.

Especially now, because their intent had come into full view. They were here to spy on his proficiency as a father.

A more sinister thought entered his mind. What if they just snatched her away? It echoed in his mind as he saw them off the property and as he walked back into the room where his daughter slept. He looked at Elenora, a woman in her fifties with kind brown eyes, and left instructions with a caution about the issue with his in-laws. Elenora had to stay with Rose, and if anyone tried to come on the property, he was to be alerted at once.

The woman nodded her understanding. Feeling satisfied, he walked to his other unofficial charge. He went to find Maureen. Needed to make sure she was okay after her accident. There had been no time to actually check on her—not with his in-laws so close by.

Striding over to the clinic—another retrofitted and well-windowed building—his pace quickened. An urgency to move filled him. The stress of his in-laws, their constant reminders of the danger of the refuge and the way he was raising Rose. It all slammed into him.

Opening the door to the clinic, the sour smell of oil assaulted him. He turned the first corner in the building to see Maureen and a gaggle of oil-soaked seabirds. When the boat tipped, oil had seeped into the water and drenched the feathers of about five birds. The refuge had rounded them up for cleaning.

Maureen worked quickly, using the Dawn dish soap generously to lift the layers of oil from delicate feathers. He studied her, once again reminded of the intense gut-kick he'd felt earlier when she'd fallen into the water. The fear of loss knotted. He hated that fear.

Maureen cooed at the birds, mimicking their squawks with absolute precision. From a distance, and if he didn't know any better, he'd felt like she was actually talking to them. A real conversation. Her heart seemed to soar with delight as every inky layer of oil was lifted from the feathers of the bird.

Easton, a few feet away in the exam room, diligently looked over every bird Maureen had expertly cleaned.

Her hair was wet and piled on top of her head in a loose topknot with a few spiral curls escaping. She wore surgical scrubs. Apparently she'd only taken a quick shower to remove the muck from herself before going to work again.

She probably hadn't even thought about getting her own ankle examined. So like Maureen. So tender.

As she stood rinsing a bird, a smile on her lips, he felt the world slip away again. Mesmerized by her grace and movements.

And so kind. That fact, her empathy and patience, it was the remedy he needed. One that might even strike favor with his hard-to-please in-laws.

Gently, Maureen worked the oil out of the bird's left wing feathers, careful not to squeeze too tightly and damage the delicate bones. Moments had fallen away before she registered someone lingering by the door frame.

Not just someone. Xander.

Heat flooded into her cheeks as she remembered the way their bodies had pressed up against each other after the gator run-in.

"Are you okay? That was quite a spill you took."

She shrugged her shoulders, tongue unable to articulate any of her whirring thoughts.

"What makes a girl—hell, anyone—want to wrestle with alligators?" He inched closer.

"They don't bite nearly as hard as the ones in the boardroom," she volleyed back, thankful to find her voice again. He unnerved her fully.

"Funny." A puff of a laugh teased against his teeth, leaving behind a serpentine hiss.

"And I can outrun them."

"Also funny. But seriously, why this career?"

A loaded question. Freedom. This career awarded her a sense of sky and life the way nothing else could. "Why any career? Why would you want to stay inside all the time?"

"I enjoy the corporate challenge and I have a head for business. Without that, places like this would close down. It almost did." A defensive edge filled his tone.

She flashed a toothy smile, raising an eyebrow as a soap bubble floated in the space between them. "True enough. And without me, places like this wouldn't exist. I wanted to be a veterinarian. I just had to find my niche."

"So someone threw an alligator in your pool and you knew?" His lips parted into an incredulous smile and she found it hard to concentrate. Averting her gaze, she turned back to the double-crested cormorant, the bird made its traditional guttural noise that sounded much like a grunting pig. Funny. Endearing. It helped her re-center, refocus on her work with the greenish-black bird that sported an adorable orange neck.

"I was actually out on a field trip for school. My work group got separated from the rest and we were lost, wandering around deeper into the moors. The fog rolled in and we couldn't see what was around our feet. It freaked out the others in the group, but I found that soup of nature…fascinating. I just wanted to reach down in there and run my fingers through the mist. I felt…connected. I knew." She gestured to the world around her. "This is what I'm supposed to do with my life."

"You are…an incredible woman."

She felt the blush heat her cheeks. His compliment shouldn't matter but it did. Her self-esteem had taken some serious dings during her marriage. "Thank you. I'm just a lucky one."

"Hard work certainly increases the odds of good luck."

"Still, life isn't always evenhanded." In fact, she felt like it was often like an out-of-balance scale. All the counterweights were askew. Looking at him now, leaning casually against the workstation, definitely riled her sense of evenhandedness. Being attracted to him was not without complications. Serious work-altering complications. And then, there was the problem of her work visa expiring.

His face went somber. "True enough."

"Oh, God." She touched his arm. "I'm sorry. I didn't mean to be insensitive."

"It's okay. Really. I can't spend the rest of my life having people measure their every word around me. I wouldn't want that for Rose, either. I want her to grow up in a world of happiness."

Searching for some level ground, she offered, "I'm sure she's being pampered to pieces by her grandparents."

His face went even darker.

"What did I say wrong?" Her stomach knotted.

"It's not you. It's just that my relationship with them has become strained since Terri died. They miss her, I understand that. We're all hurt."

"Everyone could tell how much you loved each other."

"We'd known each other all our lives." His voice was filled with a hollow kind of sadness.

"So you've known her parents as long, too. They should be like parents to you, as well."

He barked out a laugh. "If only it was that simple."

"I don't want to pry."

He shook his head. "You're not. They blame me for not taking care of her. I was working late when she died. If I'd been home on time, maybe I would have seen the symptoms, gotten her to the hospital in time…"

In his tone, she could hear how many times he'd replayed that night in his head. Played the what-if game. She knew how painful the potential of what-if could be.

"You can't blame yourself." Her voice was gentle but firm.

"I do. They do." Quieter still, he took a step forward, buried his face in his hands as if to shut out any chance of redemption. But Maureen knew a thing or two about "phoenixing"—the importance of being birthed by fire and ash.

"Easton told me the doctors said there was nothing that could have been done."

She reached a soapy hand for his, certain Xander needed a small show of comfort. Her heart demanded that of her.

"I wish I could believe that. I wish we all could."

"That has to have left a big hole in your life."

"It has."

"I'm so sorry." And she was. So damn sorry for how things had played out for him. For the burden of a future he'd glimpsed but could never have. She understood that sort of pain.

"I have our child. And I can't change things."

"Stoic."

He leveled a sardonic look her way. "The problem with that?"

"Nothing."

"Even I know that when a woman says nothing, she means something." He half grinned, an attempt at light in a shadowed spot. A good sign. A necessary one. And Maureen used that light to ask the question that had burned a hole in her mind all day.

"I just wonder who…"

"Who what?"

"Who helped you through that time?" Immediately she regretted the push for information. Stammering, she continued. "Th-that's too personal. Forget I said anything."

He waved his hand, dismissing her retraction. "Holding my daughter comforted me. There's no way to make the pain go away. Enough talk about me. What about you? Tell me your life history if you expect mine."

"I'm from Ireland." An evident truth and perhaps a cop-out answer meant to delay going deeper.

"Great mystery there, lass." He re-created a thick brogue, sounding like an Irishman in a BBC production. The gesture tugged a smile at the corners of her mouth.

"My accent's not that thick."

"True. And why is that?"

She looked up at him through her lashes as she finished the last bird's wing. "My father worked for an American-based company in Michigan for ten years."

"Is that what drew you back here?"

"Maybe. I needed a change after my divorce and this opening came up. I got the work visa. Here I am." That was the heart of the story. No lies, but nothing to sink his teeth into. Maureen was always much more comfortable asking people how they felt and what they needed than sharing her own details, especially after her divorce.

"And now it's time to go home." He tipped his head to the side. "You don't seem pleased about that. I imagine your family has missed you."

"They weren't pleased with me for splitting with my ex. They accused me of choosing my job over my marriage."

"Your husband wasn't interested in coming with you?"

"No, he wasn't. I didn't ask, actually. We'd already split by then, but my parents didn't know." She shook her head. "But I don't want to talk about that. Nothing more boring than raking over the coals of a very cold divorce." The need to change the subject ached in her very bones.

"Whatever you wish."

Time to shift back to Xander. To something of the present. "What brought you out here?"

"I need your help."

"Is there an animal loose?"

He held a hand to his chest, acting as if he'd been wounded by her insinuation. "I think you just insulted my manhood. I may not be my brother, but I can handle a stray critter."

Damn, he was too handsome and charming for his own good—or her sanity.

She considered his words for a moment before pressing further. "Snakes?"

"Sure." He nodded.

"Birds?"

"A net and gentle finesse?"

"A key deer?"

"I could chase it with the four-wheeler."

The image of Xander loaded up in a four-wheeler corralling key deer sent her giggling. She'd never seen this fun side of him before and she couldn't help but be enchanted by the flirtatious game. After all, it was safe, not likely to lead anywhere. "Gators?"

"Stay away from the gators."

She rolled her eyes. "Whatever. Quite frankly, I would rather handle the gator than wrestle the numbers and executives you deal with." She shuddered. "And living in an office? No, thank you."

"But you'll stay in the boat when it comes to the alligators from now on."

"Of course." She winked playfully at him, enjoying the lighthearted, no-pressure moment. "What did you want to ask me?"

"How's your work visa extension progressing?"

Ugh. Now that was a sobering turn to the conversation. This wasn't new information. The question confused her. "Not well."

"I can help you."

"You'll put in a good word for me?"

"I already did that and clearly that's not enough."

"Then what are you proposing?"

"That's just it. I'm proposing."

His words thundered in her brain, a reality she couldn't quite locate yet.

Proposing?

Four

The words hung heavy in the air between them. She blinked at him. Not a good sign.

Her head bobbed side to side, as if she was replaying his words. He watched as her practiced hands put the now-clean bird in a cage, the greenish hues of the feathers more vibrant, the orange neck glowing again. Astonishment pulled at her lips while the bird perched and gave its little grunting honk of joy. Maureen, however, stayed silent.

There was no enthusiastic agreement coming. He could see that now.

But that only made him all the more determined that this was the right path for both of them.

Maureen frantically scanned the room. Looking for Easton and the other technicians, no doubt, her eyes wide as she turned back to him. "Proposing what, exactly? A proposition?"

"Not propositioning you. Proposing *to* you."

"Pro...posing?" she stuttered in a shrill whisper. "To me? As in 'get married' proposing? You and I?"

"Pro-pose! Pro-pose!" screeched a three-foot-high parrot named Randy who kept watch over this workstation when he wasn't in the aviary. The parrot marched around a perch near the window, his presence somehow calming the traumatized new birds.

"A marriage of convenience. So yes, proposing we get married." This was a practical arrangement. A business deal that would suit them both. And damn lucky for them, they had the spark and heat that could make a marriage more than just a contract arrangement.

"So the work visa is no longer an issue and I could stay in the States?" Her teeth skimmed her bottom lip. He could see the reality of his offer taking root in her.

"And my in-laws won't stand a chance at taking my daughter."

Her brow furrowed. "You want a mother for your daughter? Is that fair to her to have her think of me that way and then I leave?"

"She has a mother and her mother is dead. I'm not asking you to replace her, not by a long shot. My daughter has a father who loves her more than anything on this earth and she has the best nanny money can hire in Elenora."

Maureen's shoulders relaxed down at least a little. "What exactly are you asking of me then?"

"I need my in-laws to quit threatening me. And I do know you will be a positive influence in Rose's life while you're here. I'm damn good at interviewing. I don't expect you to spend time with her if that's not what you want." He just needed a convincing façade to show the world. The appearance of cohesion. Unity. The sort of thing that would even appease Delilah. She could take this information back to their family lawyer. It'd be a helluva lot tougher for his in-laws to gain custody of Rose if a nuclear family manifested.

"Of course I would—"

Shaking his head, he leaned forward on the sink's countertop. "My mother-in-law—hell, everyone—will sense it if you're faking the emotion. It should be genuine."

"Won't she wonder why we married so quickly?"

"Let her wonder. This is a temporary arrangement. By the time your work situation is settled and my court battle is solid, then we can split. Rose'll be too young to understand. And I trust you to be kind."

She touched her forehead. "I need time to think about this. It's just so…calculated."

Xander made his fortune through careful calculations. He knew how to weigh options, to choose the most sensible path for the biggest gains. He had a knack for this sort of interaction. He couldn't help it if it appeared calculated. It was his skill set.

"You don't have the luxury of time and neither do I, so think fast. Our futures—Rose's future—depend on your decision."

All of his years in boardroom coups and takeovers had taught him two things: when someone would cave and when someone wouldn't. Examining her lip-chewing and her continuously wringing hands, he could see Maureen's resolve crumbling. Not only for her future—he knew how much she wanted to stay in the States—but also for Rose. For the child who needed to be protected. Xander knew Maureen couldn't turn her back on any living being in need. Especially not a vulnerable little girl.

Damned if that didn't make Maureen all the more appealing to him—and perhaps a bit riskier than he'd anticipated.

* * *

Xander took his seat at the head of the dining room table. Dinner with his in-laws. An informal affair, as always, since he opened up his dining room to anyone still on the grounds volunteering. It wasn't unusual for people to come and go, filling a plate of food and joining the family or making their own little groupings out on the patio area. The cost of the food was nothing to him compared to the compassionate volunteer help of the people who helped fulfill Terri's mission here.

And he appreciated the love and attention they showered on Rose. She had quite an extended family, not blood-related but connected by affection.

He was doing his best to build a life for her here and he hoped like hell his former in-laws could recognize the depth and thought he put into parenting. He did not take this responsibility lightly. Neither did his brother.

And now that Maureen had agreed—albeit reluctantly—to his proposal, all would see he had a stable environment in place here for Rose. In fact, he'd asked Maureen to bring Rose in after the little one woke from her nap to help set the stage of their connection.

The three of them.

Xander had to keep his cool and not let the threat of a custody battle cloud their visit. Even Easton was keeping his normally outrageous personality in check, seated at the other end of the table.

Xander lifted the wine carafe. "I trust your hotel suite is comfortable?"

He poured Delilah a glass of wine. Her manicured fingers touched the base of the wine stem, gray eyes steadily focused on the merlot cascading from bottle to glass.

Jake answered, "Of course. It's a beautiful hotel. Big bay windows. Polite bellman."

He cast a look at his wife. The nod she gave back was practically imperceptible, but the subtle gesture didn't escape Xander's notice.

"You know, Xander, we love Rose. We see so much of Terri in her."

Xander stopped pouring the wine. "I know. I see that, too."

"Where is she, Xander? Our visit was too short today," Delilah pressed.

"She's sleep—" His voice trailed off as Maureen entered the dining room. With Rose. "—ing."

His in-laws followed his gaze, resting on Maureen and the child. *His* child, who looked so damn comfortable in her arms. Rose's face had regained color and her eyes, finally cleared of their earlier drowsiness, sparkled with interest. Rose giggled and blew baby kisses at her uncle Easton, who winked back.

After examining the sweet expression of ease on his daughter's face, Xander's gaze drank in the curves exposed by Maureen's lilac-colored sundress. Heart hammering, he swallowed. Hard.

Delilah practically leaped out of her chair, pushing to see her grandchild.

"I'll take her off your hands. It's late and Xander shouldn't keep you here after hours."

"Actually, I'm here for dinner." If she noticed Delilah's disappointment as the woman slid back into her chair, Maureen didn't let on.

Brow furrowing, he tried to read Maureen's expression for a hint of what she was thinking. And quickly, before his in-laws read the silent exchange between them. But he wasn't going to argue. In fact, he had to admit to being charged by the way she kept him on his toes. "Yes, I'll take Rose while you help yourself to dinner." He gestured to the sideboard with the plates and supper buffet, china serving platters laden with crab-covered snapper, coconut shrimp, asparagus and diced red potatoes. Small baskets of fluffy biscuits and hushpuppies rested at the end of the line of steaming offerings.

Maureen shook her head. "It's okay. I'll hold her until one of you finishes your food. I've missed her today." With admirable dexterity, she held Rose on one hip while putting together a dessert-size plate of finger foods for the toddler—fries, a roll, fruit and cheese. Rose carried a sippy cup of milk in her chubby fist.

"Go on, eat. I really don't mind." She kissed Rose's forehead, brushed back her baby curls with her hand, and sat in the chair next to Easton. Bouncing her knee up and down, she began to sing softly to Rose. Melting his heart with every movement. And Rose… She looked so happy in Maureen's lap. So natural—as if they'd spent a lifetime together and this was routine.

His in-laws said nothing, looking at each other sidelong before heading to the buffet across the massive dining area, two more volunteers gathering up plates to head out the French doors to the lanai—Don and his wife always stayed late, such loyal helpers using their retirement to give back to the community. Lips tight, Delilah shoved up from the table to refill her plate, her husband following her. To keep the peace?

Draining his glass of wine, Xander let out a long sigh, eyes still fixated on Maureen, completely preoccupied as she adorably moved her mouth to create an exotic bird noise. Easton fished a toy bird out of his pocket.

Portia leaned toward Xander, following his gaze. "They're not like us."

"Are you saying Maureen belongs with him and not with me?" he asked softly.

His brother's assistant sipped her glass of wine, her voice low, as well. "No, just that they're alike in spirit."

"In spirit? I'm a man. Speak in less woo-hoo kind of terms." The idea that Maureen would be better suited for Easton set Xander's skin on fire. The suggestion bothered him more than it should have.

"I mean we're the organized, feet-on-the-ground sorts. They're the dreamers." She gestured with her wineglass, as if pointing to the vastness of space.

"They're scientists." He raised a brow at her. Scientists and dreamers didn't seem to go hand in hand. Too poetic.

"They're Dr. Doolittles. They talk to the animals and live on different plains than you and I. They don't care about convention or practicality. Their hearts are huge and defy practicality or reason. They're different."

And it was that difference that set him ablaze. But he saw his opening—the way to announce the arrangement. With his father-in-law in earshot, Xander said, "If you're congratulating me on the engagement, this is a strange way to go about it."

"Engagement?" Portia squeaked.

He cocked an eyebrow, glancing around the room quickly to see if anyone else had overheard.

Portia held up a hand and quieted her voice again. "Who am I to say anything about secret relationships? We all have our private lives."

Secret relationships? What could she possibly mean by that? Had people speculated that Maureen and he were... together before this? How would his in-laws feel if they caught wind of that? The last thing he needed was more tension or trouble from them.

Before giving any more thought to Portia's comment, his eyes fell back to Maureen a few chairs down at the lengthy table.

Out of her chair now, she raised Rose to the ceiling, simulating a plane sound. His baby girl's peal of laughter warmed the room.

Tipping her head to the side, Portia added, "Maureen's quite lovely."

"Yes, she is." Lovely. Unpredictable. Sexy. And the perfect business partner for this arrangement.

"Treat her well when you take her shopping for the ring."

"Why are you telling me this?"

"You'll have to sort that out for yourself. Besides, you're the boss. I wouldn't presume to give you advice." She smiled.

"Even if I asked for it?"

"No need to ask." She tapped his phone. "Add more features to your data planner and you can just look up the answers."

Maureen cut into the snapper with practiced ease, balancing Rose on her lap. Shoveling the fish into her mouth, she enjoyed the savory fusion of lemon, garlic and pepper.

A few bites later she felt satiated and cut up the biscuit on Rose's plate, feeding her small pieces. Rose devoured the food. *Sweet girl.* The return of her appetite said good things about her recovery.

Though she'd played it smoothly, entering with Rose on her hip, Maureen's nerves pulsated in her chest. All throughout dinner she'd felt the gaze of Xander's in-laws. As she cut up Rose's food, she could practically hear their running commentary assessing how well she was doing.

Rose lifted her small, chubby fingers, stretching and grasping toward her uncle. She squirmed in Maureen's lap, eyes fixated on Easton.

"Mmmmmmmmmmm," Rose blurted, bouncing more emphatically.

"Easton, I think you are being summoned," Maureen said, planting a kiss on the toddler's blond hair.

Easton turned, setting his plate down at the table. A little giggle emanated from Rose as Easton stuck out his tongue at her, his voice descending into a wild birdcall.

"I'll take her from you." Easton scooped Rose up off of Maureen's lap, zooming her like a rocket ship. Hardly the normal dinner-side antics, but Easton's free spirit was what made him a brilliant boss.

"Go on, Maureen, get seconds. Thirds. Tenths. Enjoy yourself, will ya?" Easton sat in the chair next to her. "You barely put anything on your plate."

She shrugged. The few bites she'd eaten had been enough. Her nerves were starting to get the better of her. "I'm fine, Easton. But thank you. I'm going to put my plate away."

"Suit yourself."

Maureen pushed out from her chair, eyes locking with Xander's. His blue gaze sent electricity into the core of her being. Grabbing her plate from the table, she arched her eyebrow at him, hoping he would understand.

They needed to talk. So much felt up in the air. Not that Maureen wasn't up for adventure, but she could use some bearings at this point.

She maneuvered past the conversations taking place in the dining room, entering the kitchen. Scraping the food bits off her plate into the kitchen sink, she took a steadying breath. Running the water from the faucet, she flipped on the garbage disposal.

The grinding noise stifled Xander's footfalls, but Maureen saw him in the reflection of the big window. Even in a shadowed, distorted form, he sent butterflies leaping down her spine.

"So…" His voice was a sexy growl. "You're fully on board with my proposal, then?"

Turning off the water, she grabbed an orange-colored plush towel, leaning against the counter. "Tentatively."

"Tentatively? What can I do to persuade you more fully?" He took a step toward her with a smoldering smile.

She bit her lip. "More defined terms would be a decent start." Maureen couldn't let this devilishly handsome, tall, dark and sexy thing derail her from getting to the truth.

"Hmm. Well. As my wife, you'd get to stay in the States. Continue working for my brother and doing your job here, at the refuge."

"Right. That's my benefit. What do you get? Exactly?" She pinned him with a stare.

"You'd have to help me at the fundraisers, mix and mingle at work events. A stable parental figure for Rose—" he stepped closer, lowering his voice "—and a way to keep my in-laws from taking my daughter. It's not forever. Just for a bit. Until everything settles down on both our ends."

Maureen pressed her palms into the cool granite countertop, leaning back. Considering.

"I know how it sounds. But we don't have the luxury of time." Another step toward her.

Cocking her head to the side, she crossed her arms. "We don't?"

"Your work visa is going to expire. My in-laws want Rose. If it's going to happen, we can't afford to delay. We have to close the deal. Now."

Pursing her lips, she took a step toward him. "Is this how you close all your boardroom meetings?"

The heat between them was nearly tangible. Her face was inches from his.

A haughty laugh crinkled his expression. "Things don't have to stay so...businesslike. Not if you don't want them to."

She swallowed, eyes lingering on his lips. Damn. She wanted to grab him, pull him close. Feel him against her. "So you're saying, we can get engaged, married, and... explore?"

"Explore the heat between us...see where it takes us." He drew closer, lips barely brushing hers as he spoke. The smell of sandalwood anchored her. Maureen's heart thudded. She wanted him. Bad.

"I can see where this takes us."

He touched the side of her face, running a finger down her neck. "So is that your final answer?"

Her mind wandered away from the kitchen. What would it be like to be with—even if only fake married—a man that made her so reckless with her heart? The heat between them made her want to damn caution and practicality.

"My final answer? I'll do it."

As the lightning feathered across the sky, Maureen realized there was nothing typical about a date with Xander. The first indication of his adventurous nature evidenced by an impromptu date night to Miami. Via private jet. Just the two of them.

That level of grandeur had been offset by the burgeoning storm. Even that had a certain charm to it. He seemed willing to risk, to push. So different from the life she'd had when she'd been married. Everything had been dictated for her, controlled and regimented.

No, Xander reminded her of the storm outside. Full of life and flash. A force to be reckoned with. She liked this aspect of his personality.

The dark sky didn't bother her one bit. Tropical rains were standard South Florida fare. So much for the sunshine state. And this tropical depression didn't warrant any kind of alarm. She'd quickly adopted the South Florida vibe that if you buckled down for every tropical depression, you'd never get a damn thing done. The only time to become concerned was when the bad weather turned into a tropical storm or hurricane. Not that she'd experienced either, but tropical depressions had seemed relatively minor in damages and stress.

Peeling her eyes away from outside the limo's tempered glass, her thoughts drifted back to Rose and Xander.

Rose's need for stability had lit a maternal instinct in Maureen. Sure, she'd always had a penchant for lost souls, the ones that wandered. But this was different. She'd seen Xander with his daughter, knew that the best place for Rose was with him.

So when Xander had asked her to go with him to Miami on his business jet to further stage the ruse of their engagement, she'd accepted.

Of course, that didn't mean the idea of deceiving his in-laws and the government sat well with her, but she also couldn't imagine Rose being taken from her father, from her home.

Maybe it was more Maureen's own history unsettling her. A false engagement and marriage gave her the same sort of feeling she'd gotten when she'd been talked into skydiving. The rush of adrenaline and exhilaration coalescing with fear.

He'd insisted on dinner in Miami at an upscale restaurant, Bella Terre.

He'd left his in-laws to watch Rose. And, he had admitted on the flight over, he'd left Easton and Portia to watch Delilah and Jake. An insurance that nothing would go wrong—at least nothing that his in-laws could use in a custody dispute. After spending dinner with them last night, Maureen understood and shared his concerns. They clearly loved Rose, but they wanted to manage her.

The limo stopped in front of Belle Terre, rain streaming and pooling against the window. The chauffeur popped open the door, extending a sturdy hand. He helped her out of the car, giant umbrella already extended overhead. In an instant Xander's body pressed against hers, the warmth of him teasing her senses to life as he took the umbrella from the driver and offered her his arm. She couldn't deny how damn sexy he looked, all dark-haired and charming.

As they stepped into Belle Terre, the sound of a Spanish guitar flooded her ears. Not a murmur, not a whisper or a trill of laughter pushed against the sound waves. What? That didn't make sense. Scanning the floor of the restaurant, she realized they were the only ones there. Aside from the waitstaff, of course.

Xander's breath whispered against her ear. "I rented this place. Just for us."

Her breath caught, drinking in the crystal chandelier, the rich, gold chairs.

The whole place looked like a fairy tale. Lace lingered against the white tablecloths, and as they made their way to the center of the room, she noticed the guitarist off in the corner.

He'd pulled out all the stops. So much effort, but she felt out of place in this extravagance. As he pulled her chair out for her, the scent of his woodsy cologne danced in the space between them. His fingers brushed against her bare shoulder and she stole an appreciative glance at the way his tailored suit hinted at his broad, muscular chest. Touching a hand to her neck, she fumbled with the small, teardrop-diamond necklace that rested at the center of her collarbone. The necklace, her mother's, was the finest thing she owned, and added glamour to her simple floor-length black-chiffon dress.

"You didn't have to go to all of this trouble. I already agreed to your plan."

"This engagement is going to come out of the blue. If we want people to believe we're in love, if we want to convince them all, then we need, well—" he spread his arms wide "—moments like this."

"Why not just make them up? We could get our stories together."

A true fiction uncomplicated their arrangement. But being here with him pushed up her attraction to him, made her remember the press of his body at the dance, on the beach.

Those were the kinds of feelings that needed to stay leashed to ensure the success of their deal.

As if in answer, ripples of thunder filled the room, reminding her to stay focused. A tropical depression didn't cause the damage of a hurricane. And those memories of how he felt against her? Potentially devastating.

His eyes glinted like sexy shards of lightning snapping across the table. "You must confess, this is easier and a helluva lot more fun."

She averted her gaze, tearing away from the heat of his eyes. *Focus elsewhere. Fast.* Staring at the plate of lavish food the waiter set in front of her, Maureen's stomach leaped in anticipation. Lobster. Escargot. Shrimp. "It is lovely."

"You're lovely."

"I don't smell of fish and I'm not wearing scrubs. It's likely the contrast." Her mouth dry, and needing to divert his attention, she speared a shrimp with her fork.

"What about the night you danced by the fire? I've seen you dressed up before." Flashes of the dance materialized before her eyes. Maureen wanted to press into the simplicity of that moment.

"True." She reached for her chardonnay. A sip—then two—later, she turned to stare out the window, watching the rain bubble on the thick cut of glass.

"And I noticed then. I also noticed when you were waterlogged in the swamp covered in seaweed." He refilled his wineglass.

She smiled for an instant before her mood darkened. "And your in-laws arrived. It must be difficult for them seeing you engaged again."

"They'll have to get used to it since we will be married soon. Very soon. The custody battle outweighs their personal reactions." He broke the shell of his lobster easily. "And we'll have much to look forward to with the refuge expanding."

As Xander continued to talk about plans for the coming year, her stomach knotted until she barely noticed what she ate. What type of wedding was he going to want? Her mind skated back to her own first marriage, that day in a massive church when she'd expected her vows to last forever.

Xander stroked a finger across her forehead. "Smooth that frown away. Only happy thoughts tonight. This is a new start for both of us," he said in a way that was completely truthful regardless of who listened in.

The waiter, a short man with a mustache like the Monopoly game banker, removed their dinner plates with a great flourish. In exchange, he brought molten chocolate cake to the table, served along with two gleaming silver forks.

"Happy thoughts. Of course." She forced a smile. "You're right, and you've gone to so much trouble, I must seem a horrible ingrate."

His fork edged into the chocolate cake, the melted fudge trickling out onto the plate.

Though she felt full, a small indulgence of chocolate seemed like the right call. A spoonful of sugar to help the deception go down. Or something like that.

"Maureen, stop worrying about what I think. Let's focus on you. And more thoughts about how beautiful you are now, and with that seaweed, and when you wear surgical scrubs."

Her shoulders rolled with her laughter. "You're quite a charmer."

"Not really. Not usually." He reached across the table to twine one of her curls around his finger. "You make it easy."

He tugged her toward him ever so gently. More thunder rolled.

"I'm not exactly a girly girl."

"You are entirely feminine. Alluring. Sexy."

Confused and more than a little rattled, she sagged back in her seat. He tugged her lock of hair ever so slightly before he let go. Were the compliments just for show? She was attracted to him and he knew it. Would he take advantage of that to enhance their ruse? She hated to think of all this male seductiveness serving as gossip for the waitstaff.

The cake lay in ruins on the plate. A bite left. Maybe two. He scooped up the last bit onto his fork. Lifted it to her lips. She took the cake off the fork, her eyes trained on his.

A small smile played on his lips and he snapped his fingers.

On cue, men in tuxedos and women in plain black dresses wheeled out carts that glittered like water in subdued light. Rows of velvet-lined cases glittered with wedding rings. Scores of them, each prettier than the last. Pressing a napkin to her mouth, she dabbed at any chocolate residue.

Was this actually happening?

Xander pushed back his chair and held out a hand for her to stand. "Choose whatever ring you want."

She pressed her fingers to her racing heart. "I couldn't do that."

"Of course you can." He took her hand and squeezed gently, tugging her upward.

"There's no need for you to go to such expense—" In fact, the amount of carats that surrounded her caused her anxiety. Too much. It was all too much.

"Expense is not an issue." He waved his hand.

"Or you could choose. Then I won't feel guilty." Heat torched her cheeks and she could almost feel her freckles popping all the more hotly to the surface.

He slid his arm around her bared shoulders until his mouth brushed her ear. "The waiters and jewelry staff have ears. Learn to be a better actress, my love."

He nipped her earlobe and she battled a wave of heat that was only partly from all that raw masculine appeal. Be a better actress? Oh, the man was getting away with too much. She simmered silently even as her body hummed from his touch. "Now, what engagement ring would you like?" he pressed, his voice sending pleasant shivers down her spine. "With a wedding band, too, of course. Let's make this a night to remember."

Two could play at this game, damn him. He wanted an act? She turned her face and nibbled his bottom lip, releasing slowly. "If you insist, *my love*."

His gaze tracked the movement of her mouth in a telltale sign that shot a thrill through her.

For a moment they stayed there, breathing one another's air. Locked in the drumroll moment, heat and fire building, the Spanish guitar swelling to an aching crescendo. His hand went to her jaw, his touch setting her ablaze, that familiar pull between them descending over her.

She knew then that she was no match for him in this seductive game. Her heart beat so fast she swore he must've heard it.

Her lips touched his in a perfect meet, in a kiss igniting all the sparks she had been trying to ignore for weeks. Longer even? Now those feelings flamed to life, fast and hot, coaxing a delicious warmth at just a stroke of his hand up her spine.

The glide of his mouth over hers, the parting his lips. An invitation she couldn't resist.

Five

This kiss fired his blood.

Her lips pressed into his, tongue searching and meeting until he already throbbed in response. He'd known she would be hot, that there was a connection, but this was so much more than he'd been prepared for. On instinct, his hands leaped to the back of her head, cradling and holding the kiss that seemed to kick up a notch with every passing moment.

Xander tasted her greedily, as if she might fall away off the earth if he slowed. And he had no intention of slowing. Not anytime soon.

But then a clap of thunder, one that sounded overhead, grounded him. Reminded him that they were in a restaurant. That there were boundaries in place.

He could—and would—have more of her later.

Another crack of thunder, more intense than the last. It reverberated through him, blending with his pulse. Pushing him. He felt a storm rage in his chest, building with intensity, building to get his hands on Maureen.

Xander cradled her face in his hands, passion still pumping through his veins. "How did any man ever let you go?"

A slight retreat shone in her eyes. So quick, he'd almost missed it as she spoke. "Why does anyone get divorced?"

"You don't need to brush off the statement. I'm serious. You're an incredibly smart, fascinating, sexy woman."

"I appreciate you saying that. And I could feel that attraction a few seconds ago." Her voice turned husky and low, eyebrows arching.

He liked her this way—fiery and challenging. She'd been so quiet at the beginning of dinner he'd wondered where this strong, determined woman had gone. She seemed overwhelmed by the more traditional, lavish gestures, and he'd made note. Next time, he would try to find a way to romance her that was more in keeping with her hands-on, passionate personality.

"That's more than attraction. It's damn near twenty-four-seven fascination." And even that description felt like an understatement. He drew his chair closer to hers.

"The feeling is mutual." With preternatural grace, she grazed her fingertips along the top of his thigh. Tempting. He eased back into his chair. "I'm seriously trying to talk here."

"And I'm trying to distract you from discussion." She scrunched her nose.

"Why?"

"I don't want this to get complicated," she said tightly, easing back. "We've made it clear this is a deal."

He angled his head to the side, his eyes narrowing.

"What happened to make you so closed off, so defensive?"

"Are you calling me insecure?" A hint of her Irish brogue slipped out. Exotic and powerful.

"If I wanted to use the word 'insecure,' I would have."

A moment passed. The world so still as she considered him, and in the spaces between breath, he could hear the steady drumbeat of the rain.

She bit her lip, looked him up and down, then eased back, relenting. "I shouldn't have snapped." She gestured around the dining room. "You've made everything so lovely tonight."

The hint of insecurity in her tone felt foreign to him. Maureen always had an air of confidence to her actions, even her subtle movements. Had this layer of vulnerability always been there, somehow latent and overlooked?

"Maureen, snap all you want. If I say something that upsets you, let me know. Fire up that Irish temper."

"That's a stereotype."

"Not with you."

Her lips pursed tight.

"What did I say wrong?" The evening was devolving before his eyes. He needed to figure out how to diffuse this. "Maureen? Tell me."

Leaning back in her chair, she loosened a chest-heaving breath. "I don't want to be the bitter woman who talks crap about her ex until other people yawn or run for the hills."

"You aren't. For that matter, I can't recall hearing you say anything more than irreconcilable differences."

"It was. Totally irreconcilable. I thought when we said 'till death do us part, in sickness and in health,' that's what it meant. He apparently thought it just meant until you get on my nerves and I'm just not 'happy.'" She glanced up. "I told you I can sound bitter."

"That had to be hard, having someone you love walk away for no tangible reason. He sounds like an ass."

He wanted her to know that he would never judge her for any degree of bitterness about someone so willing to walk away. That wasn't his style.

"He was an ass. Which makes me feel worse for putting up with a man who belittled me that way. The more he criticized me about getting on his nerves, the harder I worked to make him happy and the more he complained." She drew circles on Xander's shoulder absently. "I guess neither of us was very happy."

"I refer back to my original statement about him being an ass."

"There are two sides to every breakup and I'm sure he has his." Her gaze went past him, far past him. As if she was imagining how that breakup might be partly her fault. Taking the blame and somehow internalizing it.

"I've watched you this past year with the animals, with my daughter—hell, even with the way you put up with my brother. You're a good person."

"Thank you." She swallowed hard. "That means a lot to me."

"You deserve to hear it often."

"I definitely don't want to sound pathetic." Her hands flew to the sides of her temples, red curls twining around her fingers.

"You don't. You sound caring. You are kind." He cupped the back of her neck, his thumb caressing her cheek. "And you are very sexy."

"As are you." The more familiar smile and lightness edged back into her voice.

"Even if I'm all buttoned up and not the type to wade around with alligators?"

"I've seen you work with a diaper. That's far more impressive—and fearsome." Her freckled nose crinkled.

"I would have to agree. Scary stuff."

Her shoulders braced as if she'd been waiting for the right moment to broach a difficult topic. "I do want to be clear, just because we're engaged and that kiss was…undeniably full of toe-curling chemistry, that doesn't mean we'll automatically be sleeping together."

"I can't say I'm not disappointed. But then, I did state this is a marriage of convenience. When we have sex is your call." This whole marriage proposal was surreal enough for him when he'd expected to stay single for life. But he couldn't deny the lust he felt for Maureen, and the timing was right for them to help each other.

"If," she said. "If we have sex." The defiance and correction felt loaded with electricity.

A practical challenge he wanted to meet. "When."

His hand wandered back over her cheek. She leaned into his touch, eyes fluttering shut.

He brought his lips just out of reach of hers and he felt the sigh ripple from her body to his. "Time to choose your ring."

Helping her up from the table, they walked past the rows of diamonds. He watched her expression as she studied the options. Her eyes seemed to linger on a pear-shaped diamond. A pause he caught. She pushed past that ring and pointed to a small, round diamond. Traditional. Plain. The smallest one of all the ring cases.

"This one is beautiful," she said, smiling. She sent a small eye flick back to the case where the pear-diamond ring sparkled.

"Anything for you, my love." He gestured to the attendant. "We'll take the pear ring from case number three. The one in the middle."

Maureen's face flushed as the man handed Xander the ring she'd been eyeing.

He knelt down, sliding the ring on her thin finger. Eagerly, he put his lips to her finger, kissed the placement, then her wrist. When he stood, he kissed her gently on the cheek, wanting the moment to be special for her. And also knowing that if he went further, he might lose control altogether.

He pushed aside memories of Terri and what they'd shared. He had to. This was too important for his daughter.

Maureen's eyes were soft. Words seemed to press at her mouth, but found no audible track.

A familiar sound pushed against his pocket. His brother's ringtone. Immediately, Xander reached for his phone, hoping Rose was okay.

"Easton? Is Rose all right?"

Maureen's face grew pale so Xander put the phone on speaker.

Easton continued, "She's fine. But the weather's been upgraded to a tropical storm and it's predicted to be a bad one. You need to get the plane off the ground right away while it's still safe, if you plan to come home, which I assume you do. We really need your and Maureen's help to lock down the clinic and deal with any aftermath at the refuge."

Damn it. These kinds of storms could wreak havoc on wildlife, something Maureen understood, as well, as she was already reaching for her purse.

Xander extended a hand to her as he finished with his brother. "Say no more. We're leaving now."

* * *

The return flight left Maureen wrestling with a tangle of ragged nerves and stress. Was it crazy of her to be just a little bit grateful for the storm because it had distracted them from the attraction raging as fiercely as the winds outside the jet? Of course. And yet she couldn't deny as much anxiety about her feelings for Xander as she experienced about the worsening weather. The turbulence and reality of a storm coming for their refuge left her queasy and uneven.

When they'd made it back to the house, Xander's in-laws were gone. Easton said they'd blamed their departure on the weather, but they'd been upset over Xander and Maureen's engagement. Not that she could blame them.

She didn't have long to consider their reaction, though. They didn't have long to secure all the animals. Hurrying into her office, Maureen changed quickly out of her evening gown into pants and a shirt she kept stashed in a locker, piling her flowing hair into a tight ponytail.

Randy cawed from his perch, his feathers ruffling when the thunder boomed loudest. She spoke softly to him as she grabbed a rain poncho on the way out the door.

Xander and Easton were already pulling tarps over a few cages that could remain outside under the deep eaves of one of the buildings, leaving enough of a gap at the bottom to ensure fresh air even as the tarps kept out the more severe weather.

The three of them moved silently through the yard, reaching the main animal shelter.

Wind whipped at her, stinging her cheeks. So there was a huge difference in pure fury between a tropical depression and a tropical storm.

On rote memorization, she secured the animals. Talked to them in soothing tones.

Putting the storm shutters down in the avian center, the feel of the cool metal of her engagement ring pressed on her finger.

An odd feeling, really. After her divorce, her finger had ached in her wedding band's absence. So much had been promised with that little piece of metal. When she'd taken it off after her divorce, the ring's absence had left her with a lot of questions.

The clang of her ring sparked something in her. It felt strange to have another promise around her finger. At least she knew the bounds of this one.

While wings flapped nervously and the new arrivals squawked unhappily, Maureen checked all the birds, making sure they had food and water to tough out the hours of a tempest's barrage.

Through the sheeting rain, she could hear Easton trying to coax one of the big cats into the sheltered portion of their habitat, but Sheekra wasn't having it. Most cats hated the rain, but the cougar liked to sit in a tree during a storm. Xander was latching the door to the coyote shelter while Maureen dragged some of the goat feed under cover so it wouldn't spoil. Once the animals in the clinic and outdoor sanctuaries were secured, the trio raced back to the house to the storm shelter, rain pelting furiously on their backs, urging them inside.

Dripping wet, they made their way to the shelter at the center of the main house on stilts, which was protected from rising tides and secured from glass breaking through. As they ran, water puddled behind them.

Easton tossed towels at Maureen and Xander. She pressed the fabric to her face, mopping water beads that clung to her skin.

She glanced around the storm shelter. Rose sprawled on Elenora's lap, fast asleep as her sitter dozed lightly in a fat rocking chair. Looking at the child, Maureen could have almost forgotten the storm outside. The little girl epitomized peace.

The well-equipped room featured a few sofas, a generator and a fridge filled with drinks. A shelving unit pressed against the back wall was stocked with a variety of food. A reminder that these were the other kinds of dangers of living in Florida. Natural predators aside, the weather could turn life-threatening.

Easton weaved past Maureen to Portia. She sat at a table, pencil pushed into her hair, papers scattered in front of her. They began talking quietly, inventorying the status of the refuge.

Xander motioned for Maureen to join him on the blue-and-white-striped overstuffed sofa.

A crash that cut to Maureen's core pulsated above them. A low whistling sound seemed to respond. Destruction. This was the sound of destruction.

Her body shook of its own accord.

Xander pointed to the well-secured windows and the supplies. "You're okay here in the storm shelter. This place is solid. We have a top-notch generator."

Did she really look as shaken as she felt? "I understand in theory. And I researched all about hurricanes and tropical storms before I moved here, even after, because of the care needed for the animals. I just didn't expect it to be so…much."

So much? Ha. That was an understatement. From beyond the walls of the storm shelter, she heard the sounds of branches scraping against the house. The burnt smell of up-close lightning wafted into the room.

"You don't need me to tell you this isn't even the

worst." That casual feeling about storms in South Florida left her. Pressing herself into him, she let his presence steady her.

The warmth of his strong arms slowed her racing pulse and helped her to take a deep breath. "Thanks."

"No problem." He tucked her closer, his soft cotton work shirt carrying a hint of his scent—a blend of something smoky and sandalwood.

"I can't believe Rose is sleeping right through this." Safer to think about his daughter than the way he smelled, even if it made Maureen want to bury her nose in his shirt.

"Storms are soothing for some. Lucky for us, she's one of those people." He rubbed Maureen's arm, his touch steady and sure. "You should try to rest, too. There will be a lot of work to do afterward, cleaning up and taking care of trapped and displaced animals."

A reminder that straightened her spine.

"And that's the reason I didn't let the storms scare me away. There's a challenge and a need here. A lot to be learned and good work to be done." How were the animals doing? Concern for them ripped through her soul. She might not like the storm, but she could rationalize it. But the animals? They didn't have that benefit.

"True enough." His voice seemed distant, and his attention drew away from her. She could feel it in the way he shifted on the sofa.

"Is there a problem?"

"I'm just thinking, remembering."

"About when your wife volunteered here."

He nodded. The pain of her absence visibly hit him as his eyes lingered on Rose.

"She wasn't scared at all, was she? Her daughter's just like her." A palpable thunder rattled through Maureen.

"Terri grew up in Florida. We all did. So while we have a healthy respect for the fickle weather, we understand it."

The internalized environment. It made sense to her. The cold of Ireland, the natural state of overcast skies and misting rain. It was a part of her. So she understood how his environment molded him. How could it not?

A crash seemed to shake the shelter. Perhaps a tree falling? It sent her closer to him, to the muscled planes of his chest. His arms pulled her close.

They were a hairbreadth apart. Lips so close. Just like they'd been in the restaurant. All she wanted was to lose herself in him, indulge in more kisses and enjoy the bliss of that courtship of the mouths, something she'd lost over the span of a controlling and ultimately loveless marriage. She wanted to have the storm fade as she found courage to trust in his embrace.

But with so many people here with them, she held herself at bay.

Rose awoke to what Xander had identified as a falling tree. She was bleary-eyed, calm, but definitely awake.

Maureen had taken some animal figurines off the shelves and brought them to the floor. Rose climbed into her lap, clearly interested in the menagerie.

His daughter. Maureen. What a sight. Long red curls curtained the little girl's face as she played. Maureen's knees bracketed her and Rose used a chubby hand to steady herself on one of Maureen's legs.

He couldn't keep himself from thinking about Terri, though. His thoughts fell back to his life with the wife he'd lost. On the future he'd imagined for them since they were kids. She'd left him. Not by choice, of course, but her absence created a space in his life that, even fourteen months later, he felt. Phantom pain encircled him the way an amputee still felt a missing limb.

More than that, though, he'd lost his mother shortly after. Not in a permanent, delineated way like with Terri. Growing up, Xander and Easton had been well-traveled, following his parents on adrenaline-fused adventures. Adventures that made him feel like the world had magic in it. When Xander's father died in a mountain climbing accident, his mother had been like a ball that suddenly lost its tether. She'd skidded and skirted out of his life. Hadn't even checked on him when Terri died. Wasn't there for him. Or Rose. She'd simply checked out, a bohemian spirit that refused to settle. Another fracture, another point of departure that ripped into his soul.

He didn't want anyone else leaving his life.

Under no circumstances could that happen with Maureen.

Rose's infectious laughter colored the room. Easton and Portia and some of the other staff stirred from sleep.

"Shh-hh. Shh-hh. We have to make quiet noises. What sound does this snake make?" Maureen asked, lifting a rubber snake in front of Rose.

"Hisssssss," Rose said proudly, taking the fake snake in her hand. She wriggled it in the air.

Xander moved from his chair to sit on the ground in front of her. "You're good with her."

Maureen flashed a smile his way. "Thank you."

"I know I've indulged her."

She stayed quiet.

"Okay, I've spoiled her."

Maureen shook her head, giving Rose a quick hug. A grin bloomed across the toddler's mouth. "You've loved her. She lost her mother. She needed to feel secure and she's attached to you."

"And she's spoiled."

"And you'll do something about that at the right time."
She handed Rose a rubber tiger. The baby made a growl-ing noise.

"You handle her tantrums well."

"I'm not her parent."

"Her boo-boo lip protruding doesn't move you the way
it tears me apart." And it did. All that talk about being
able to resist his little girl's charm had cracked.

"It moves me. I just—" she shrugged "—think it's
easier for me to be the bad guy."

"That's a nice way to put it. I'm working on it, though.
I have to. I'm just still finding my footing on parenting.
It's tougher than I could have known. I don't want to spoil
her, but I want her to feel loved and confident."

"For what my opinion is worth, I think you're doing
a great job. Every child deserves as good." A heavy sigh
passed through her and her gaze fell away from his with
hesitancy and resignation. He recognized that look. Had
seen Terri exhibit a similar reaction.

"Your parents were critical?"

"Strict. The divorce was difficult for them to accept."
Maureen's normally full lips thinned.

"I'm sorry. You deserved support."

"Thank you for the sympathy but, honestly, it made
me stronger in the end. I'm here, forging a new path."

This woman embodied resilience. He admired her for
that. Wanted to drink that into his essence. Starting a new
path wasn't easy. Especially when he'd thought his life
had been planned out.

"I'm sorry the stress of getting engaged to me brought
back bad memories." He hadn't anticipated what it might
be like for her, his plans taking shape around his own
needs and a desire to keep her working at the refuge.

"Nothing to apologize for. You're saving me from having to give up the work I love. Thank you for filing the paperwork so quickly." She heaved a sigh of relief. "You kept me from having to go back to all the reasons I left in the first place."

"Are you hiding here until you're ready to return?" Maybe the question wasn't fair. But he needed to understand her motivations. Maureen's veiled past made it difficult to understand her full perspective.

"Hiding? That's a harsh word. I'm not sure if I plan to go back. I just know my destiny is here for now."

Stroking Rose's feathery hair, she added, "One day at a time."

Perhaps that sentiment was her marching orders. Kept her from feeling the weight of forever.

"Fair enough." His hand found hers and he stroked her palm, his thumb moving along the band of the ring he'd placed there what felt like another world ago. He could sense her tiredness, her fraying. "Do you mind if I ask you one last question?"

She eyed him warily. "Okay, shoot."

"Can you help teach me that trick for getting my daughter to stop pitching a temper tantrum?" He tried for levity, adding in a grin for good measure.

Her shoulders lifted with her laugh. A good sound. A needed one. He had this well in hand, damn it. Friendship and attraction. Just that. Good. Satisfying. Not dangerous, not something that would shatter his world again.

"I'll try my best." She took Rose's hand in hers and played with her pinky finger. "But I suspect we may have to work on how tightly she has you wrapped around that tiny finger of hers."

"You may have a point."

The still room seemed to inhale and hold its breath.

Everyone slept. His eyes met hers and her lips parted slightly. His desire and longing for her returned.

They were engaged now and kissing her would sell the cover story even more. But beyond cementing their story, he wanted to feel her against him. Craved it. Ached to have her in bed, to be inside her, to wake up with her next to him and see all that magnificent red hair splayed across the pillow.

He nearly took his chance on his wife-to-be but then the radio blurted emergency signals.

The room burst into life as the radio host gave an update on the tropical storm. The worst had passed them by, moving on toward Miami. They could re-enter the main part of the house now.

And maybe even find some privacy.

Six

The tropical storm had ruffled the landscape of the refuge. Xander surveyed the grounds, noting the damage. An uprooted tree from the east of the property found a new home just outside the bird sanctuary. Speaking of which, glass speckled the ground outside the aviary. That'd been the first place Maureen dashed to. She'd wanted to make sure those birds that couldn't survive on their own in the wild were safe.

The busted glass was thankfully the most substantial damage any of the buildings sustained. Xander made a mental note to put the hurricane shutters for the newly constructed part of the refuge on rush. The tropical storm's damage reminded him a hurricane would be devastating by comparison. They needed to make sure all of the windows were secured.

Of course, other miscellaneous pieces of shrubbery decorated the lawn. Palm fronds, bushes, branches and garbage scattered the area, looking like discarded wrapping paper after an eager child's Christmas morning.

Alongside Easton and Xander, volunteers began reclaiming the space. A crew had arrived on-site early, setting up a tent with bottled water and boxed lunches for the group, acting as command central for the cleanup efforts. By now, most of the new arrivals were either piling up debris or acting as company for some of the more unsettled animals. While cleaning up after the tropical storm frustrated him—he hated lugging and stacking branches—he'd been glad for the minimal damage. Tree branches were annoying, sure. But if they'd lost a building and the animals inside? That would be much harder to come back from.

Xander worked in silence, stacking palm fronds one on top of the other in what looked like a woodsy edition of Jenga. Easton added to the pile, too. The other volunteers spread out around the yard, giving Easton and Xander a small degree of privacy.

He'd always been close to his brother. That's how he knew Easton was weighing his approach to something he wanted to discuss. His indecision rendered itself visible in the way he carelessly tossed the branches and licked his lips.

Easton cast a sidelong glance at Xander, jaw set and voice quiet. "Are you sure you know what you're doing?"

"I can lift a branch and work a saw. It's not like I never leave the office." He could still steer this conversation.

"That's not what I'm talking about and you know it."

Xander kept working silently. He wasn't interested in advice right now and if his brother wanted to confront him, he would have to work for it.

Easton tugged off his heavy-duty work gloves. "Come

on, brother. You're not really going to pull that old silence act, are you? You pretend like I don't know you."

"Say what you want."

"You got engaged to Maureen to ensure your custody of Rose is secure."

"I'm marrying her." No discussion. Just the matter-of-fact delivery that had made him such a success in the business world. Xander chucked another piece of a palm tree onto the wobbling stack.

"For real? And what does she think about this—" He sighed. "She gets to stay in the States. Aren't you worried about the legal implications of a fake marriage?"

"It will be a real marriage." The words pressed out of his clenched teeth. This was *his* life, not his brother's. He didn't have any right to comment.

"What does Maureen think? How honest have you been with her? Because I'm not buying for a second that you're in love with her." Easton held up his hand once he saw a protest form. "Oh, I get that you're in lust with her. But love? Nope. I've seen you in love before."

Pain lanced Xander at the reminder of all he'd lost. Damn it.

"What makes you think anything Maureen and I discuss is any of your business?"

"I'm family." He folded his arms across his chest, staring.

Xander inhaled deeply, drawing closer to his brother. Undaunted. "Then be supportive, damn you."

A command and a warning all at once.

Easton nodded, but his body tightened into hard lines. "I'm your brother, so I'm the one person not afraid to stand up to you."

"Maureen and I understand each other." The arrangement benefited them both. She'd chosen to accept his offer.

"Do you realize how vulnerable she is?" Easton's octave dropped, eyes scanning Xander's.

"I know her past with her ex-husband."

"Then tread warily. Because you may be my brother but she's my friend, and if you break her heart, I will kick your ass."

"I'm not going to hurt her and you're not going to kick my ass."

"If worse comes to worst, I have the gators on my side."

He playfully slugged Xander on the shoulder before stepping away toward a group of volunteers.

Xander watched his brother walk away, but his eyes settled on Maureen. She emerged from the bird sanctuary. Hair piled high into a ponytail, gloves and trash bag in hand. Ready to work. Even now, she looked stunning. This storm-torn element reflected a truth about Maureen, he noted. That her heart sung for these moments of reconstruction, that her earthy vibe and huge heart rendered her beautiful.

His mind wandered back—had it really only been a few hours ago when she'd spoken of her ex-husband?—to the pain and calluses he'd uncovered.

He warily regarded his brother's warning about hurting her. He didn't want to be so significant to her that he could cause her emotional pain.

And yet, their engagement, his proposal…it had to be right. He needed to keep custody of Rose and Maureen needed to stay in the States. He'd put them on this course and had to see it through. They were too far in to go back now.

And besides, he wanted to take that kiss to its very satisfying conclusion in bed.

* * *

Cleaning up after the storm had left everyone sticky with sweat and dirt. In her short time in the Keys, she'd learned a shower wasn't the first way to clean up after muck and grime attached to skin. The ocean, now settled and calm, claimed the first rite of cleansing.

This system of ocean cleansing before an outright shower jibed with Maureen's sensibilities. If nothing else, it'd proved an excuse to literally immerse herself in this landscape. Two years later and Maureen still found the water enchanting. She loved how there were multiple incarnations of water on this small island. The boggy area she'd fallen into represented only part of what Key Largo offered. That swampy ecosystem supported specific types of creatures, had its own scent and flavor. And then there was the ocean access—unreal colors of turquoise sparkling in the sun. For such a small island, Key Largo's nuances fascinated her.

As she looked around, she felt suddenly aware of how the wildlife refuge had become its own ecosystem, one she felt part of. The group of dedicated volunteers who had showed up today astounded and humbled her.

They'd waded into the water, too, ready for a little bit of fun after a morning that had everyone's muscles aching. The whole area seemed alive with chatter and laughter. No one had bothered changing, charging headlong into the water, clothes and all. A minor form of recklessness she enjoyed.

Even Portia had joined in the impromptu beach excursion. Maureen watched as a wave fell against Portia's back, soaking her clothes. Easton's whooping laugh filtered on the breeze.

Maureen's breath hitched a bit as Xander approached. Self-consciously, she adjusted the strap of her green tank top. When she'd started the cleanup this morning, she'd been in a T-shirt and shorts. The Florida sun had warmed her, prompting her to discard the black shirt in favor of the tank top. Layering clothes was a leftover habit from Ireland she'd yet to break.

As he approached he discarded his shirt, tucking it into the pockets of his shorts. Heart quickening, her eyes fell on his muscled chest. Why did he have to be so damn sexy?

His smile caught her off guard, pairing nicely with his dark hair. He had that old-school-movie-star glamour, effortless charm.

Just like that, he made his way to her. Their bodies so close. And she became aware of just how thin their physical barriers were.

She flashed him a grin as he took her hands, leading them deeper into the ocean. The small waves caused them to brush more and more against each other. And move farther away from Easton, Portia and the volunteers. A semblance of privacy.

Maureen splashed water at Xander, trying to maintain a lightness in their communication that ran counter to the unease mounting in her gut. "What a relief that we're all okay and the refuge only suffered minor damage."

"We've been lucky this hurricane season."

"I read up on the storms before moving here, preparing myself, and so far I feel over prepared."

"The time will come you'll use that knowledge, now that you're staying." His hand brushed her cheek, sending shivers down her spine. The warmth of his fingertips almost made her forget what had plagued her mind all morning during the cleanup.

She raised her eyebrows. "Maybe there won't be one during my time here, since I'm not staying permanently."

Her forehead creased. "We never did talk about how long this marriage is supposed to last."

She stared down at the ring on her finger where her hand rested on his forearm, her skin so pale next to his while the diamond sparkled in the sunlight.

"We can figure that out later. This isn't the time or the place to discuss it, anyway, when someone could walk up and overhear."

"Of course, you're right." She curled her toes in the soft white sand.

He wrapped his arms around her waist. "We should be persuading people we're a couple, an engaged couple, a totally enamored couple." His hands skimmed up and down her back, inciting pleasurable shivers. "It's not that difficult to be convincing. You are a gorgeous woman, Maureen, and that smart mind of yours is every bit as sexy."

His words held her spellbound. He stared a moment at her and she felt the press of the waves knock them even closer. As if by instinct, his grip on her waist tightened. The squeeze encouraged contact, underscoring her desire to get closer. His wet thigh brushed hers, igniting a rush of longing so strong it threatened to pull her under faster than any wave.

And so she kissed him, tasting the salt on his lower lip. Warming up to this moment she'd been thinking about— no, *hoping* for—all morning. His right hand cupped her head, keeping her with him. As if she had any thought of backing away. Anticipation fired hot inside her, deep in her belly, radiating out to tremble through her limbs. Making her weak with desire.

He drank her in, pushing farther with his tongue until the space between his body and hers melted away. So much so that they were unaware of the approaching wave.

It rocked them, pulling them gently underneath the water, but their bodies remained entwined. Eyes closed, lips still pressed together. Even with the water closing over her, the only tangible relationship was the feel of his body and hers. How she wanted to luxuriate here, in this feeling of weightlessness. To surrender full control to the moment as his body pressed more firmly to hers. Her breasts ached for his caress and she could feel him against her, broadcasting how much he wanted her, as well.

An urgency for air disrupted that need, however. They pushed their way to the surface with quick inhales.

And then he pulled her back, folding her into him. Kissing her deeply. Hungrily. The sounds of the seagulls and volunteers returning her to the moment in a way she didn't want. For a secluded refuge, there sure were a lot of people around all the time.

Don, a volunteer with spiked hair, shouted in their direction, "Get a room, you two."

She thought that sounded like a brilliant idea. And, oh, God, what was she thinking to let herself get so aroused in a public place? She could barely catch her breath.

Xander lifted an eyebrow at her. "Interested in a room?"

She splayed her hands along his chest, trying to slow her racing heart rate. "I thought you said I would call the shots on the issue of when—or if—we sleep together."

"I did ask."

"True." She looked down at her hands, her engagement ring sparkling in the bright Florida sun, a reminder that she needed to think carefully about her decisions when it came to him. "But this is all so new to me. Let's take our time."

"Ah, the lady would like to be romanced."

She laughed lightly. "Perhaps the man should be romanced, too."

"We chase each other?"

"We do have a wedding to plan." This romance would leave her with whiplash if she wasn't careful. She needed to remain in control of the situation.

"Are you suggesting we wait until the wedding night?"

"Is that such an outrageous idea? Especially considering how quickly this all came about?"

Cupping her face, he let out a groan. "Sounds like an incredible invitation to foreplay. But keep in mind, we get married in a week."

"Not much time to plan a wedding."

He rubbed a thumb along her bottom lip. "And an eternity to get you into my bed."

Sleep held Xander in the hazy world of the past. In that most vulnerable time, when there were no safeguards in place to stop the memories that could slay a man, he was tormented by memories he'd been fighting hard since the word *marriage* became a part of his life again.

He stood at the altar of the church, eyes trained on the big oak door. Waiting for her. Anticipation of the future coloring his stance, making his heart palpitate. The moment stretched before him like an eternity. Easton leaned in next to him. "Delilah's straightening out the flowers on the pew. For the third time."

Was she? Xander hadn't even noticed. His sole focus had been on waiting for Terri to come through those doors. So they could start their lives together.

"Today I don't even care." He meant it, though he did avert his gaze to see Delilah fuss over the lilies by their parents. Xander's mother looked at him, joy painting her

face in a serene, eye-shining smile. She squeezed his father's hand. Xander nodded at them, his father winking in response. Perfection. This was what it looked like.

"I know. I just thought it'd help distract you. Dude, you look intense right now." *A small, nearly inaudible laugh.*

"Ah. Always looking out for me, aren't—"

The doors opened. This was the moment. The organist began playing "Here Comes the Bride."

All of the air was knocked from his lungs. Terri radiated as she approached, her slender frame accented by the A-line skirt. Her blond hair styled in perfect ringlet curls.

Jake walked next to her, looking at Xander with a fierceness.

"Take care of my baby girl," *he mouthed to Xander.*

In response, Xander nodded. Of course he would. He'd shield her from anything.

Grasping Terri's hand, Xander had never felt more certain about anything in his life. That they'd live happily ever after. Have kids. The works.

But then she started seizing. Shaking. On the ground. Voices pushed against him.

Paramedics appeared. An aneurism. That's what they were saying.

This was all wrong. Not like this.

And it wasn't like this. Where was Rose?

He looked at Terri, her body stilling after the seizure. Life flooding out of her eyes. Pain flooding his. The pink rose she'd been holding lay limp in her hands.

He went to pick up the rose, but it fell away from his grip, becoming—

Sheets?

Blinking, Xander kicked aside the blankets in his California King bed and took in his surroundings. He heard the steady beat of waves against sand, the feel of his Egyptian cotton sheets and his tossed pillows.

A damn nightmare.

A helluva way to cap off an exhausting twenty-four-hour period. Sweat soaked his sheets and even trickled down his chest.

No way he could stay in bed after that piece of the past shredded him. Space and air. That's what he needed. Anything to get those images out of his mind.

He'd never been much of a runner. Instead he'd found swimming to be what set his mind right. In times of stress, personal or business, he'd found a few laps brought him solace.

And he needed that now.

Quietly he slipped out of his room to the grand pool. He'd brought in a special designer, wanting this to be a kind of sanctuary for Rose, too. So he'd pulled out all the stops. Salt water and Olympic length, he'd also had a faux water cliff constructed on the back wall. Waterfalls had been added, giving off a very distinct lagoon feeling. Even the hot tub had been incorporated into the tropical feeling. Live palms were interspersed in the design, shading the hot tub and adding texture to the cliff.

As he closed the sliding-glass door behind him, he noticed he hadn't been the only one with this idea.

Water rippled behind a redheaded mermaid. The hair webbing behind her, parting to reveal a topless Maureen.

While swimming topless was a European custom he appreciated, his desire ramped up. Without a second thought, he shucked his blue shorts and dove in after her.

Seven

Water flowed over Maureen's body, washing away the tension of the day, the storm. Her desire for a man still in love with his dead wife.

A man Maureen had agreed to marry.

What had she been thinking?

Why couldn't he have been a troll?

She swam harder, faster, desperate to wear herself out to the very last atom of energy so she could fall into a dreamless slumber. She was a strong swimmer, a part of not only her job but also from having grown up on the craggy shores of a waves-tossed Irish village. She wanted to swim in the ocean tonight but fear of sharks and riptides had kept her in check at the last minute, opting for the pool instead. No one stirred this late at night, anyway. She could be alone with her thoughts.

A whoosh of water rippled over her. From the fountain or water features? She opened her eyes and realized…

Xander swam in front of her, side-stroking, studying her through the crystal waters. God, he was so muscular and broad-chested.

He matched her pace, stroke for stroke. Tendons in his arms rippled with each strong sweep through the crystal water. Definitely nothing troll-like about this man. Instead he exuded power and seduction with every ripple that broke against his tanned skin.

Not ready to come to full reality, to words, Maureen pushed on. Since their impromptu dinner at Belle Terre, they'd yet to be alone together. Even at the restaurant, waitstaff and musicians had stood at an attentive, audible distance. Now this midnight swim felt different from that night.

Cresting the water for a moment, she stole a glance at him and the lanai beyond. Alone. They were actually alone. No Easton or Portia or volunteers.

The thought simultaneously thrilled and terrified her. Never before had two equal but opposite forces begged her muscles for movement. So she kept swimming, kept doing her laps, all too aware of the throaty sound of his breathing, of his lips searching for air.

A phantom trace of the kiss from the ocean lingered in her thoughts when she pushed off the side of the pool, more determined than ever to keep swimming. As if swimming in this pool with him and not throwing herself at her very sexy, fake fiancé would prove to Maureen once and for all that she was in control.

He kept time with her. To an outsider, they must have looked like synchronized swimmers. Every so often, on the lap exchange, she'd catch his eye. A watery grin and challenge arched in his eye. They went on lapping until Maureen lost count, until her lungs and limbs burned with exhaustion. Finally, they both stopped at the side by the water feature.

Gasping, she asked, "What brought you out here tonight?"

"What brought you?" he asked back, not in the least winded, which almost made her roll her eyes but also gave her a moment of pleasure to appreciate his strength.

Treading water, she shrugged, keeping energy in her limbs. "Trouble sleeping. I guess I'm too ramped up from all the stress of the storm and cleanup. Relieved, too, but over-revved. And you?"

"The same. Adrenaline."

Xander pulled himself out over the pool's lip and into the hot tub, settling on the far wall. She followed, aware of him and appreciating the way his gaze lingered on her exposed breasts.

But the appreciation also made her aware that she needed to be more careful. Put boundaries up. Though the water teased and wrapped just above her breasts, she scanned for her bikini top. Too exposed, too quickly.

She nibbled her lip and reached for her stretchy Lycra top on the concrete. And wrapped the front tie bandeau around her again.

Xander smiled, his eyes heavy-lidded and sexy. "Damn shame to cover up such beauty."

"Someone else could be awake. I shouldn't have been so reckless. I forget I'm not in Europe sometimes."

"Well, I won't so easily be forgetting the loveliness I saw, regardless of what you're wearing." His lips tipped in a crooked grin, eyes lingering from mouth to bikini top and finally flicking back to her eyes. Rattling her to the core.

"I'll simply take that as a compliment, you wicked

man." She flipped her red hair that already had begun to form little ringlets.

"I'm your wicked fiancé." He floated toward her, the movement of the water sending anticipatory chills down her spine.

"Yes, you are, and we agreed this is in name only."

She was telling it to him as much as she was telling it to herself.

"How long do you think we'll be able to hold on to that sterile farce with all this attraction and chemistry damn near electrocuting us as we sit here in the water?" He motioned lightly with his fingers in the space between them, the light tremors pressing into her chest. How she wanted him to actually touch her. But she needed to keep her head. For both their sakes.

"I believe sex would complicate things tremendously when we have to say goodbye."

"It doesn't have to, not as long as we agree to get on as amiably as this, friends. It could be fun, exciting… Think of the adventures we could have in this exotic locale."

Oh. Was she just a way to live out what never was with Terri? The thought gutted her like a fish at market. That would never work, not for either of them. It wouldn't be fair to Terri's memory or to Maureen's world. "I won't be a part of you replaying your past."

His face went somber. "I wouldn't dishonor either of you that way. Anything between you and me is just that, about the two of us. New experiences. New adventures."

"I want to trust that." And she did want to trust that. But, damn, their scenario exploded with complications and unhealed wounds. A dangerous combination.

"You want to trust me. You want *me*. Because I sure as hell want you."

She glanced down, his thick erection visible enough through the material of his shorts and the hot tub swirls. "I can tell."

He grinned. Definitely wicked.

She splashed him. "Wipe that look off your face."

He tossed back his head and laughed and Lord, that was every bit as enticing as his smile, his face.

His body.

"Maureen, I truly meant what I said. We'll take our time. Wanting and acting on those desires are two different things. When you're ready, clearly—" he glanced down with a wry smile "—I'll be ready, as well."

"And meanwhile?"

His thigh grazed hers. "I'll be doing my best to romance you and entice you to make that night one to remember."

The dwindling golden rays of late afternoon glinted off the deck of the glass-bottomed section of the yacht. But nothing looked more radiant than Maureen.

She stood a few feet away from him, her wild hair ablaze in the light, loose curls against ivory skin and a green shift dress. Slow, smooth jazz stirred on the breeze, coming from the small band stationed at the end of the yacht in front of the makeshift dance floor where high-powered couples pressed cheeks.

Xander watched her eyes take in the fish darting in and out of the coral. A bemused smile on her lips.

For him, this sort of gathering felt stale and stifling. At least it had for the last fourteen months. He'd always found excuses for attending the minimum amount of social gatherings since Terri's death. Too many questions. Everyone gave him a sympathetic headshake.

With Maureen by his side? Everything changed. He

wanted to show her a fine evening, to romance her. She deserved that. So he'd confirmed his RSVP for the company's glass-bottomed boat charity event.

He scanned the crowd, noting the sheer variety of movers and shakers. A lot of these guys were politicians whose plastically constructed trophy wives made the Stepford wives look like a leper colony. Local celebrities from the Miami sports teams sipped champagne, huddled among the wealthiest people Miami-Dade County had to offer.

A glittering world. Xander could almost forget there'd been a tropical storm as he looked toward the shore. A few knocked and battered trees, but most of the lush greenery remained intact. A tropical oasis beckoning.

A part of him worried he was letting go of Terri's memory, yet he also couldn't help but indulge in Maureen's company that reminded him he was still alive, something he'd avoided thinking about or feeling since Terri's death.

And the people on the glass-bottomed section of the yacht were all potential partners, investors and promoters. He turned to the bartender, handing over his downed bourbon-on-the rocks glass. An older man and his wife sidled past Xander, bumping in to him.

"Oh, so sorry, love," the older lady with gray-blue hair crooned. Her voice sounded real and genuine, something often lacking at gatherings of the elite and wealthy. She and her husband looked like the kind of people he liked to chat with at events like these.

"Not a problem at all," Xander murmured, waving his hand.

Her husband, an older gentlemen dressed in a fairly modest black suit, cleared his throat. "You and your girl remind us of, well…us when we were younger. Hold on to her," he added, winking before walking away with his wife.

"Thank you, sir." Xander knew he and Maureen were selling the engaged couple act well. Truth be told, she made it damn easy. Maureen's natural beauty, her kind heart. Their intense chemistry. The role seemed like a perfect cast.

Looking back toward Maureen, he realized he wasn't the only one appreciating the way her body curved. A tall blond man approached her, eyes hungry.

A wave of jealousy coursed in Xander's blood, bubbling in his stomach. He cut the blond man off at the pass, planting a kiss on her forehead, placing his palm possessively on her spine.

"Dance with me, my love," he breathed into her ear.

She nodded, her slender hand folding in his. He pulled her to the dance floor, his hand finding purchase again along the small of her back. She was his. He didn't want to question why he felt that way, not now. He just wanted to hold on to this moment, this attraction. He just had to pick the right moment to make his move to win her over into his bed.

"You reminded me of the Little Mermaid a few moments ago."

"For real? So you've had a Little Mermaid crush since you were, like, ten years old?"

He choked on a laugh then shook his head. "Maybe. But make no mistake, my feelings now are one hundred percent adult, feeling drawn to the siren song of a luscious adult mermaid."

"For real? That's…intriguing." Her voice was a sigh on pink lips.

"Yeah. When you were standing there, looking at the

fish with the coral backdrop. You looked like part of that landscape. Like I said, a siren."

"Mmm."

Her subdued response tipped him off that her mind trailed elsewhere.

"What's wrong?"

Pulling back slightly from the intimate slow dance, she squared to look at him. "This is your life? Full of parties and gatherings with the wealthiest people in the country?"

He mentally regrouped, trying to gauge where this was coming from, where it might be leading. And what that meant regarding turning the page on his past with Terri.

"I'm a person with a chance to make a difference. I do that my way. You do the same in your way."

"What about all the waste here?" Heat entered her syllables, infusing them with accusations and distaste.

"Be more specific." He couldn't address her concerns until he understood them better, but he recalled her discomfort at Belle Terre, almost as if she didn't dare enjoy the opulent dinner.

"The decadence? You know, like endless escargot and party bags with gold and sapphire jewelry."

"They chose how to spend their money and that money went into a business's pocket, feeding back into the economy. And the majority of the people on the yacht donated heavily to charity, as well." He couldn't help his defensiveness. He knew the people here could solve a lot of the world's problems with the kinds of checks they wrote. And they frequently did just that. "So your problem is?"

He glanced around the deck, taking note of Jerry Ghera, the world-famous surgeon who'd given up his private practice to be part of Doctors Without Borders.

Sure, the lights, the band, the food was lavish…but a lot of these people were kind and generous.

Pausing, she nibbled her bottom lip. "I sounded judgmental, didn't I?"

"Were you being judgmental?" Every time Xander thought he'd pegged Maureen, figured her out, a surprise leaped out at him.

"What did Terri think of this lifestyle?"

The tempo quickened so he increased their pace, spinning her around and then back to him. "She wasn't comfortable in large groups."

"So it wasn't the money for her, just so many people?"

"Basically, yes. Her parents are quite well-off." A problem only because of the power that came with their wealth and what it might mean for his daughter. He'd never given their wealth—any of the wealth—much thought before.

"I didn't realize that."

"Terri's money is all in a trust for Rose."

"And Rose's maternal grandparents?" She pressed into him, leaning in as he led her toward the center of the dance floor.

"They could pitch one helluva battle for custody of Rose if they decided to dig in deep."

The Irish anger leeched from her face. Concern touched her brow, causing it to furrow and her eyes to widen. In a lower voice, she asked, "Have they been in touch or made threats?"

"No. Nothing since our engagement announcement." He thrust his hand through his hair. "I want to find a way to trust them so they can spend more time with her. But I'm terrified they'll leave the country with her."

"Do you seriously think they would go to illegal lengths?"

"They loved their daughter and I understand that. God, I understand a parent's love for their kid. But Rose is my daughter. My child." He closed his eyes for a moment. There'd be time to deal with all of that later. He sighed hard before continuing. "Enough of that kind of discussion. You're supposed to be having decadent fun."

"It is a lovely party," she admitted finally, although it was obviously not the kind she'd ever throw.

He winked. "I enjoy the way you dance."

"Are you teasing me?" Her head titled to the side, a strand of hair falling into her face.

Lifting his hand from her side, he tucked the curl behind her ear.

"Your moves are sexy as hell, lass. I would never tease you about that. In fact, now that I'm thinking about it, maybe I don't want them seeing you dance."

An overpowering stillness rippled through Maureen's body, like someone had fastened her with a pin like a Victorian moth. Her normal grace and fluidity vacated her features, a retreating shift he felt as tension rippled through her.

"Maureen? What's wrong?" Trying like hell to read her face, to understand what had happened.

"It's nothing." Her lip jutted, brow furrowed, and her voice sounded distant and cold. Not a terribly convincing liar.

"Clearly, it's something."

Her eyes, filled with rage and resignation, met his. "My ex had a jealousy issue. A bad one."

Damn. His brother's veiled warning about how bad her ex was entered his mind again. "Did he hurt you?"

"Physically? God, no." She held up her hands. "Forget I said anything. Really. I don't want to talk about this."

Maureen pulled back, shifting her weight onto her slender heels. Leaving the dance floor and him.

He needed her to understand that he shared little in common with her ex. He'd never been the kind of man to emotionally or physically hurt a woman. Didn't have it in him for that level of manipulation.

Determined to make his point, he searched the crowd for her until he found her chatting with a group of women around a champagne fountain. Her glorious red hair drew him like a beacon. Lightly, he touched her arm, fixing her with a stare.

A shudder unfolded beneath his fingertips, but she stayed. In the truest way he knew how to convey his understanding, he kissed her. Lightly, on the forehead. Then softer still on her mouth. The tension in her stance eased.

Xander held out his hand. "Keep dancing with me. We won't talk. Just…dance."

In response she drew closer in his arms, practically melting into his body. The light scent of her jasmine perfume enveloping him as a sigh ricocheted through her body.

Damn. This woman… She could become a living flame, and when she burned, it was bright and fearsome. He admired the hell out of her spirit. And her willingness to stay here, pressed up against him, meant he might be getting through to her. Winning her over, after all.

With a week left until the wedding, he hoped Maureen would begin to trust him. To separate him from that scumbag ex of hers. If he played all his cards right, kept that boardroom bravado, she would be his.

And he would have to learn to overcome the twinge in his gut—in his heart—that suggested he was somehow betraying Terri. Because no matter how many times he told himself he and Maureen were just helping each other out, he knew damn well he wanted her.

Wedding planning.

Words that normally involved a small group of girl-friends pouring over websites and bridal magazines, mimosas in hand. Picking out decorations that reflected the couple's collective personalities.

This meeting with Portia? Opposite of that.

Not that Maureen minded. She'd done the months-of-planning wedding before. And her real wedding had ended with real pain, despite the hours of primping and making her wedding day look like a spread in one of those magazines.

Even with Portia's assistance, and the knowledge that somehow this wedding wasn't real, she still felt nervous. For a variety of reasons.

The biggest of which? Her conflicted but ever-present attraction to her fiancé. Her *fake* fiancé. A reality that continued to crash into her soul.

"So talk to me about what you'd like your wedding to be like. The vibe you are going for. I'm great at organiz-ing and getting things done quickly," Portia said, taking a seat next to Maureen. Portia clicked her retractable pen and wrote the wedding date at the top of her legal pad.

A week to go until the wedding. A week and nothing planned yet. *Not a big deal. Not a big deal.* If she told herself that enough times, would it become true?

"The exact opposite of my first one," Maureen quipped, folding her legs into lotus position. She ran her fingers on the light fabric of her capris, thinking back to her wedding.

"What was your first one like?" Portia asked.

A loaded question. "In a nutshell? Too big."

And not by Maureen's choice. Her parents, her now ex-husband—they'd all wanted the big white wedding. A huge bridal party, a guest list of over 200 people. A wedding dress that had practically swallowed her whole in yards of fabric. A cathedral-length train. She wanted this wedding—real or not—to feel nothing like that.

"You don't strike me as the big wedding type, anyway."

"I'm not interested in replaying the past in any capacity. Which reminds me—" a blush burned on Maureen's cheeks "—I should extend the same courtesy to Xander. Any chance you know what his wedding was like?"

Portia chewed at her lip, shaking her head. "No. Do you want to call and ask him?"

Oh, heavens no. Maureen had to think quickly on her feet. "I don't want to bother him at the office."

Portia laid the pen to the center of her chin. "We could always look at his wedding album. It's in the family room."

"Great. That'd be perfect." Maureen exhaled a little too quickly. Portia's eyebrows inclined slightly, but she didn't press.

"I'll be right back." Portia set her pad and pen on the driftwood coffee table, flitting out of the room. Moments later she returned, album in hand.

Moving the chairs together, Portia and Maureen sifted through the album. For a moment Maureen felt intrusive, looking at these photos.

Her heart burst as she took them in. His smile, bright, unfettered by heartbreak. She wished he could still look like that, feel like that. Terri and Xander had been a beautiful couple. Their wedding, also very traditional, had been set in a large church.

"Oh, look at Easton," Portia said, laughing at the picture of Easton dancing next to Xander's in-laws. Always a ham.

Maureen's emerald eyes slid to the next picture, the one that showed the huge dance floor filled with couples.

"I think it's safe to say, you and Xander both did that big white wedding before. So, what's the opposite?" Portia said, closing the album.

"When I was a little girl in County Cork, I always wanted to get married at one of the old, mossy country chapels. Something situated in nature. And something that only has room for the few people that actually matter," Maureen said wistfully, recalling the green and mist.

Portia snapped her fingers. "There's a small, old, Spanish-style chapel on one of the nearby barrier islands."

Nodding, Maureen said, "That could work. Can we check it out?"

Portia shrugged. "As long as we don't take a dip with any alligators, I don't see why not."

Within about fifteen minutes Portia and Maureen had made their way to one of the smaller boats. Portia took up her familiar boat position—clinging to the railing and concentrating on filling her lungs with air. Maureen laughed, admiring her friend's willingness to constantly fling herself into the jaws of anxiety.

The Sunday-afternoon sun stretched long rays in front of them, singeing warmth into Maureen's skin. She drove the boat with a steady hand, anticipation rising as the shoreline of the small barrier island drew closer.

Visible from the shore was a small Spanish chapel. Climbing ivy shrouded the curved façade of the building, with the exception of the wood door. An elaborate bronze cross jutted from the curved roofline. Exotic tropical plants surrounded the chapel, flanking it in natural beauty.

As Maureen anchored the boat, Portia stood on wobbling legs. "What do you think?"

"It's perfect. This is definitely the place." A true smile pushed loose.

"So now that we are here, tell me your vision. I'll help make it tangible."

Maureen blinked, letting her Irish imagination have full rein and dance before her.

"Small. The family and some of the full-time staff for the guest list. Will you be my bridesmaid?" Maureen asked.

"Of course, I will. That's an easy enough request. What else? Colors you have in mind?" Portia pressed, pen to paper.

"Light and natural colors. Orange flowers. They feel like they could have come from this landscape, don't they?"

Portia nodded, scribbling on her legal pad. "Dress?"

Maureen took a moment, letting the image wash over her. "I want Rose to be in a flowing white dress, one with peonies that ripple out of the fabric by her precious feet."

"Gorgeous. What about flowers for her? Perhaps a flower wreath headband?" Portia offered, trying to ride in the direction of Maureen's vision.

Maureen nodded in agreement. "Yes. A beautiful flower crown of orange and white flowers with nice green leaves twined together."

"And how do you envision your dress?"

A pause. Her first wedding dress had been stifling and rigid. The landscape here beckoned for something more natural. "Something strapless. And with ruffles from the waistline down. The kinds of ruffles that look like cascading waves."

"Now *that* I know we can find. And you will look like a fairy-bride in a dress like that. I'll make a few calls to bridal shops as soon as we get back. This is going to be a beautiful ceremony."

Maureen's eyes lingered on the chapel. The echo of a childhood plan rendered real. Or real enough. She could practically picture Rose as the flower girl and Xander, all tall, tan and handsome, standing with her in that chapel.

Tears threatened to blur her vision, a lump pushing in her throat. She knew the wedding would be stunning, and go off without a hitch.

But the wedding night… That was another story. What would it be like after a day of fairy-tale romance? Could she resist Xander when it was just the two of them?

Or, better yet, did she want to?

Eight

Xander slipped on his aviator sunglasses as he stepped outside. Looking for Maureen.

Less than a week until their wedding. Until he could have her. But for now, he'd settle just to see her. Maureen's presence had a steadying effect on him, like a constant drumbeat in a song.

He had a sneaking suspicion of where he'd find her today. His paces eating up the ground fast, he made his way to the wild bird sanctuary and rehab facility. The covered screen area rose high as a palm tree, maybe about twenty feet tall. Maureen worked in the screened area, every bit the sexy wood nymph.

Her hair twisted on her head in a messy ballerina bun, she wiped beads of sweat from her brow. The Florida sun worked overtime, heating the air, turning the midday afternoon sticky with unbridled humidity.

And she still looked damn good.

Xander stood back a moment, drinking her in. She hadn't noticed him yet. He recognized one of the birds from the boat oil spill. The bird seemed to test its wings, stretching them as it perched on her arm.

She cooed at it. Patient. Encouraging. The bird cocked its head at her, as if trying to understand.

"There we go. You've got it." As if in response, the bird bristled its chest, white feathers puffing. But it made no attempt to leave her arm.

"Maybe later, love." She sat the small bird down on a nearby branch. It chirped at her as she turned her attention to an African gray parrot. One with a splinted broken wing. She scrutinized the wing, nose crinkling as she inspected it.

As he approached, Xander noted the way the days out in the sun had left her skin slightly pink. A sunburn, but it colored her fair skin in the appearance of a fixed blush.

Stepping up behind her, he cleared his throat. "Shouldn't you be planning the wedding?"

"We could just go to a justice of the peace."

"We could, but we're looking to make this appear as legit as possible for both our sakes. Need I remind you how high the stakes are for you and for Rose?" The words came out sharply, but damn it, she needed to take this seriously.

Stroking the African gray's feathers, she returned the bird to the low branch.

Casting him a glance over her shoulder, she replied, even-keeled as ever. "You can calm down. Portia and I have everything mapped out. Portia and I already called the caterer and florist this morning. All will be taken care of."

"And your dress?" The dress he wanted to see and then promptly relieve her of.

She chewed her full bottom lip. "I, uh, I'll have one."

"I certainly hope so."

"I have evenings to shop." Her voice wavered and her hands went to her hair, a sign of fraying nerves.

"There are parties planned, you know. As my wife, there will be more functions to attend. It will be good for the refuge, too."

"I understand and I can handle it."

He hooked his arms around her. "Part of this whole deal is appearing like a couple. Starting now."

The heat of her sunburn radiated warmth between them, adding to the electric nature of their embrace. He pulled her closer, bodies practically one. His hand traced up the small of her back, gently outlining her spine, hinting at her generous curves. He wanted her. Not a week from now. But now.

Ever since that night in the hot tub with her, the level of his craving had ratcheted up too high to ignore.

She blinked up at him flirtatiously. "Are you asking to kiss me?"

"Do you want me to?"

Her eyes went sultry. "Well, in the interest of being a good, engaged couple."

He laughed softly. Angling his head to hers, he kissed her. Slowly and thoroughly, long enough to feel her body go limp in his arms. A victory that only made him ache.

Before he lost his senses, he pulled back, away from the fierce temptation her mouth presented. "I have a wedding gift for you."

Her eyes went wide. "You do?"

"Easton and I hired extra help for today so you can have the afternoon and evening off with Portia and your friends here."

"Doing what?" She nibbled her enticing bottom lip, trying to ferret out the information.

He grinned, wishing he could work on that lower lip of hers himself, but he knew that kissing her again would be his undoing. "It's not a gift if it isn't a surprise."

The owner of Je T'aime, Darling passed out five flutes of champagne. Maureen nodded her thanks to the shop owner, wishing it was socially acceptable to down the whole glass before the toast.

Nerves jumbling in her stomach, she surveyed the women that accompanied her as she searched for a picture-perfect dress. Portia sat next to a thin, athletic, brunette woman in a yellow sundress—Allie, one of Maureen's good friends and one of the hardest-working volunteers at the refuge. Jessie, the wife of Don the security guard, reapplied bright pink lipstick before taking the champagne off the tray. Two other volunteers sat on the couch. Maureen's impromptu wedding-dress-shopping gang assembled.

"Now, Portia called ahead and let me know the styles you were interested in. And your size. I've pulled a collection of about five dresses for you to try on. We can add from there." The shopkeeper smiled warmly, pointing to a dressing room. "I'll be standing right in the main area if you need me."

With that the woman turned on her heels, disappearing in a rustle of chiffon behind pale pink curtains.

Maureen smiled at her collection of friends, still apprehensive about picking out a dress.

"To Maureen, the beautiful bride," Allie said, raising her glass.

"To Maureen!" the ladies echoed, full smiles as they raised and clinked their glasses together.

With a practiced, steadied hand, Maureen raised and clinked her glass, slamming the champagne back.

"Well, go on. We want to see you in those gorgeous gowns!" Portia grabbed the empty flute from Maureen, ushering her to the dressing room. "Just remember, we can have anything rush-altered. I've got seamstresses on speed dial."

"Is there anything you don't have covered?" Maureen laughed, slipping into the oversize dressing room. Eyes catching immediately on the floor-length mirror, she noticed how the five gowns were each carefully laid on their own hooks. All waiting for her to try.

"No, not if I can help it." Portia squeezed her hand before returning to the couch with the other ladies.

Maureen gravitated toward the gown in the right corner—a strapless, mermaid-cut ivory dress that had ruching all the way from waist to the floor. She slid out of her blue sundress and into the mermaid gown. Taking a glance in the mirror, she twisted her face in displeasure.

Because this dress pressed the unreal reality of her impending wedding on her? She couldn't tell.

Still, she gathered the dress in her hand, walked out to stand in front of her friends.

"It's a beautiful gown," offered Allie, eyebrows rising as she sipped her champagne.

"But?" Maureen pressed, needing further clarification.

"It hides your pretty curves. So restricting, too. You're like the ocean, love. Movement and passion. You need a dress that shows that exuberance, reflects you," Jessie said, fluffing her blond bob.

Maureen nodded, chewing her lip. She did want a gown that spoke to the vibe of this place she loved so much. The untamed, unstructured grace. "I'll try another."

Back into the dressing room. This time she selected an A-line cut. It, too, was strapless, but a true white. An attendant came out with a series of belts to add to cinch in the waist, starting with a simple braided ribbon. Not right. Then more of a low-lying chain, which wasn't quite right, either.

Then…yes, the attendant placed a wide belt of intricate beads along Maureen's waist, cinching it with ribbons in the back to give the right effect until the band could be fitted and sewed on. From beneath the belt, waves of fabric coalesced, folding in and out like sea water.

She didn't even bother to look at herself in the mirror before striding out to her group. "Well?"

Maureen glanced at her friends on the couch, and then past them, to her reflection in the mirror.

The dress was…

"It's you. Someone stole your spirit and made a dress out of you," Portia breathed, smile widening. All the ladies nodded.

Admiring herself in the mirror, Maureen spun, luxuriating in the swish of fabric, the freedom it promised.

"Can you go tell the shop owner I've made my selection? I don't need to try any more."

"You've got it." Portia stood up from the couch. "And Xander has booked the spa for us. That's up next."

After Maureen changed into her clothes and paid for her dress, the group of ladies found their way back to the limo. The chauffeur set a course for the Oasis Spa, an exclusive resort known for their Swedish massages, kelp-based facials and gel mani-pedi combos. An afternoon of pampering for her and her friends, courtesy of Xander Lourdes.

The limo ride went quickly. Maureen did her best to concentrate, to stay present and calm. But guilt crept into her thoughts. All the levels of deceit gnawed at her ability to enjoy such a kind gesture.

As they entered the marbled room, Maureen's jaw dropped. A water feature trickled down a rock wall, the soft babble of water soothing her along with the scents of lavender and eucalyptus in the air. Calm guitar music melted into the background, layering luxury into the very air. A spread of chocolates, grapes, chocolate-dipped fruits, pastries and cheeses covered a long table. Five plush chairs were arranged in a circle, primed for conversation.

First up, pedicures for the ladies.

"You know, Jessie, I always knew Xander and Maureen would hit it off," Allie said, a sly smile playing on her face.

"Did you, now?" Maureen asked, popping a grape in her mouth.

"Oh, yes. You balance each other. The timing just had to be right. But I saw the spark months ago."

Months ago? He hadn't even been on her radar then. Not in a real way.

"Oh, yes, I can see that, too. He's always had that intense gaze for her, hasn't he?" Jessie agreed, clearly enjoying the pedicure. Her normally tensely furrowed brow seemed to release all tension.

"Ah, yes. And here they are today. Inseparable. In love," Portia added.

A bit *too* quickly, Maureen noted. Wondering, briefly, if she knew the nature of the ruse.

Best not to dwell on that. Instead, Maureen focused on relaxing. Living in the moment, drinking in the layered scents of incense and nail polish. Letting the conversation fall away as her personal attendant shaped her nails.

While their face masks were still setting, her friends told her to close her eyes. More surprises?

"Okay. Open them." Portia urged, placing a shirt in her hand.

Eyes blinking to readjust to the light in the room, she read the shirt. *Bride.* She willed her mouth to smile. "Thank you. It's so kind."

And a lie. But for a minute she wanted it to be true.

"That's not all. We've gotten you something to make your big night and your life together just a little sweeter," Allie said, pulling a perfectly wrapped box out from under her chair.

"Or saucier." A wicked grin escaped Jessie's lips.

Oh, Lord. She was worse than a liar. She was a downright fraud. All of the effort these women had put in on such short notice…

"You all…you all didn't have to do this." Maureen's voice cracked, a hint of shimmering tears beginning to line her eyes.

"Of course, we did. It's not every day you get married. And it's certainly not every day you get married to such a handsome, generous man," Allie chided, unaware that this, in fact, was not Maureen's first jaunt down the aisle. The first wedding had been in earnest and ended in flames. Could a wedding constructed in falsehood somehow fare better? She shoved that thought away.

"Anyway, I want you to open mine first," Jessie said, pushing her silver-wrapped box in front of Maureen. Jessie took a bite of chocolate fudge, motioning Maureen to hurry up.

With shaking fingers, touched and humbled by the attention of these kind woman, she tore through the wrapping paper, lifted the cardboard lid to reveal five smaller boxes, all with little cards affixed to the lids. Each card had a jingle about panties—when to wear each pair. One for the honeymoon. One for their first fight. One for Valentine's Day.

Maureen's face turned upward, light dancing in her eyes. "This is hysterical."

"I thought you'd appreciate them." She winked, biting into a chocolate-covered strawberry.

Maureen unwrapped the rest of the gifts—a few pieces of delicate, lacy lingerie, an embroidered pillow with their names and wedding date, and a tiny, glittering frame.

"Thank you so much. I really appreciate all of this."

"Of course, Maureen. We wanted you to have a special, albeit hastened, bridal shower. Which reminds me. I wrote down all of your reactions to your presents. It's a list I like to call 'Things I Will Say to Xander on Our Wedding Night.'" Portia's smile reached her eyes.

"What?"

"Oh, just listen. 'Things Maureen Will Say to Xander in Bed.' Ahem. 'This is hysterical. This is so precious! Lord, this is so tiny! Beautiful and delicate. What a pretty shade of pink!'"

Peals of laughter erupted from around the spa room. Her fake bridal shower had been so much more spontaneous and comfortable than her real one. After another two hours of massages, the limo arrived to take them all back to the refuge. Back to Xander. She wanted to thank him for his kindness, to show how much she appreciated him.

She rushed back to her room, slipped into a backless black dress. The front was a deep cowl neck that tastefully nodded to the nature of her curves. Ready to see him. Ready to unwind from the day together.

So eager to see him it almost scared her.

* * *

Two hours later, and dinner on the water still made her heart sing. Xander had made reservations at a small, local restaurant. They'd eaten the catch of the day on the deck, watched the sun sink heavy on the horizon and exchanged stories about their childhoods. Gotten to know each other.

The night offered them a degree of comfort—stars dipping in the sky. The lack of true light pollution meant the stars were out in full force, crowning the end of a pretty amazing day. Maureen felt like she lingered on in a fairy world. A slumber that she didn't want to wake from. The whole day had been wonderful. Brilliant.

He helped her into the Mercedes. The touch of his fingertips leaving her wanting. He closed her door, loosened his tie on the way around and climbed into the driver's side. The ride back to the refuge was about five minutes. Too short before they'd part.

Xander parked the Mercedes in the driveway and turned to face her. An eternity passed between them and she stared at his lips, his eyes. He looped his tie around her neck and tugged her toward him. Melting into the feel of him, Maureen inhaled his spicy aftershave, rich with sandalwood and spices and *man*. Greedy with need, their mouths met, parting instantly as they tasted each other for the first time after denying the attraction for so long.

As Xander tunneled his fingers through her hair, it slipped loose, tumbling around them both in a sensuous cloud. Strands spiraling midway along her back tickled down her spine, tingling along her already sensitive skin.

Maureen gripped the lapels of his jacket. Her fingers clenched tight as she strained to get nearer, desperate to deepen the closeness she felt with him, blocking out the rest of the world. Twining her fingers in his hair, she held his face to hers, devouring him, ravenous after what felt like an eternity of waiting. Had this attraction been lurking even longer than she'd allowed herself to acknowledge?

A low groan rumbling in his throat, Xander's leg pressed against hers, the muscles firm, exciting. He covered her body with his, muscled arms lowering her into the corner of the seat. His hand trailed up her leg, stopping to grasp her hip and pull her against him, hard with need.

Maureen arched her back as something uncomfortable prodded her spine. When her body bowed upward, Xander groaned in response and pressed her deeper into the cushioned seat.

"Ouch!" Maureen reached behind her back and tossed a pen case aside.

"Sorry," Xander mumbled against her lips, groping to locate any other possible sharp objects that might distract her. He tossed the pen box over the seat to land in a thudding heap on the floor on top of his briefcase.

"It's okay." Maureen pulled his face back for another mind-drugging kiss.

Xander slipped her dress down one shoulder and cupped her breast, brushing a thumb across the tightened crest, sending sparks of desire through her. When he lowered his mouth to replace his hand, Maureen couldn't control the desire to roll her hips against his. A new music coursed through her as they resumed their dance.

She pushed away any concerns, wanting to revel in him. She'd spent enough time pretending. She wanted something real.

She wanted him.

"Birth control," Xander moaned.

His chest heaving, he rested his head against her

breast. Puffy gasps of air dried the damp peak, the painful chill almost as stimulating as his warm, moist kisses.

"You have my mind so muddled I can't think straight half the time." He raked his fingers through his mussed hair. "I can't believe I let things go this far in the driveway, where anyone could walk up on us. Give me a minute to clear my head and figure out where we should go."

Maureen struggled to control the passion singing through her body as she watched Xander, his eyes closed, his breathing ragged. She'd been so determined to wait, but something, maybe the edginess of the storm or the visions of him with his family or just his magnetism altogether, created a different storm inside her and she knew.

She didn't want to wait any longer.

"My place."

"What?"

"Go to my place." Maureen cupped his face in her hands and explained with urgency, "It's private and I have condoms."

His eyes opened wide as realization dawned. "Yes, ma'am."

Rolling off her, Xander turned on the Mercedes and slammed it into gear just as she snapped her seat belt into place. Their labored breathing filled the luxurious car as they made record time through the dirt roads to her cabin. Every stop sign became a sweet temptation as they stole hot, passionate kisses, becoming more familiar with the flavor of each other at every intersection.

After four years of abstinence, she owed it to herself not to wait one minute longer. She stroked up his arm. "Drive faster."

"And you have condoms?"

"An unopened box of a dozen."

"Twelve!" Xander's brow creased into deep furrows

while he stared at the road as if pondering a quadratic equation. "Well, at least that's in the ballpark if you give me a couple of days. It is a weekend, after all."

"If only you had one in your wallet."

With a low growl of sexual arousal, he put the car in Park and reached for her again. "You're driving me crazy."

The second Xander slid to the middle of the front seat, Maureen straddled his lap. She couldn't remember when sex had been fun. And this was so wonderfully abandoned and impulsive, and a huge turn-on.

The skirt of her dress hitched up as she knelt, her feet dangling off the edge of the seat. She fumbled with his belt, having difficulty managing even in the luxury sedan, leather creaking as she moved.

Xander's jaw slid open.

Even though it couldn't go further until they reached her place, the thick press of his arousal through his pants pressed against the core of her, sending sweet sparks of pleasure through her.

Not one to lag behind, he slid his hand under her dress and skimmed his fingers along the edge of her panties.

When he gripped her hips, his fingers grazed across her stomach. She grabbed his wrists and moved his other hand to cup her breast under the silky fabric flowing around them both in a fiery cloud.

Tap-tap-tap.

Maureen flinched.

Xander's head pivoted toward the sound.

Someone with a flashlight strobed the beam in their direction, illuminating Xander's eyes, full of heat and desire. Xander's hands snaked from under her dress with lightning speed.

"Good evening. Is everything okay?" Don, a volunteer, shouted through the window. The older man had worked security detail for a major corporation before retiring, and now volunteered those skills to patrol the refuge at night.

Maureen pressed the electric button, thankful the Mercedes was still running. Easing off Xander's lap, she almost toppled over when he clamped his hands on either side of her dress to hide the considerable evidence of his arousal. The exotic scent of tropical flowers in the night air drifted through the open window as the security guard shuffled his feet.

"Hi, Don. Uh, nice weather." She shifted, sitting on Xander's knees and praying very hard that this nightmare would end—soon.

"Yes, ma'am, mighty nice." Grin spreading across his craggy face, Don thumped his flashlight against his palm, the beam flickering through the dark like a laser show out of control.

"Uh-huh." Maureen unclenched her hands, tight with building desire.

Xander injected into the awkward silence, "How's little Donny Junior?"

"Just fine. He and his wife have a baby on the way."

Maureen felt Xander's glance her way as she focused with undue concentration on the files littering the floor of the car.

Xander cleared his throat. "Tell them I said congratulations."

"Sure will." Don tapped a foot against a tire. "Night, Mr. Lourdes. Good evening, Miz Burke."

She nodded and smiled awkwardly.

Xander waved. "Good night, Don."

With a low chortle, the volunteer security guard turned and strode off into the darkened parking lot.

Maureen raised the window and turned back to Xander just as he adjusted his pants. She clenched the armrest, unsettled by the interruption and by how quickly she'd been swept away by desire for this man.

"Maureen, don't you think you could have helped me out with Don?"

"Nope. I can still barely put two thoughts together." Maureen pressed a hand to her mouth, a hysterical giggle bursting free.

"What?" An indignant expression stained Xander's face as he flopped back against the seat.

"Think about it, Xander."

His shoulders lifted and fell, chuckles rumbling low in his chest. "You make me act like a sixteen-year-old again, making out in a car."

"You must have had a very different life at sixteen than I did. Sorry I didn't consider Don when I, uh, jumped you."

"Don't worry about it. We have a dozen condoms waiting for us at your place."

Nine

From the Mercedes to the cabin door seemed to take an eternity. She stepped in front of him, her slender calves visible in the subdued moonlight, teasing him even more. The promise of her skin against his drove him to madness as she fumbled to slip her keys in the door.

And each step gave him too much damn time to think about the step he was taking—sleeping with a woman for the first time since he'd lost Terri. But she was gone, and he had to move forward with his life. He shut down thoughts of the past that threatened the present.

He wanted this, and Maureen deserved his full attention.

The lock clicked open like a gunshot starting a marathon race, spurring him to action. They stepped through the frame and he kicked the door closed behind him, kissing her deeply. The soft press of her body against his sent his passion into overdrive.

Her hands wandered over his shirt, undoing each button. Shrugging off the fabric, he broke their embrace. To look at her. To *see* her.

Maureen's wild red hair framed her face, falling just above her breasts. A hunger danced in her green eyes as she stood, pressed against the white wicker sofa in the center of her small living room. The modest cabin was filled with photographs of exotic locales and remnants of her Irish roots in the form of a Celtic Cross centered on the wall behind her. A woman who knew no real borders.

He approached her again, kissing her exposed shoulder, running his hand to the zipper on the back of her satiny dress edged with the gentle rasp of lace. He wanted nothing between them. He couldn't remember when he'd felt so out of control as he'd been in the car. That wasn't his style. He ran the show, called the pace, took things slow and careful. Yet they'd almost forgotten birth control.

Above all, he had to remember to be careful with her, to think of her needs. He didn't want to think about Terri now, but she'd been so delicate. Hell. He shoved thoughts of her aside and focused on this moment and what Maureen wanted. What Maureen needed from him. What he needed from her.

Not that reasonable thought was any easier to find now than in the Mercedes.

She felt exquisitely smooth and soft to his touch. Memories of her bare breasts the day in the hot tub grotto blared into his brain, a vision seared on the backs of his eyelids that he couldn't wait to re-create. Tugging her dress down, down, he unveiled her delicate yellow bra, an expanse of sheer lace with strategic roses stitched to cover the rosy tips.

With a groan, he stripped off the yellow ribbons that

served as straps, letting the lace peel down and away. Her back arched, tilting those beautiful breasts toward his mouth. Inviting his kiss. He palmed one creamy weight in his hand, lifting her for a taste.

She hissed a sigh between her teeth, her knees giving way as she fell deeper into him. He anchored her waist with one arm as he rolled one taut nipple between his teeth—gently plucking and licking. Her hair spilled over his arms as she strained to get closer. He molded her waist and hips with his hands, dragging the dress fabric down and off.

Their clothes fell away in a trail on the way to her bedroom, pooling haphazardly on the wood cabin floor.

Entering her bedroom, she pulled out a box of condoms from her driftwood nightstand. They were still sealed. She made no further moves as he joined her near the bed.

He looked at her, questioning. Hoping she still wanted him.

A mischievous look entered her eye. "You can ask."

"Ask what?"

"When I bought them. Why I have them. I bought them after your proposal."

"For this?" He lifted his hand to her face, touching the softness of her wild curls.

She leaned in, kissing the outline of his top lip. "It's been inevitable."

A roar of victory filled his brain as finally, finally, she understood what he'd known in his gut since that impulsive proposal burst from his mouth.

"Nice to hear you acknowledge what I've felt since our first dance together," he said, skimming his lips over hers.

She teased her fingers along his bristly jaw, then back

around to the back of his neck, stroking up into his hair. "Because I want you as much as I believe you want me."

Pulling her closer, their bodies pressed together, he reveled in the brush of their bare flesh against flesh, their legs tangling. One hand between her shoulder blades, his other against her spine, he lowered her onto the thick duvet and covered her body with his. The mattress gave beneath them, her curves molding to his, sending his need into intense overdrive.

The ceiling fan stirred gusts of air over their rapidly heating flesh as his hands learned the terrain of her every curve. As she reciprocated. It was so natural. So right.

And so well lit, thanks to the bedside lamp.

He couldn't have dreamed anything more perfect. And he wasn't sure how much longer he could wait.

Just when he thought he'd reached the breaking point, he saw her pat the bed for the box of condoms and, yes, he was more than happy to assist. Quickly.

At the last instant she snatched a packet from his hands and tore it open. Maureen sheathed the throbbing length of him with deliberate—oh, so deliberate—control. Slowly. Almost torturously slowly, and her smile said she understood well how close she danced to the very hot flame of desire.

His hands tangled in her hair, he kissed her, thoroughly, sealing their lips, their tongues mating as he pushed inside her body for the first time. Felt the hot clamp of her around him, drawing him in, welcoming him.

Bringing him such intense pleasure he almost flew over the edge right then and there.

But he held on, holding still until he had enough self-control to move again, with her, in and out, thrusting and guiding her hips with the rock of his against hers.

He took each kittenish gasp of pleasure into his mouth, grazing kisses along her jaw, then her neck as her head flung back, exposing the graceful arch. Her riotous red hair splayed over the pillow like a fire he would never forget. Ever.

She pushed against his shoulders, rolling him to his back, her magnificent hair draping forward in long, tangled curls over her shoulders, skimming the tops of her breasts. His hands slid from her hips up to cup the weight of her, his thumbs grazing her until her nipples tightened into peaks of pleasure.

The *hmm* of bliss rolling up her throat and between her lips encouraged him as much as the roll of her hips as she rode him, drawing out the pleasure between them.

He pulled her closer to him, needing to feel the curve of soft breasts in his palms. Leaning forward, she kissed his neck, breath heavy and urgent. Hand slipping on her back, pushing her farther. Needing more of her.

He gritted his teeth to hold back the urge to come. Now. Hard and fast. But he wasn't finishing without her. He was determined to see the ecstasy of release stamped on her face, flushing her bare flesh.

Audible moans rose from her, encouraging him to hold on longer. The long red curls that shadowed her face a moment ago flipped back. She arched in pleasure as her body throbbed around him with ripples of her orgasm, massaging him into a release that sent his head pressing back into the pillow.

Then in a flash, he rolled her to her back again and thrust once, twice more, drawing an additional moan of pleasure from her.

He sighed deeply, pulling her to his chest. No words, just the sound of labored breathing growing calm. Her leg snaked around his, breasts and thighs against his side.

She mumbled against him, kissing his shoulder. "That was…perfect."

He skimmed his mouth along the top of her head. "Damn straight it was and the next time will be even better if possible. I have plans for you, lady."

"Hmm—" she hummed against him "—I like the sound of that…" Her voice trailed off.

"Maureen?"

"Yes," she said in a whisper.

"Are you with me?"

"Uh-huh," she murmured. "Just deliciously mellow and recharging for the next…round…"

Maureen's breath slowed more, sleep finding her.

Sweat trickled on his brow, cooling him physically.

Emotionally? He revved up thinking of the next time he'd have her once she woke. For now, though, he couldn't help but be glad for the chance to get his thoughts together. Because his world had just been rocked. He hadn't felt this way in a damn long time.

Not since Terri. He hadn't had sex since his wife had passed away. Fourteen months and it all had come down to this moment. A moment he had angled for. Wanted. And, more importantly, *enjoyed*.

But that didn't change the fact that conflict swirled like a burgeoning hurricane in his heart. Maureen rolled slightly away from him, the sudden space between their bodies sending a brief chill through him. Already aching over that absence, he knew his feelings for Maureen had transitioned. Not tonight, exactly. He couldn't tell when it had happened.

Xander was starting to experience more than just lust for her. Something so much more. Something that scared the hell out of him. He felt disloyal to the memory of Terri as he lay in bed, tangled with Maureen.

And for Maureen. Would this complicate how she approached their marriage of convenience?

His thoughts picked up force, that familiar tightness in his gut howling.

Distance and space. He needed that now. Needed to sort all of this out. Carefully, Xander pulled his arm out from beneath Maureen. She stirred but didn't wake. Even sleeping, her expression seemed kind.

The last thing he wanted to do was hurt her. Gathering up his clothes, he dressed. Taking one last look at her, he noted the way the covers dipped with her hourglass figure. His eyes slid to the box of condoms. Eleven left. Part of him wished he could have used more tonight. He wished a lot of things and had damn few answers to his questions.

Dressing the next morning, Maureen told herself she wasn't upset Xander hadn't been in bed when she'd woken. That was fine. Really.

She'd curled up beside him again and drifted often, expecting a morning of leisurely wake-up sex. And instead found a cold pillow that still carried a hint of dampness from his showered hair.

Maureen went through a rational list of reasons why he'd left before she woke up. He did have a child. And with his in-laws breathing down his neck, he probably needed to make sure he didn't appear negligent or selfish. That explanation seemed satisfactory.

Besides, even though she and Xander were technically engaged, his early morning departure effectively eradicated the possibility of too much gossip around the refuge. Another aspect she greatly appreciated. Appearing engaged and in love was one thing. Having people watching him slip out of her cabin and fill in lurid details was another altogether. This was all still so new to her.

She refused to let her mind wander to more sinister reasons. There'd be no good in that.

Over the past few days he'd been so kind to her. Filled her hours with surprises—the spa day with her friends, dinner. Maureen desperately wanted to do something for him. So he'd know how much she appreciated his gestures and actions. Before this all fizzled away and she was forced back to reality with only a couple of days left until the wedding.

Her wedding, the reality that she would really be staying in the States, reminded her of her home in Ireland and all of the things she'd left behind. She was committed to staying here, wanted to stay in the States, but daily she'd had to remind herself that might not be possible. It still might not be possible for any number of reasons if—when—she and Xander split. If she were to survive that transition, she wanted to make sure she and Xander parted as good friends. Maureen needed to build her fake marriage on something real.

She and her ex were like an arsonist and a lit match. While the flaming love sounded poetic, its reality manifested in destruction. Damaging. The ashes of that life still swirled around her.

After her fake marriage ended, she didn't want to find herself again in a burn pit of ruins. *After.* The reality of *after* bit at her, nipped at her mind.

What did she want after? To really return to Ireland? To leave Xander and Rose? The refuge?

So many pounding questions she couldn't deal with. Instead, she dressed in coral-colored shorts and a flowing white top, and went to pick up pastries for Xander. A small surprise, but food always had a way of easing tension between people.

Knocking on the door to the main house, pastries in

hand, Maureen's thoughts entered the now-familiar circle in her mind. Xander. What did he do for fun? He didn't appear to have any hobbies. His interests seemed to be work and caring for Rose.

Part of her wondered if he didn't allow himself any quiet time. Time when he'd have to face realities he seemed desperate to escape. Or maybe that was just her. She'd always pushed into work in moments of stress and uncertainty. Maybe he did the same.

The door swung open, interrupting her thoughts. The afternoon sun soaked into Xander's cool blue eyes and tanned skin. Sexy still. Her belly did a little backflip, nerves prickling her face into a smile.

"I brought pastries." She extended the box to him.

"You'll be bringing those to go. I was actually headed to come surprise you. I've got a whole afternoon and evening planned for us. And Rose." There was a lightness in his voice that didn't fully reach his eyes.

Maureen blamed it on the strength of the sun, taking the gesture of an impromptu date more seriously than the lack of sparkle in those eyes. She tried to guess the nature of the date from his clothes: khaki shorts, a polo shirt that matched his eyes and leather boat shoes that finished off his casual look so different from his office suits and formal tuxedos.

He'd been prepared for her. Within five minutes, the little trio packed into the limo. The nanny had already left ahead of them to set things up in the hotel. Rose chattered in her car seat, grabbing for Maureen's hair. They set out for a tiny neighboring island where a street market filled with entertainment and life flourished like a school of vibrant fish.

Maureen carried Rose on her hip, relishing the smile on the baby's face. She liked the way Rose drank in the scenery, cooed at the street musicians. So aware for one so young. A natural-born observer, perhaps a future scientist in the making.

"Xander, last night was…beautiful," Maureen said softly, her gaze focused away from him, "but I can't help wondering why you didn't say goodbye."

He paused for an instant before answering. "I didn't want to wake you."

"Hmm," she said softly. "That sounds a bit like a cop-out to me."

His shoes thudded along the boardwalk. "You're a smart woman. So, okay, I'll be honest. It was the first time I've been with anyone since Terri died and I needed to gather my thoughts."

She glanced up at him. "It was a first for me, too, since my divorce. That takes a lot of trust on both of our parts, I'm thinking."

He nodded. "I believe you're right."

Silence fell between them again, more comfortable in some ways but also more intense as they both openly acknowledged the shift in their relationship. This wasn't just about Rose or paperwork or interfering in-laws anymore.

Xander stroked Maureen's back as they walked. For a few brief, shining hours she felt a sense of togetherness. Like they were a real couple, a real family. Like she'd actually gained entrance into this world. That there wasn't a fake marriage tied to her pear-shaped ring that glittered in the fading light.

They paused on the brick-paved street. Maureen leaned into Xander. Wrapping his arm around her shoulder, they watched a street performer juggle a pineapple and a sword. The action made Maureen a little queasy, but the juggler moved with a dancer's grace. A small, collapsible black table stood in front of him. With break-neck speed, the juggler tossed the pineapple to the table, grabbed the sword by the hilt and sliced open the fruit.

"Impressive," Xander murmured right as Rose began to cry hysterically. Maureen's maternal instincts stimulated, she began to rock Rose, speaking in a soothing voice.

To no avail.

Glancing at his bronze-faced watch, Xander cleared his throat. "I think she's exhausted. It's a little past her bedtime. Come on, let's go to the Dolphin's Tale and meet the nanny. She'll put her down and we'll have time alone. Just you and me. No more talk or interference of the past."

The promise of his words struck a chord in her, reassuring her.

They walked down the street, to the quaint but well-appointed bed-and-breakfast. The dying light sinking into the ocean seemed to absorb the fair pink color of the building, making it part of the sunset. Elenora was waiting in the lobby for them.

"Shall we?" Xander extended his arm to Maureen. She grabbed it, nodding. "I hope you don't scare easy." A laugh rolled off his tongue like a stray wave on a calm day.

"Why?" She squeezed his arm, having enjoyed the day more than she possibly could have imagined a couple of weeks ago.

Not that she would have imagined any of this two weeks ago. Could it be real so fast? Or was it as simple as the plan he'd stated at the outset?

Old insecurities were difficult to shake.

"You'll see." He maneuvered them toward a party boat

designed to hold a couple dozen tourists, the craft moored at a nearby dock.

They boarded the boat and the guide began telling legends of ghosts and vampires. Tracking over to a smaller island's shore, the tour group followed the guide on the sand, huddled close to hear about gruesome deaths and hauntings that chilled Maureen, making her hold tighter to Xander.

"What made you think of this?" Maureen asked on the way back to the main island, wind causing her hair to have a life of its own.

He shrugged, looking at the water below the railing. "I tried to imagine the date a scientist would have never considered."

"Vampires. Good guess."

"So you've never been to Transylvania." He laughed but his gaze seemed to travel past her.

What was he thinking? Were his thoughts drifting back to his dead wife in spite of what he'd said earlier?

"Can't say that I have. I still remember coming to the States as a child and realizing how the size of everything is…overwhelming. But in an amazing way. I love my home country and I miss so much about it, but the space here, the expanses and vast differences in terrain that offer so much for my mind to ponder…I feel at home here, as well. It wasn't hard to run here when I needed to leave."

"God, Maureen…" Night wind tore at his jet-black hair. "I'm sorry taking the job on Key Largo happened under duress." His answer seemed more rote than governed by feeling. This couldn't all be in her head. Something was definitely off.

"I don't want to talk about that. I love my job. I love being here. And we had an amazing night out." She tried to shift the focus back to the positive. Putting them back into the moment of this lovely night. They both seemed to need that.

"Okay," he said, turning to her, the light entering his eyes again as he rejoined the lighter mood she'd sought, "so no Transylvania trip as a kid. What about vampire crushes as a teenager?"

She smiled, toying with the button on his polo shirt. "What teenage girl hasn't read some kind of vampire hot-hero story and imagined being in love forever?"

"That's the appeal? The forever part?" He guided her onto an empty bench seat, shrouded in a bit of darkness and privacy from the other passengers.

"And the sexy charisma. The machismo. You have that—without the fangs."

"I can still bite. Lightly, of course, and in just the right places." He kissed her neck, playfully nipping it.

She shivered. "You're bad."

"I thought I was a starched-shirt businessman."

"You're a...surprise."

"That's good. I used to wonder why you and my brother didn't end up together." Was this why he was distant? Fear of a crush on his free-spirited younger brother? That kind of fear she could squash.

"Three reasons."

"Care to share?"

She sipped the bottle of water the guide had distributed earlier in the evening. "We're too much alike. There's no chemistry. And I think he has a thing for Portia."

"Portia? For real? They can barely stand working together. I've never even been sure why he keeps her on the payroll other than the fact most people wouldn't put up with him. I'm even more bemused as to why she stays."

She cast him a sidelong glance as the boat drew closer to the dock. Could he really be that oblivious? "And that should tell you something."

"Good point."

Leaning against the rail, she inspected her leather bracelet as the boat pulled up to the dock. The boat came to an abrupt stop, causing Xander to press against her slightly.

"I'm not sure and, certainly, I've never seen anything concrete. It's just an impression I get sometimes," she said as the crew finished tying off the boat and placing the debarking plank so the passengers could leave.

They made their way to the exit, falling into line with the others in the group.

"You have good instincts. That's clear." He helped her down off the boat ramp, his grip light and loose.

"Thank you. That's a lovely thing to say." While he hadn't stopped touching her all night, she could hear the distance in his voice.

"It's just the truth." Grasping her hand, they meandered on the sidewalk. Bars filled with loud, live music jumbled together. Their discordant mingling reminding Maureen of the play she'd studied while at university—*The Rites of Spring*. The disorientation extended beyond the framing of the various bands' sounds. She didn't know how to ease whatever troubled Xander.

"Still, thank you for the compliment."

"You deserve it and so many more. You're an incredibly resilient, compassionate and accomplished woman—which all makes you even hotter than you already are, which is mighty damn hot."

Playfully shoving him away, she stopped on the corner before the Dolphin's Tale, eyebrows raised incredulously, more than a little concerned. A horribly failed marriage could do that to a person. "Are you for real or playing me?"

"I hope you know me well enough to realize I shoot straight from the hip. I always have. Dishonesty in business and life gets you nowhere fast." He closed the distance, grabbing her hand. His intense eyes fixed on her, undoing her doubts slightly. This was the most honest he'd been all day. She could tell he meant it.

"I have to agree. Honesty is crucial. Dishonesty always comes back around. Karma's a bitch."

"A bitch with vampire fangs." He gave her a long, sensual look of promise.

This evening's date had clearly brought up more questions than answers, leaving her more confused and unsure than ever. She should be content. All would be well when it came to enjoying their short-term marriage of convenience.

She twisted the ring on her finger and wondered at the odd squeeze of her heart that warned her she could be getting in over her head.

Leading her up the wooden stairs of the Dolphin's Tale, he noticed a shift in Maureen's demeanor. She seemed subdued. A far cry from the siren in the pool the other night. Or from the woman he'd taken to bed last night and, damn it, that was his fault—for bailing on her after their night of sex. He'd let his own mixed emotions about making love for the first time after Terri's death lead him to disregard Maureen's feelings.

Unforgivable.

Thoughtfully, he opened the pale yellow door, stepping into the main lobby of the bed-and-breakfast. Tasteful experimental coastal art framed the room; it had a lot in common with an art gallery showroom. The harpist played in the back corner, her fingers nimbly pluck-ing an old crooner's song about paper moons and love.

Placing his hand on the small of her back, he led her to their room, sending her inside. Stepping up to the bamboo drink cart, he opened the bottle of chardonnay, pouring Maureen a glass. She lingered a few feet away, absently placing her soft brown purse on the glass liv-ing room table. Leaning against the overstuffed couch, she stared into the bedroom off to the left. The plush ma-hogany four-poster was framed in billowing white tufts of sheer fabric. An inviting space.

He laughed softly. "I brought my own this time."

She turned on her heel and looked at him through her eyelashes. "I like a man who thinks ahead. Impulsive is nice, too."

"I can do that. Think fast on my feet. But keep in mind I'm the analytical type, the kind who has a very distinct plan to bring you complete and utter bliss. Soon. Very soon."

Her lips parted, driving him wild. "I'll be right back. Don't go anywhere," he replied huskily.

Slipping from the room, he checked on Rose and the nanny before rejoining her. Elenora reported Rose had fussed, but slept soundly now. On her way out of the room, the nanny handed over the baby monitor. He smiled, ready to return to Maureen.

Pausing outside the door, he thought about where this—all of this—was heading. He could sense that Mau-reen felt how he'd coiled like a pygmy rattler today. Xan-der's retreat had had little to do with her, though. Mostly, his distance had been from a lifetime of too many end-ings and partings.

Hand on the decadent crystal doorknob, he focused fully on this moment. This woman.

He needed more than just sex from her and a business deal. He needed the oblivion being with her could bring. A tangible, incredible connection between them. Something to stand on. Her caring heart, her banter. Maureen's empathy made him want to be better. Opening the door, he smiled at her. Ready to try harder than before. Feeling as light as the breeze that drifted in from the window overlooking a blackened sea and dew-dripped stars.

When he returned, she stood, sipping the glass of wine he'd poured for her, lingering at the threshold of the bedroom. He approached her, eager as ever. He took the wineglass, set it aside and eased her back on the bed, her legs draped off as he skimmed her dress up.

She laughed softly. "The wicked man is back."

"Do you want to talk?" He nuzzled the inside of her thigh. "Or do you want to see just how bad I can be?"

He snapped the edge of her panties.

"Talking finished," she said succinctly just as he nuzzled between her legs.

He swept off her satin underwear and found the core of her, inhaling her feminine scent of jasmine and desire. With a flick of his tongue, he heard her moan, caught a glimpse of her twisting her hands in the covers. He continued to push her, feeling her hips pulse up to him beneath his tongue. Her breath growing more clipped, more hitched. His own desire ramping up—

Only to be interrupted by the nursery monitor shrieking to life. A deep wail blared through, followed by another. And another, each more urgent than before.

Ten

Rose's wails tore at Maureen's ears, spurring her limbs to move. Xander snapped back, gaze flying to the baby monitor and then to Maureen. He pulled on sweats and a T-shirt as she yanked her panties on, trailing after Xander out of the bedroom, heading for the door. As she passed the couch, she grabbed a robe, feeling the need for more coverage, but she didn't break stride.

The urge to make sure Rose was okay flooded Maureen's awareness. Popping open the door to the baby's room, Maureen tightened the robe's tie. From the corner of her eye, Maureen noticed Elenora's sleep-bleary face emerge from the bedroom as the woman headed for the crib.

Maureen's gait broke into a near-run, needing to check on Rose herself. Lifting Rose out of the crib, a relief washed through her.

Elenora extended her arms. "I'm sorry she disturbed you both. I can take her."

Maureen shook her head. "I've got her. Truly, no worries. It's okay, Rose, sweetie." Lifting the toddler to her shoulder, she patted her back. Maureen had never spent much time around babies, but there seemed to be a natural maternal instinct she must have tapped into.

Elenora stepped away, waiting in the shadows.

From a distance, Maureen had watched Rose grow up. She'd known Rose for the baby's entire life. But over the last few days, and especially tonight, a chord had been struck. A shift, perhaps, as she realized the larger role she would be playing in this little girl's life. One that represented every complicated aspect of her relationship to Xander.

Maureen would be moving into the house, living with Rose, would become her stepmother. And inhaling the baby shampoo scent, feeling that soft little cheek against hers, Maureen realized that stepping back when the marriage ended was going to be far more complicated than she'd considered in the mad rush to the altar as a way to solve their immediate problems.

Nevertheless, a new feeling of closeness, affection, love for this little life twisted in her heart. She made *shush-shush-shushing* noises as she rubbed soothing circles on Rose's back, the cotton footie pajamas soft against her palm.

Xander walked up behind Maureen. She could feel the heat of him before she heard him, felt his hand on her shoulder.

"Is Rose okay?"

Maureen felt the baby's soft, plump cheek. Turning to face him. "She doesn't feel feverish. Maybe just a baby dream or gas pain?"

Elenora, reaching for Rose, added gently, "I can take her now."

Maureen glanced at Xander and saw the answer in his eyes, an answer that mirrored her own instinct. "We're going to stay with her until she falls back asleep, and then we'll keep the monitor with us. Please, you go ahead and rest."

Xander slid his arm along Maureen's waist. "Yes, please, rest. We'll need your help with Rose tomorrow since we'll be busy with company and finalizing wedding plans."

Maureen's stomach fluttered. Wedding finalization? Only two days left until they exchanged vows. Until their lives were tied. Until this little girl would be her stepdaughter.

And Xander would be her husband. At least temporarily.

Back home again the next day, Xander sat on a beached piece of palm that had probably floated in with the storm. Elbows on his knees, his blue eyes scanned the lapping turf in front of him. A few gulls added their sounds to the rhythm of waves and the soft laughter of Rose.

The objective of the early afternoon? Wear Rose out so she napped soundly since she'd snagged a catnap on the trip home this morning. That would free up some time to finalize wedding details with Maureen.

Wedding details.

As he thought about the ceremony only two days away, his heart tightened. He hoped Maureen felt welcomed and like a part of his small, fractured family. He wasn't sure why it was so important, but he needed her to. Even as he still grieved over the loss of Terri—he would always love her—he knew he had to do this. Hell, he wanted to. Maureen was a good fit in his life. She'd helped him wake up again. This was good for him and for Rose.

So far, his in-laws had made it clear they wanted no part of seeing their son-in-law get remarried. And while he was sad they felt that way, at least the decision was made. He hoped over time they could have a more amicable relationship and accept Maureen.

A vision filled his head of how at ease she was with his child. When they'd spent the night at the bed-and-breakfast, Maureen had sprung for Rose with feline grace and a mother's power. A natural-born nurturer.

A fact Xander had always understood about her, but in that moment he'd seen how deep that inner chord vibrated.

Even now, on the beach, he watched Rose's easy smile. A trusting one. Her shining eyes on Maureen's delicate face. No doubt about it. A bond had been forged between the two of them.

Maureen sat crouched in the shallow crystalline water of a recently developed tide pool. She splashed the cool water on Rose's legs as unadulterated laughter erupted from his daughter's lips.

The scene seemed perfect. Downright natural. He scraped sand between his toes, understanding gathering in his mind as a gust of wind knocked into his chest, the salt heavy on the air and the faint spray of water finding his cheek.

When Maureen left…

Lord. The thought scared the hell out of him. No, she wasn't Terri. He knew that. But Maureen was a woman who deeply cared for Rose. Showed her love and support. Bonded with Rose.

And when she left after the end of this fake marriage? What would happen to Rose?

Devastation.

He knew the feeling. Even though his own mother had

left him in his later years, he understood what kind of vacuum that created. A damn hole that billowed open, the result of trusting in a vanishing act.

Maureen caught his gaze, a smile gracing her fair skin, tugging all the way up to her eyes. She began to sing an old Irish song to Rose. In her pink-and-white swimsuit, Rose clapped her hands together, enjoying the sound of Maureen's soft voice.

Damn. That gaze. That heart. He didn't want to lose that. They'd begun to forge a real friendship and their banter made him feel alive. He didn't want to lose that, either.

No, he had to find a way to convince her to stay. And not just for a year. Or even five.

Maybe forever? Something he damn well should start thinking about. The thought gave him qualms, no question, because the thought of having her around permanently sounded good. Too good. It was getting harder and harder to convince himself he was just doing this for Rose.

Xander leaped from log to shore, going to join the ladies who held his heart captive.

Checking her watch, Maureen looked at him. "Time for Rose to nap already?" Her eyes scrunched, squinting in the sunlight.

"It appears that way. I'll carry her." Xander hoisted Rose into his arms. But she grabbed for Maureen.

"I've got her," she said, glowing slightly. "I'll put her down, and I'll be back soon." Taking Rose on her hip, she squeezed his hand, that familiar electricity pulsing in her gaze. Dropping both his hand and gaze, she made her way back to the main house.

Xander put a palm to the back of his neck, massaging it gently as he watched her walk away.

A low whistle sounded behind him. Easton. He'd forgotten his brother was coming to meet him to go over his best-man duties.

"Dive, shall we?" Easton said with a theatrical wave of his hand, alluding to the water in front of him. He had two sets of gear slung over his back.

A dive would probably clear his head. "Done."

They suited up, pushing into the crystal water, heading to the reef.

Once submerged, Xander did his best to feel present, notice the parrot fish, the flow of the anemones and smaller tropical sea creatures. The reef looked like the home of a mermaid queen—and that brought his mind straight back to Maureen.

He motioned to Easton to go back up to the surface. Xander loved the way the sun looked like stained glass from beneath the water and how, since he was a kid, breaking the surface always made him feel like he busted through glass.

Once they both reached the surface, they began treading water, removing the gear so they could talk.

"Know what I love?" Easton said, voice cutting into the air.

"A good, adrenaline-filled vacation?"

Easton's lips curled into a smile. "Well that, obviously, but that I'm a best man twice to my big brother. Seriously. How are you doing and what do you need from me?"

How was he doing? What a loaded question. Xander stayed quiet for a moment, considering how to answer.

In the pause, Easton continued. "The flavor of the speech would be a good place to start."

"Oh, well, nothing that will turn my bride scarlet. Or me, for that matter."

"So I shouldn't mention the run-in with Don the security guy?" Easton winked, devilish mischief in his eyes. Xander stared at him, laughing slightly. "I'm kidding and you know it. My toast will be funny but tasteful. Just like last time."

"But this isn't like last time." Xander breathed, arms moving through the water with more determination than before.

"I know it's not. Mom's not going to be there this time."

Xander had known this, but the reaffirmation of her absence cut still. "Do you think she'll ever stay in one place?"

"Mom is the actual embodiment of wanderlust. I know we all traveled a lot, but I get the feeling Dad had reined in Mom's tendency for that vagabond life." Easton tilted his head, started heading for the shore.

"Yeah. I think you are right. He balanced her out. Grounded her." Xander kicked his feet beneath the water, gaining forward motion, slinging seaweed.

"Listen, I know I accused you of just being in lust the other week…but something seems to have shifted with you two."

"Something has. I think." But was it enough? The women in his life wandered in and out of his story so easily. Too easily. Terri. His mother.

He wouldn't add Maureen's name to that list.

The ground buzzed with movement. Volunteers with flowers, tables and chairs flooded the grounds, transforming the great yard of the refuge into a beautiful rehearsal dinner area.

Maureen sat perched on the edge of an oversize wood chair on the main house's balcony. Watching her fairy-tale wedding come together. And it was a fairy-tale wedding, wasn't it?

She had to keep reminding herself this was scripted, fictional, fabricated. Her heart could not take any more abuse or ache. Still, she couldn't stop the rush of attraction—and more—that caught her unaware every time he walked in the room.

Even when his name was mentioned. She was completely and totally infatuated with this man. She liked him, respected him. Found her daydreams drifting to thoughts of him and plans for ways they could spend time together, ways to help him find more fun in life so she could see that smile spread across his handsome face.

She caught sight of Portia and Easton directing the catering company around. They'd be up here soon, to finalize details. To make sure the whole event went off without a hitch.

Xander set down his tall glass of lemonade on the table, calling her back to their plans.

The honeymoon.

"So, we've narrowed it between Greece and Sicily. But, my Irish lass, I want you to have the final say." He grabbed her hand, stroking his thumb over hers.

The warmth of his gentle touch made her belly flip. She kept thinking she would get used to this—the incredible way he made her feel every time he put his hands on her. But, if anything, each time they were together amped up her attraction. Tilted her whole world on its axis until she seemed to always lean toward him.

"So much pressure, sir."

He looked at her sidelong. "You can handle it."

She chewed her lip, looking at the two vacation itineraries before her, both of which would start with a night in a local cabana before a flight somewhere romantic the day after the wedding. "Sicily."

"That's what I was going to pick, too." He raised her hand to his lips, kissed it gently, sending sparks through her.

Still holding on to her, he looked at her, blue eyes as soft and clear as summer. "Have you ever thought about having children of your own?"

The question became a harpoon lodging in her chest, and she let herself collect her breath by glancing at the wedding preparations: a floral arch being delivered, exotic blooms unloaded in sprays from a truck, and the food van—so much food.

Finally, she turned back to Xander to answer his question, which had caught her so unaware. "Of course I've thought about it. But after my divorce I realized my work is my family. The animals I save and work with are, in effect, my children."

"But you could still have a baby, too."

She shook her head. "I'm not marrying again." Her heart couldn't allow it.

"You already have." Xander gestured to the bustle below.

"I meant after we finish our arrangement."

His dark eyebrows knotted, a storm descending on his face. Shifting to a serious tone, he leaned forward. "But this—as you call it—*arrangement* is going well. We get along. We're compatible in bed and out. You're fantastic with Rose. We could build a family."

Build a family? A fake family?

She wanted him. Cared for him and Rose. But to be with a man who didn't love her. And to be with a man who wouldn't ever love her? She couldn't do that. Couldn't break again like that.

"You're backing out of our agreement."

He blinked at her. "What?"

"You're scared of losing Rose so you're trying to bribe me into staying longer." That had to be what this was about. No other explanation seemed logical.

"Damn it, no. You've misunderstood my meaning altogether. I was being honest. I think we could build a great life together."

Her Irish temper surged, a storm of her own infusing her voice with anger. And pain. "And so you're offering me a baby if I stay?"

"You're twisting everything I'm saying. We're going to be married. Why not stay that way? You said you're not waiting for another man. So let's share our lives. Be friends."

"Friends?" The last time she checked, marriage was about more than friendship. *Love.* There had to be love, too.

"With benefits and a ring, and a family and common interests. It's actually a stronger foundation than most marriages out there. Think about it tonight."

So, the stiff-shirt businessman returned. The engagement and marriage had been calculated. Sure. But this? A whole new level.

He leaned in to kiss her. But feeling deceived, she angled away under the excuse of conferring with the florist, wondering if she could really go through with this, after all.

The next morning Xander stood outside Maureen's cabin, rolling the simple gold band between his fingers. Maybe it was bad luck to see the bride before the wedding, but he needed to look into her eyes before they said their vows. While he didn't expect the unrestrained joy of his first wedding, things still felt too unsettled.

He'd been trying to reconcile his feelings for Terri,

a love he feared he might never know again. But then, too, he was afraid to let what he felt for Maureen really flourish since it seemed like he would be robbing his first marriage of the bond he'd always felt for Terri and he didn't want to let go of that for Rose's sake.

After their seaside argument, Xander had wanted to run for the hills and stay a single man forever, parent his child and hire the best damn lawyers possible to reach an amenable arrangement for his in-laws to safely visit their granddaughter. He would live a satisfying life watching his daughter grow up, work the hours he wanted and watch football games on a wide screen TV with his brother.

Later that night, Xander had thought through his options as he lay in bed staring at the ceiling, missing Maureen. Though a calculating businessman, his rationale for wanting Maureen to stay had little to do with logic. But to persuade her, he needed to present it in a way that made practical sense. Rose grew more and more attached to Maureen by the day. To rip her away from Maureen would completely fracture Rose's young life.

And, damn it, he wanted Maureen in his life, too. He couldn't deny that. They had a solid friendship. Chemistry. A mutual desire to stay here. Tons of things in common. She was the one he wanted to vent to and laugh with. He'd become quite fond of the way her nose crinkled, and her fiery spirit. That didn't diminish his love for Terri. The women were different. Comparing would be unfair to both of them.

Standing outside Maureen's cabin on their wedding day, with the sun beaming in a cloudless sky, he still couldn't decide what it was about her that entranced him beyond the normal realm of sexual attraction. She wasn't at all his type. Yet when they were together, he felt alive, happy…in a way he hadn't in a long time.

In the midst of all the confusion, one thought remained clear to Xander. He wanted Maureen. He wouldn't let it take anything from his marriage with Terri, but he would enjoy being with Maureen.

Xander tucked the ring into the inside pocket of his charcoal-gray suit coat. He rang the bell and stepped back, leaning against a porch post.

Maureen answered, half dressed. She wore a pale blue satin gown, her makeup soft and natural, accenting her Irish eyes. Everything about her glowed, Xander thought, as his gaze swept down.

Even her nail polish shimmered.

Looking more than a little nervous, Maureen wiggled her toes, emphasizing that sparkly pedicure. "You caught me before I had a chance to finish dressing. Portia and Jessie are inside. Don't let them catch you."

Relaxing into the safety shield of banter, Xander resumed his lazy position against the post and gestured with a small nod of his head. "Come here and they won't, lady."

Maureen smiled stiffly, unsettled by his words. "Who me?"

"Yeah, you."

She padded across the porch, stopping just in front of him. A breeze blew the skirt of her dress across his legs. The scent of her shampoo and her jasmine perfume teased his senses.

He skimmed his knuckles across her velvety cheek. "Do you mind if I muss you up a bit?"

"Please." Her arms rested by her sides as she pressed her full length to his.

Xander slipped one hand behind her head and cupped her neck. With the other, he palmed her waist, his hand tightening instinctively as the feel of her tingled up his arm. Maureen slid her hand inside his jacket, her fingers spreading wide against his chest, digging past his shirt, imprinting his skin.

He guided her face to his, pressing his lips to hers, flicking his tongue along the seam of her full mouth. She opened, begging for more, needing the reassurance of connecting on any level they could find after their tense, uncertain time apart. With a gentle moan, Maureen slid her arms around Xander's neck, deepening their kiss. Their mouths mated with the familiar yet unexplainable frenzy both had come to accept as inevitable.

And in less than two hours they would be married. For better.

Or worse?

Eleven

In the end, Maureen ditched her shoes just before entering the chapel, wanting instead to make her vows in the ruins of the old church with the soles of her feet pressing into the cool stone slab of the floor. She needed to ground herself in reality, even if only through the sense of the ground beneath her feet.

This wasn't a real wedding.

They were entering this union for practical reasons only.

She couldn't afford to forget that. Her heart couldn't take another round of marital rejection.

Nerves dancing in her stomach, she held her small bouquet of white peonies as a trio of guitarists began playing, their stringed music filling the space with a harp-like quality that carried a hint of local flair. Perfect.

Except, was it really?

Her mind floated back to a letter she'd been terrified to read but had read anyway. Moments before the ceremony—a choice she regretted now. A wildlife refuge in Killarney had offered her a job.

A job in her home country. She'd applied when she'd thought the expiration of her work visa was inevitable.

She didn't even want the job. Not really. But knowing she had this option—a plan of her own that could have been in play—knotted her gut with tension and fear and the realization of how high today's stakes were. How important it was to make the right choice.

Her growing feelings for Xander made her feel out of control. Filled with an urgency to flee.

But she knew better. She had to go through with this for so many reasons, not the least of which being that she couldn't let Xander and Rose down.

Portia stood just ahead of her, ready to do her maid of honor walk down the aisle with baby Rose on her hip. Before they began the trek to the altar, Maureen leaned down to kiss Rose's cheek and handed her a mini bouquet of peonies. The flowers complemented the floral orange-and-white crown in the girl's golden curls. As the two walked between the benches of volunteers, friends and family, Rose giggled, her bouquet bouncing like an erratic orchestra conductor's baton. Those baby giggles elicited a lot of clucks and laughs from the guests in the pews.

The butterfly nerves picked up speed in Maureen's tummy as she stood alone, just out of sight of the church's occupants. This was different from her first wedding in so many ways. Unlike her last wedding, her father wasn't here to escort her down the aisle. She tried to bury the thought, will it back to the dark recesses of her mind and think of the reasons this marriage was right. Good. Safe?

Her hand wandered up to her own flowers. The stylist

had woven them seamlessly into her hair. To her relief, it seemed like they weren't going anywhere.

The setting, the music, those ancient stones, made her feel like a fairy princess from all the Celtic stories she'd read as a child. If this was to be her fabricated narrative, she wanted the story to have some degree of authenticity, to represent her wildness. Would Xander find that part of her too impractical over time? Would the friendship and passion withstand day-to-day living?

As she made her way to Xander, her bare feet taking in the cool stones along the aisle, her heartbeat roared in her ears. He stood at the altar, a genuine smile radiating from his lips to his eyes. Damn, he was sexy in his suit, with his blue eyes and dark hair. This tall, looming alpha male who'd somehow become such a huge part of her life.

A light breeze carrying the scent of salt and blooming flowers seemed to urge her toward him, tousling her hair slightly, making her feel truly like a water nymph in her dress that mirrored the waves of the ocean, and for a moment, her nerves stilled.

A moment only. Was his smile real? Or was he hiding thoughts of his first wedding? An ache over the loss of his wife? Maureen swallowed hard and pressed forward.

Easton stood next to Xander and shot a quick wink her way. He shifted on his feet, shoulder brushing against a lush green leaf that poked out from the side of the old Spanish-style ruins.

Hibiscus plants and vibrant flowers in sunset hues lined the aisle in homage to their tropical location. Out of the corner of her vision, she saw the smiling faces of the volunteers. They pressed up against each other, hands held to mouths and ears, bowing and flowing like marsh grass. Wisps of words like "She's stunning!" and

"Look at the love in his eyes!" caressed her ears. A fairy tale indeed.

Portia smiled at her, holding Rose still on her hip. Her one-shoulder coral gown complementing her fair complexion, the light breeze pushing loose strands of her hair.

Maureen reached the altar, gave herself away, and took her position next to Xander as they both turned to face each other. His hands were warm as they clasped her chilly shaking ones.

Out of the corner of her eyes, her gaze flitted once more to the crowd of people, and she counted those who weren't actually there. Xander's mother had sent an email from Tibet, confirming her inability to attend. She wondered, as the last few notes of the music reverberated, if Xander felt sad about that. Or if, since this was an arrangement, after all, he felt indifferent.

Also missing were his in-laws. Or, his former in-laws. Once Maureen said "I do," their definition would shift. Another way for him to lose more of Terri.

Shoving that thought aside, too, Maureen looked at Xander. He reached for her hand, his touch reassuring and stabilizing. Anchoring. The leap of her pulse only scared her more with fears that she'd let him mean too much to her, too fast.

Rose fussed in Portia's arms, pointing toward Maureen. She lifted Rose from Portia, smiling as the little girl's face lit up, glowing as bright as the sun. Xander touched Maureen's cheek with a gentle stroke of fingertips and emotion in his eyes, a gratitude that she'd allowed his daughter to share in the spotlight of this big moment.

They'd opted to write their own vows rather than go the traditional route and repeat pledges of forever love that would have resembled their first weddings—and also wasn't truthful to their reasoning for this marriage. They'd opted for promises to keep. Honesty.

Maureen had labored over what to say and was relieved that Xander went first. "Maureen, I promise to be here for you. To pledge my every effort to take care of you, to keep you safe, to remind you daily what an incredibly fascinating and alluring and giving woman you are."

"I promise to make you laugh and remember to enjoy life outside the office, to live life to the fullest." She smiled, planting a kiss on Rose's forehead.

The remainder of the ceremony reminded Maureen of a dream. Before she knew it, she locked her lips on his, the strength of his embrace pressing into her. The sparks were there, no question.

Would it be enough?

Flower petals were tossed over them as they left the church to go to the outdoor reception set up just off to the side near the shore. Her toes skimmed over the bright white rocks. Seagulls danced above their heads, circling.

As they moved toward the reception area outdoors, by the ocean, her place of peace, Maureen took in the sounds of the waves crashing, the contained chaos of an unfolding reception. Portia calmly directed people to their tables, smiling, handling the crowds with grace. Maureen appreciated Portia's presence.

Maureen felt like one of the dolls in "It's A Small World"—a smile painfully painted on her face. Volunteers and guests lined up to see her and Xander, offering their congratulations.

All of the smiling and handshaking had her feeling a bit like an animatronic version of herself. The gestures occurring by rote.

Xander and Maureen had split up at the reception to cover more ground to say thank you to their guests. Her hands slid to grasp and hug guest after guest, but her mind focused on that letter she'd gotten in the mail last night.

The lilt of a brogue snapped her attention into focus, her eyes searching for the owner of the voice. Andrea Yeats, the only one of her friends who had been able to fly out for the wedding on such short notice. They'd grown up together, filtering in and out of church together—a dynamic duo.

Andrea raised the glass of merlot to her plump lips, sipping as she nodded at Xander. Shaking her chestnut, curly hair, Andrea lowered her voice, stepping closer to Xander. "I'm so happy for the two of you. You know the old saying there's fault on both sides of a divorce? Well, in their case…she did everything she could to hold that marriage together."

A knot lodged in Maureen's throat. She didn't want to talk about Danny, not this way, and especially not in front of others.

"Andrea—"

But her friend pressed on. "Maureen, you can play nice and be the bigger person, but I don't have to. He was a narcissistic ass. There's no other way around it. He was mentally abusive. He belittled her to death with a thousand paper cuts. It took a lot of courage for her to break away and come here."

"What precipitated the move?" Xander's interest manifested itself in his body language. In the way he leaned on the table.

Maureen had heard enough. Time to take control. "My parents passed away in a ferry accident. Something seemed to click inside me and I moved on. Now, let's move on from this conversation and enjoy the day."

Andrea turned scarlet. Not even her thick, constella-

tion-like freckles could mask the embarrassment gracing Andrea's cheeks. Sheepishly, she wrapped Maureen
in a quick hug. "I'm sorry. My mouth ran away with me,
love. I just adore you and want to make sure this fella
knows how lucky he is to have you." She smiled at them
both. "Congratulations. Truly."

With a nervous nod, Andrea excused herself, a preda-
tory swagger in her step as she approached Easton.

With the ocean echoing in the distance at their outdoor reception, Xander slid his arm around her waist and
stayed silent, sensing that Maureen didn't want to talk
about what had just happened. She was right. This day
should be about happiness.

He'd finally claimed her as his own.

Yes, he'd had thoughts of his first wedding today and
he would always miss Terri, but Maureen had helped
him move forward with his life. Her beautiful, bold personality had shaken him from his fog and brought him
back to life again.

He just hated that Andrea had made Maureen so uncomfortable, hurting her with reminders of the past. And,
yes, he felt vaguely guilty for prying into her history, but
she'd said so little and he wanted to know.

Maureen played with the tips of her curls, fidgeting as
her brow furrowed. "Andrea didn't care for my ex-husband." Cool indifference laced her words. She grabbed
his hand, pulling him aside, toward the edge of the crowd
at the bar.

"Everyone should have a loyal friend." He pulled Maureen close, his hands trailing along the soft exposed skin
on her back.

She nodded, chewing on the edge of her bottom lip.
"I'm glad she came to visit."

"Are you homesick?" He searched her eyes. Tried to figure out what had her so distant. Learning about the death of her parents… It had changed the way he regarded her. How traumatic that must have been to lose her parents and realize her marriage was a shambles all at once. She'd been truly alone in the world. No wonder she'd made such a large move to start over somewhere fresh without reminders of all she'd lost.

Perhaps she felt their absence acutely today. He felt the absence of his mother like a deep twist of a knife in his gut. And at least she was alive, just not in the picture. He'd missed his dad today, though. The finality of him not being here hurt Xander deeply. He imagined that feeling would intensify if both of his parents were deceased. Guilt stabbed at him now that he'd never thought to ask details about her family, her past. She'd listened to so much he'd shared, drawn him out more than anyone else had been able to.

"Are you homesick?" he repeated since she'd ignored his question the first time. He would be better about listening to her from now on.

"Obviously, I'm trying to stay away from there. I went so far as to marry you, didn't I?" She turned away from him, pulling out of his grasp.

"And a horrible fate that is, right?" He skimmed his knuckles gently across her cheek.

She looked around at the crowd with nervous eyes and linked fingers to draw him behind a palm tree a bit farther from the guests so they wouldn't be interrupted. "Xander, I'm sorry for what I said. That didn't come out right."

He wrapped his arms around her, his back blocking them even further from others in hopes of making it clear they wanted this time alone, if anyone did stumble on them. "You don't need to apologize. I was only teasing." His voice faded to a lull as he realized he really needed to start things off with her by being honest. "What she said about your ex—"

"I told you he walked out on me."

"You didn't tell me he was abusive."

"He never laid a hand on me."

His hand swept over her cheek again, keeping his touch gentle even as anger pulsed through him at the man who'd treated her so poorly. "That's not the only way to abuse someone."

"Andrea talked too much. I'm fine now, happy here, feeling confident and like myself again." A dismal tone edged her voice. She crossed her arms over her chest, shutting down on him.

"You're safe here." He glided his hands down her arms until she relaxed, then pulled her close. "I want you to know that."

"I do." She swallowed hard. "What made you such an expert on emotional abuse?"

"I'm not an expert, but I'm human. And I've dealt with some employee situations…" Her head pushed off his chest to stare at him, eyebrow raised, a bemused smile on her face. He continued, a laugh on his lips. "That sounds lame and impersonal even as I say it. Why don't you tell me about your situation?"

She buried her face back against his chest, shaking her head, a sigh shuddering through her bones. "Andrea said enough. It's in the past. I'm working to restore my life and rebuild my career. Now, can we really stop talking about this? Haven't I said before that I don't want to be one of those individuals who vents nonstop about the ex," she muttered against his shoulder.

"We're married now. This is about making our history." Xander wanted her to feel comfortable talking to him about anything. Everything. The small stuff. The details and stories that shaped her. He wanted her to trust him deeply.

She pulled away from him, her eyes lined with phantom pain. "He was…charming in the beginning. And I fell fast. Looking back, I can see signs I should have paid more attention to."

"Such as?"

"We really should have talked about this before, and maybe this isn't the right time."

He held up a hand, walked over to the waiter and took two champagne flutes, hoping to ease her nerves. His own anger was boiling just below the surface at the man who'd hurt her, but he would keep that under control. For Maureen. He would listen and learn and make sure she had a better marriage this time.

Xander brought the drinks back and guided her farther away from the crowd for even more privacy, finding a bench under a swaying palm in a dim corner.

He passed a drink to Maureen and said, "Maybe we should have talked more, but I would argue we've covered a lot of ground in a week. Now we have plenty of time."

He clinked his glass with hers, and encouraged her to continue.

"My family was so volatile with what you would call a stereotypical Irish temper." She traced along the crystal base, circling with one finger. "Danny kept things light, funny. He was witty. Sarcastic sometimes, but so very witty. I was charmed. We fell fast. Married just as fast. Before long I realized 'light' meant he didn't appreciate deep discussions, especially if that meant addressing a problem. Sarcastic wit turned biting. Hurtful.

Anything to shut down a conversation that challenged his perceptions."

Xander could see how much the memories pained her. He'd give anything to make her feel better. "And if avenues for discussion were shut down, I imagine that made it tough to express your frustration or hurt."

She shrugged lightly. "I used to think it was my fault for being unable to take criticism." She looked at him. "I thought I loved him, or that at least we could find that love again. And then, out of the blue, he told me he wasn't happy, and left. It hurt, but I'm a stronger person now. Much stronger."

"That strength shows. You're strong and compassionate." He met her honesty with his own. He had seen firsthand how deeply Maureen cared for those around her... how much more so she must have felt for a man she'd been in love with. Those feelings didn't just erode overnight. The death of a marriage—for good reasons and bad ones—still had consequences in the heart.

"Thank you." Tears pushed at her eyes.

He pulled her closer, needing to show he cared.

"The breakdown of a marriage is tragic." The end of love hurt. By death or divorce. He knew that too damn well.

"But I truly am better off."

"I believe you are." He kissed her cheek. Her nose. Her lips. She sighed, falling into him more before continuing to speak.

"It just galls me that I didn't see the truth sooner. That made me doubt myself for a very long time."

"And now?"

"I'm doing better."

"Getting married again must have been difficult for you," he said, his hands roving over her arms.

"But this isn't about love. That gives me a level of emotional protection."

Her words felt like a wall coming between them.

He didn't have time to process that. Not now. Easton and Portia approached them.

"It's showtime." Easton's words slurred slightly.

Portia laughed, adjusting her one shoulder strap. "What he is trying to say is that it's time for us to send you lovebirds off."

She gestured to the crowd, which parted like the Red Sea, leading to a stretch beach buggy with a chauffeur waiting to take them to a cabana on Key Largo for their first night as man and wife before departing to Sicily for a proper honeymoon. All the trappings of romance intact.

After watching the chauffeur disappear down the thin, sandy lane, Maureen turned to face Xander. Her husband.

God, how strange that word felt. This day had been surreal enough without Andrea showing up and eliciting that whole conversation about Danny that Maureen just wasn't ready to have yet.

And then there was the job offer still looming over her that she hadn't told Xander about. Not that it mattered now. She wasn't going to take it. But she should tell him.

Before she had time to process all the tumult of the day, much less their new roles, Xander swept her off her feet. Literally.

Six hours as man and wife. She knew him as a boss. A friend. A lover. But this? This was…beyond anything she would have considered happening.

Moonlight bathed them in silver as he carried her toward the door of the cabana. The ocean provided the soundtrack—a mounting sound of waves and night birds.

Each step up to the cabana caused him to draw her

closer, the scent of sandalwood intoxicating her. Over the threshold and into the cabana, he took her.

Xander let her slide out of his arms, her bare feet touching the grain of the wood. He pushed her gently against the wall, kissing her deeply.

She wanted more of him. Angling into his kiss, she pushed farther. He pressed his hand on her hip, sending an electric pulse through her limbs.

She raised a hand to his jawline. He leaned into it for a moment, her fingers taking in the way his chin curved. His head tilted to the table at the center of the living room.

She followed his gaze, settling on the baskets filled with gifts—a collection of jasmine and vanilla massage oils, lotions and rainbow-colored condoms. A gift from Easton, according to the tag.

A bucket filled with ice and champagne took position to the left. Another basket brimmed with chocolates and dried fruits.

Platters of exotic cheeses, grapes, chocolate-dipped strawberries and crackers covered the remainder of the table. True decadent indulgence.

Xander picked up a chocolate-covered strawberry and fed it to her. Eyes on him still, she bit down into the fruit, enjoying the contrast of bitter dark chocolate and sweet strawberry. He discarded the top of the strawberry, brushing her top lip with his thumb before grabbing one of the oils and a condom from the basket.

"Coming?" His question came out breathy. She nodded, following him to the bedroom.

Rose petals speckled the ground and the bed. He kissed her hand, traced the edge of her collarbone, sending shivers down her spine. Helped her out of the gown.

"Let me spoil you. Pamper you." He gestured to the bed.

"You're too kind," she mumbled, climbing onto the silken sheets. He rubbed the oil between his hands and then pressed into her shoulders.

"Relax, Maureen. There's no reason to be so tense." He worked on her shoulders, releasing the tension with every stroke. "Everything's going to be okay. More than okay."

He began kissing her neck, back, hip. She turned over to face him, propping herself up on her forearms to kiss him.

Xander pushed her back down, hand grazing her thigh. His mouth sought hers, body pressed against hers. Urgency entered with his tongue. Roving hands teased her nipples.

Her hand wrapped around the length of him, stroking, caressing, her thumb rubbing along the tip of him until he growled with the intense pleasure of just how perfectly she seemed to know how to move him.

His desire for her grew with each movement. She became slick with feminine want. Their normal fire and frenzy changed tonight, replaced with a calm burn. A steady burn.

He kept kissing her. Her hands pulled him closer, raking lightly down his back. Her nails scored his skin ever so lightly, just enough to relay her desire.

Xander eased inside her, each thrust slow and deep as his eyes held hers. Her hips rocked against his, every move of their bodies releasing the sweet scent of the shared fruit mixed with a growing perspiration of need. Building desire. She slid her heels up the backs of his calves, higher still until her legs locked around his waist.

The urgent need to find completion built inside him, along with the realization that once—hell, twelve times or more—wouldn't be enough.

The need was becoming greater with each passing

day. The sweet clasp of her body around his sent his pulse pounding in his ears, his heart pounding against his chest. His whole body throbbed from want of her. Maureen. Her name echoed in his mind again and again.

Even while he burned to reach completion, still he took them to the edge—holding back then pushing her closer until she was wild with need. He reveled in the flush of desire spreading over her flesh, attesting to her pleasure. Her hands twisting in the sheets and rose petals alike until he brought her to a crashing release. His final deep thrust and hoarse shout made it clear he'd followed her over that edge with every bit as much bliss, their bodies connected as they rolled to their sides, panting.

As their breathing slowed to a more even pace, chests rising and falling in time together, her heart grew heavy. All of the complications of this arrangement came crashing down on her. With a weighty realization. She loved him.

She loved Xander.

And what scared her in the pit of her stomach was that even though he cared for her, even though she suspected he might one day come to love her, he would never care for her as much as he'd loved Terri. The thought rocked her.

"When was the last time you went stargazing?" he asked, kissing her.

Hesitancy flooded her. "Um. Ages ago."

"Let's change that." He handed her a silk robe out of the closet and put his clothes back on. Xander disappeared for a moment, returning with the basket full of chocolates and dried fruit in hand.

"Come with me." He opened the balcony door of the cabana. She followed, wrapping the silk against her bare skin, taking in the mesh of starred horizon and cool ocean, her revelation knotting in her stomach.

On the porch there were two oversize chairs. Maureen sank into one and Xander reached for her hand, staring at her with dreamy eyes. Melting her heart a little bit more. The world unbalancing.

Until a masculine brogue cut through the air.

"I've come for my wife."

Ice chilled her blood. She didn't even have to look over her shoulder to know.

Andrea wasn't the only person from her past to have come to the States today.

Danny had arrived.

Twelve

Maureen went rigid next to Xander. She'd inhaled sharply, eyes falling in the direction of the voice.

In the muted light of moon and stars, the form of a somewhat muscular man manifested. He approached them, features coming into focus with every step.

Danny.

Maureen's ex. Fists tightened, more than ready to slam the guy's teeth through his face if it became necessary. The urge to send Maureen inside wailed in Xander's head. Standing up from the chair, he looked down at the man, unwilling to resort to violence unless absolutely necessary.

Damn, but he hoped it would be necessary.

Danny's bronzed, buzzed hair practically glowed in the moonlight. Xander noticed how his handsome face seemed to be chiseled by bitterness.

How in the world had he found them? For the last two years Maureen had flown under the radar. He racked his brain. No matter what, he'd make sure she was safe. That thought coursed through his mind on full-blast.

"What are you doing here? And, more important, who the hell do you think you are to call yourself my husband?" Maureen lobbed pure fire at him, blazing and glorious.

"Fine, ex-husband. But I've come here to win you back, love. I miss you." His brogue was thick and deep. But Xander thought the man's swagger was a bit cartoonish, as if he was trying to put on some kind of machismo show.

Through clenched teeth, Xander said tightly, leaving no room for doubt, "She's not just engaged. We got married today."

"I'm too late?" Shock pushed his mouth into a faux grin dripping with malice. He took a few steps closer. "I heard she was engaged and the wedding was soon, so I came running. But married? Already? I screwed up the time change or something, I had plans for—"

The jackass had actually planned to burst into their wedding? Xander's eyes narrowed. "How did you even know about the engagement?"

Maureen sighed. "Andrea. Tossing it in your face that I've rebuilt my life."

Danny sneered. "She enjoyed every minute of crowing over that."

Xander put a protective arm around Maureen, damned determined she wouldn't be facing this demeaning jerk alone. "I'm her husband. She and I got married." He held up her hand to show off her ring. "It's official. Ring, certificate and all."

Danny whistled lowly, his attention narrowed on Maureen. "That is quite a rock. You landed a big fish. No wonder you don't want me."

Maureen stepped forward, her chin tipped high and proud. Strong. "Danny, I didn't want you before. I don't want you now. And the feeling was mutual, so I have no idea what you're doing here. I believe it's best you state your business and go off somewhere to sightsee or something."

Xander tucked her back at his side. Even knowing she could handle herself, he didn't want her to think she had to do this alone. He wanted to support her, to protect her. To let her know how amazing she was and how undeserving of this kind of jerk show. "Clearly this is a surprise to you, but this is how things are. Now, if you'll kindly leave—"

Danny shook his head, tapping his chin. "Something's fishy and I'm not going anywhere until I get some answers to—"

Glancing at Maureen, Xander noted the way her body had begun to shake with anger. Distress marred her face, but she wasn't backing down. Damn it, she didn't have to face this alone. No one, especially not Danny, would ever harass Maureen. Not while he was around. "You're on private property. You will only be allowed to stay if my *wife* wants you to be here." He turned to her and cocked an eyebrow. "Maureen?"

She shook her head.

Xander shrugged. "It's final, then. Your visit is done. If you wish to speak with my wife, you may, of course, call, or better yet, send a certified letter."

Danny's voice became more agitated, louder. "But I'm the one that left—"

Standing her ground, Maureen stared him down with strength and fire in her eyes. "And you'll be leaving now. Having you out of my life is a blessing. I moved forward. I have an amazing job." She leaned closer to Xander.

"And a wonderful husband. You and I no longer have any connection. So please, don't contact me again."

A calculating look entered Danny's steely eyes as his gaze moved from Maureen to Xander and back again, a laugh lodged in his throat. "Your job… And this is your boss." A slow, smarmy smile ticked at the corners of his mouth. "Convenient you got married right before you had to come home. Wasn't that job offer you got from the university big enough for you?"

Xander took him by the arm. "This discussion is over. I'm calling security."

With admirable speed, Don, still wearing his suit from attending the wedding, came to pick Danny up. Xander helped Don secure the man in the car, closed the door and watched him drive away. Satisfied to see him gone. And return to Maureen.

He wanted to make sure Maureen was safe. And not just tonight. But forever. He wanted to shield her as best he could. Because he…because he loved her. Truly and deeply loved her. It took nothing away from what he'd felt for Terri. In fact, Terri had taught him to love and he knew now that the greatest gift he could give her was to let love into his heart again.

And without question, he loved Maureen every bit as deeply as any love he'd ever felt before.

Tears cascaded down Maureen's fair cheeks. She shook uncontrollably, hands wrapping around herself. "I feel awful. He all but said we married for my green card and he's right."

Xander touched her lips then thumbed away her tears. "I needed a mother for my child to ensure she stays with me."

"Great. We pulled a fast one on the courts twice."

"Do you believe Rose is where she belongs?"

"Absolutely."

"Are you happier married to me than you were to him?"

"That's not even a fair question. I could be happier married to just about anyone."

"Then are you happy here, in the house..." He leaned closer. "In my bed." He touched her mouth again. "You don't even need to answer that. I heard your joy loud and clear that night before we stepped out on the porch."

Her cheeks flushed. "Loudly?"

"Delightfully so. And I look forward to making that happen again and again."

A part of the conversation with Danny gnawed at him. She seemed calm now, but he had to ask, had to know if she was making arrangements to leave him. "So tell me what he meant about that big job offer at the university."

She shook her head. "There's nothing to discuss."

"But it's a big deal," he pressed, hoping to get something out of her.

She shrugged.

His body chilled all the way to his soul. "Are you taking it?"

"No," she insisted quickly. "Of course not."

Then he asked the question he had to know. "If the job had been offered earlier this week, would you have accepted it?"

She looked away quickly. Too quickly for his liking. "Uh, Xander, I should double-check my suitcase for our trip."

He clasped her elbow gently. "Are you sure you still want to travel after the upset you've just had?"

She finally met his eyes. "The fact that you're asking offers the answer already. Maybe it's best that we delay any honeymoon plans."

"Is that what you really want? No honeymoon? Not even an attempt at starting this marriage off on a positive note?"

Her eyebrows shot up. "This is already nowhere close to a positive note. I think we both need to stop this discussion before we say something that can't be taken back. This is a marriage of convenience. Let's not lose sight of that."

She tugged her arm free and walked away, closing the door with a finality that echoed to his toes. He was losing her before he'd even fully had her.

Not her, too. He couldn't lose another wife. He couldn't go through that again in any way.

He couldn't lose Maureen.

A familiar sound buzzed in his pocket. Easton's ringtone. Of course.

He fished the phone out of his pocket, sliding to accept the call.

"This is your best-man courtesy call. Your jet is fueled and ready for the Lourdes party of two first thing in the morning."

"Forget it. Cancel the flight. Maureen and I had a disagreement." He sank onto a chair, running his free hand through his thick hair. Wondering how he'd gotten to this place so quickly. He didn't want to lose her.

"A fight over what, if you don't mind my asking?" Easton sighed. "You didn't do something dumbass like murmur your first wife's name during sex…"

"God, no. Thanks for the vote of confidence," he quipped back with a levity he was far from feeling.

"But you still love Terri." His brother's question was more of a statement.

"I will always love her." There would never be a moment where he'd be able to stop those feelings. But he now knew that he had a bigger capacity for love than he'd imagined.

"Of course you will."

"I'm not sure how another woman would feel about that," Xander admitted.

"If she were alive today you would still be married."

"We would." Xander snagged a grape from the fruit basket and rolled it between his fingers.

"Of course you would. But you also need to ask yourself honestly…will you be able to love another woman as much as you loved her? Because no woman wants to be second best."

Easton's tone was level but firm. Perhaps this was what Easton had been hinting at when he'd promised to beat Xander's ass if he hurt her. Because Maureen, a woman whose past marriage had been filled with emotional games, had developed a callus around her heart. She'd become accustomed to not being enough.

And just making that connection—realizing that he had, however unwittingly, treated her the same way as that ass of an ex-husband he'd met tonight—made Xander furious with himself.

Having heard every damn thing he needed to, Xander ended the call, understood with crystal clarity that he needed to follow after her. Now.

Tossing the grape into the waste can, he charged through the cabana to find her sitting on the overstuffed pale peach chair, her delicate legs tucked beneath her. Palm to chin, she gazed absently into space. Years of pain were written in her posture. The letter from the university hung limply in her hands.

"I don't know how much I have inside left to give. But I'm trying, Maureen. I want this to work between us. I want to give it a real try. The question is—" he tapped the letter "—do you?"

Her hesitation, her lack of an answer, was all he needed. Whatever she felt for him, for his daughter, for this island, didn't come close to what he felt for her. But then, when had she been shown how deeply a man could love a woman? Certainly not by that jackass she'd been married to the first time.

She wrapped her arms tightly around herself. "I think it's best we cancel the honeymoon and go back to the house."

Watching her close him out, Xander realized that he could lose her, really lose her. Forever, in fact, if he didn't put his heart on the line and let her know how much she meant to him.

Rattled.

Unsettled.

The feelings coalesced inside her, becoming a pressure system of anxiety. She'd known this wasn't at all the right time to travel and maybe some of that had to do with the shock of seeing Danny again. She knew Xander was a far better man. But that didn't mean he loved her and it didn't change the fact that they'd entered this marriage for convenience's sake only.

So Sicily? Now? No. She wouldn't have been able to enjoy herself or their time together.

She'd told Xander they should go back to the house and rethink their plans.

They'd told the volunteers and family she had a sinus infection and couldn't fly. Not a tough sell since her sinuses were stuffed after she'd cried her eyes out in the shower.

But with work covered, she had nothing to do, so she'd

sought comfort in playing with Rose at the beach. They sat together on a blanket with a pile of blocks.

Rose sat in her lap, humming a made-up tune that seemed to mimic the sounds of the nearby parrots. A call-and-response of innocence and wonder.

This little girl had quickly taken up residence in her heart. Made her want to stay.

Scooting out of her lap, Rose picked up the building blocks and began stacking them together. Smiling back at Maureen, still singing her little ditty.

Handing over a block, Rose giggled. "Yooouuu." Her bell-like voice was small and sweet.

Maureen stacked her yellow block on Rose's green one. The little girl clapped, bobbing her head from side to side. Clearly amused and satisfied by the progress they'd made.

But Maureen didn't share in the toddler's delight. The fight with Xander had left her shaken and heartsick. When she'd seen Danny, standing there in the moonlight, the life she'd fled crashed back around her.

All the strength and healing fell away in that moment. She knew Danny didn't care about her one damn bit. He'd showed up only to unsettle her. To beat her back down. Just another move in his emotionally abusive chess game.

He'd been forcibly removed from the property and given a restraining order.

But the damage to Maureen had already been done. Before he'd left her, she'd become unsure of her place and worth. Those feelings returned, fully visible, in the heated exchange with Xander.

Xander. Whom she loved.

That thought scared her, rendering her completely vulnerable. The jumble of insecurities stilled her tongue when she should have spoken up.

Of course she wanted to stay. Wanted to be in Rose's life. And Xander's.

The block tower had grown quite high and, with a devilish look in her eye, Rose pushed on the middle pieces. The whole thing tumbled, eliciting peals of laughter from Rose.

How appropriate.

But then Rose began to build the tower again. Maureen admired her tenacity. Her willingness to simply start again.

Handing over a green block, Maureen said, "Parrot."

Rose took the block, nodding. She picked up a yellow one, handing it to Maureen. "Puppy."

"That's right, love," Maureen said softly.

A rustle of sand caused Maureen to turn around. Xander approached, plopping down on the beach blanket next to them. He was dressed in khaki shorts and an old white T-shirt, and there was something decidedly off about him. His face was tense, his eyes sad. "We need to talk."

Her stomach flip-flopped with a sense of dread. "Should I take Rose back to the house?"

He shook his head. "If you don't mind, she's happy. Let's let her keep playing."

"Okay, then. What did you want to say?"

He tossed a block from hand to hand. "I had a talk with my brother. He has a brilliant mind and some damn good insights, ones I always listen to when I remind myself that I should do more listening."

"Were you always close?" Maureen asked, watching the movements in his eyes. "You don't talk much now, so it's tough to tell."

"We're both so wrapped up in our work there isn't as much time. We work all hours. We've talked more in my time here than… God, in I don't know how long." His hand went to his hair, a shrug in his shoulders.

"And when you were children?"

"Our parents were very into letting us learn through experience."

The statement gave her pause. "What do you mean?"

"They weren't helicopter parents, other than the fact they strapped us into helicopters at a young age to tour the Andes. We were homeschooled for real, except home was around the world."

A bohemian lifestyle. It explained so much about Easton's approach. Even the way he talked to people. "That sounds like your brother's style, but not so much yours."

"Are you insinuating I'm uptight?" Arms immediately crossed over his chest.

Rose hummed louder, chanting random words into her melody. Maureen handed the baby another block, which she took as fast as a snapping turtle.

"Not by a long shot. You're sexy and exciting. But you're a businessman and a family man. Not a hippie veterinarian." And, honestly, she enjoyed that about him. He was her naturally occurring counterweight in so many ways.

"I realized that fast and made my own plans accordingly."

"What kind of plans?" Maureen added a block to Rose's tower. Rose high-fived her, then toppled the tower.

"Lots of plans, some better than others. I planned to go to college and get my business degree to start my own company. My brother was clear he wanted to be an exotic animal veterinarian."

"Which you both did. What were some of your other boyhood plans?" In the span of five minutes, some of the harshness of the morning ebbed away. She felt as though, for the first time, he trusted her with the vulnerable bits of his life. Maureen wanted him to keep sharing.

"We decided to catch the biggest fish for a local contest. The grand prize was five thousand dollars."

"Wow, that's a lot of money for a fish." She knew fishing contests drew a lot of attention, but hadn't really understood the appeal.

"It was for the serious fishermen, but we had big dreams and bigger egos. We were certain we could make it happen."

"And did you?" Resting her face on her palm, she leaned forward.

He waved, a smile tugging at his lips. A bit of the Xander she knew and loved peeking through. "Wait for the story. Give it time to breathe."

"You're seriously telling me to slow down and relax? Mr. Fast-Paced Executive?"

"I'm learning. Anyhow, I built the boat. My brother researched the fishing channels. I adapted the dynamics of the craft to his calculations." He picked up a block, handing it to Rose.

"How did the competition turn out?"

"We caught the most fish, but not the biggest. We lost by two ounces."

"Seriously? Only two ounces? That must have been a huge fish." The tropical fish of Florida astounded her. So different from the fish in the streams and lakes of Ireland, so vibrant and mammoth.

"We ate well. We filled the freezer with the extra, then started a campfire to grill the rest for Mom and Dad by suppertime." He gestured with his hands, as if drawing that freezer back to the present.

She tried to picture a younger Easton and Xander hauling in the fish. The image made her laugh.

"That's really thoughtful."

"Um, Mom turned white and passed out and Dad gave us one helluva lecture about going out on the water without an adult."

"How old were you?"

"Ten and eleven." That sly smile returned. He looked at her sidelong, his blue eyes complementing the state of the sky. Piercing and intoxicating.

"What did they think the boat you'd been building was for?"

"They assumed it would be for local villagers on our latest family expedition. And it was. Once we finished with it."

She nodded, thinking she understood. But she wanted clarity. Time to be brave. "Where were you going with that story just now?"

"I was making a couple of points, really. The first point, the less pertinent one, is that for a long time I thought you and my brother might be an item because you have so much in common."

Shock rippled through her, then amusement. A laugh of disbelief snorted free. "Me? And Easton? Seriously?"

He nodded.

"Clearly you realized that's not the case at all. No disrespect to your brother. He's a brilliant veterinarian, but he's a friend and a work companion. Nothing more."

"Okay, I believe you."

She took the block from his hand, reading hesitancy in his eyes. "But what?"

"He's the sort of person you would be with at that university job, the world you're from." He paused, inhaling deeply before continuing. "Are you taking the job?"

"No," she said without hesitation. "Of course not. We made promises to each other."

His hand fell to rest on his daughter's head, his eyes still searching Maureen's. "So you're staying because of Rose? So she doesn't risk a custody battle?"

And in a flash she realized, holy hell, he was every bit as insecure as she was when it came to giving his heart again. She lifted his hand from Rose's head, linked fingers with his and went out on the biggest limb of her life. "I'm staying because of you and what's happening between us. I hope you believe me."

His throat moved in a long swallow and he squeezed her hand. "Obviously I haven't been thinking with the clearest of minds for a while, not since Terri's death. I will always love her, but I hope you understand that doesn't mean I can't fall in love with another woman just as deeply."

Her heart leaped at his words, at his implication. Could it be? Her hearing intensified, causing her to lean closer, hand touching his thigh.

"Once I realized how close I was to losing you, to your work visa expiring and your leaving for Ireland, I acted fast. Just like with the boat, I knew on some level what had to be done."

"But your in-laws? They were a threat—"

He waved a hand dismissively. "They're coming around, I believe. They love Rose, but they don't want to be parents again. They already sent flowers this morning with a congratulations and a request to come for a lunch visit to discuss how to be helpful, involved grandparents." He tapped his temple. "On some level, I knew they would see reason."

"But I didn't." She eyed him. "You manipulated me?"

"I did what I needed to in order to make you stay. To

give us this chance at a life together, because, Maureen, I love you. If we waited here while someone counted every grain of sand on the beach, there wouldn't be enough time to explain how much you mean to me. And if you'll give me a chance, I'll prove it to you and, hopefully, with time, you'll come to love me in return."

Relief coursed through her as she saw the truth in his eyes. She'd spent so long telling herself not to believe in the fairy tale, but maybe it wasn't a fairy tale. The truth had been building all along and she'd been so worried about being hurt again, she hadn't allowed herself to see it.

She caressed his face. "How beautifully lucky for us that I already am in love with you."

Urgency filled her. She'd found courage again. Leaning in to kiss him, she angled her head below his. A tender kiss transferring from her lips to his. Electricity melded with comfort, the kiss feeling like a long-overdue homecoming.

His hand braced her chin, fingers soft.

Maureen felt a smaller hand touch her cheek three times. They broke the kiss to see Rose beaming at them. She kissed Maureen's cheek, then Xander's. A ripple of laughter passed between them all. Everything settling into place. Together.

Xander scooped up his daughter and wrapped an arm around his wife's waist. "What do you say we put Rose down for a nap and we make new honeymoon plans? Together."

She leaned against his shoulder, her arm sliding around his waist, as well. "I like the sound of that, husband. Very much."

* * * * *

MILLS & BOON®

Desire™

PASSIONATE AND DRAMATIC LOVE STORIES

A sneak peek at next month's titles…

In stores from 8th September 2016:

- **The Rancher Returns** – Brenda Jackson *and*
  The Black Sheep's Secret Child – Cat Schield

- **The Pregnancy Proposition** – Andrea Laurence *and*
  His Secret Baby Bombshell – Jules Bennett

- **His Illegitimate Heir** – Sarah M. Anderson *and*
  Convenient Cowgirl Bride – Silver James

MILLS & BOON®

18 bundles of joy from your favourite authors!